Deceptive Men

Preview an Excerpt from
Another Novel by Alina

mrs. deveraux

Nothing is as it seems…

Coming soon…

Visit **Alina** at
www.alinabooks.com
or
www.alinaswritings.com

Deceptive Men

Stealth, Wealth, and Lies

By Alina

ALINA BOOKS are published by

Alina Books, PO Box 1323, Round Rock, Texas 78680-1323

Alina, 1974-
    Deceptive Men / by Alina

ISBN – 13: 978-0-578-00189-0
ISBN – 10: 0-578-00189-6

Printed in the United States of America

Book design and jacket illustration by *Angel Allen*

Thank You

For my mother, Yvonne
Who always believed in my abilities!

For my sister, my niece and nephews,
Thank you for being there along the way.

In loving memory of my aunt, Eather Jackson
She instilled values that could not be forgotten.

I love you all. Thank you for your support.

Chapter

1

Months Before the Annual Meeting

STARING THROUGH the windshield at the billowy forms subtly surrounding the descending sun, overwhelmed by an endless overcast sky, unique thoughts entered Evelyn's mind as she drove down Manchester Drive. The rain seemed only miles away. The distinctive scent of downpour weighed heavily in the evening mist. She could see the darkness moving closer. She blinked and instantaneously, the rain came thundering down flooding her windshield. Blinded by the sudden darkness, her auto-lights turned on, but still she struggled for some visibility. She frightfully fumbled to regain control of the vehicle, which she immediately lost as a river of water swallowed her windshield, obstructing her view. In a panic, she activated her left turn signal trying to flip on the windshield wipers. Her car veered across the road just missing an oncoming SUV. Passing horns were heard, but no visual. She leaned over the steering wheel hoping to see past her drenched windshield, but the dotted white lines that separated the two lane street remained invisible. The sky she had embraced was no longer a spectacle of her immediate view. The trees that once crowded the street on either side had disappeared. The blackness overpowered her thoughts—she shivered, suddenly remembering disconcerting events from her past. She couldn't explain why, but the intensity of this very moment led her mind back to Clarence.

Envisioning his blood covered body lay next to her nearly comatose body. The thought lingered just as if he had died yesterday. Only fragments of the event went through her mind on this day. His brown, almost gray and ghostly like still eyes staring back at her. Motionless. This she could clearly visualize. The stab wounds across his chest that dismantled a tattoo that said, *"Cody"* underneath two baby doves, *which represented his three month old son that died in his arms.* Oh wait…Clarence didn't have a son that died. Or did he? Her mind started to question her thoughts. She couldn't understand it. She contemplated on this thought for a moment; then the warmth of his smile came crashing through her heart smothering her lungs, as she forcibly tried gasping for a breath. Still the thoughts would not elude her. She could not understand why her mind unexpectedly became wrapped around these horrific memories.

Just as the wipers splashed through the flood, she gained a clear vision of the car charging ahead in full speed as if the rain was not a challenge. Her eyes widen and no thoughts escaped her brain. She froze. Hastily, she slammed on her brakes and her back tires slid across the pavement, veering to the right. As her car danced across Manchester Drive, she blinked again to regain some stability within her thoughts. Then she opened her eyes, a moment later, which seemed like an hour—all was new. No rain. No frantic windshield wipers swaying back and forth. No speeding car flying ahead. Nothing. She glanced at her surroundings and noticed that she was horizontally positioned at a standstill, with her right foot still on the brakes, in a neighboring home's driveway. She shook her head slowly in disbelief. She was only moments away from the club but she didn't think she would make it that far. She sat in wonder for a few minutes, then noticed something unusual up ahead.

A man standing about ten feet in the distance next to one of the mature trees in the neighbor's yard caught her eye. The face seemed familiar, but Evelyn wasn't sure. Her eyes glittered rapidly trying to regain focus on the image ahead. She put the car in park and proceeded to exit the vehicle. She opened her car door and tried to get out but she couldn't. She looked over her chest and noticed her seat belt was still fastened. Evelyn unsnapped the seat belt and exited the car. Just in that brief moment, he was gone. She looked frantically across the road, then back into the yard where the man had first appeared. She studied for a second then concluded that it was probably someone from a landscaping company, although she did not see any other vehicles on the road besides hers. Evelyn deliberated for a moment, then sat back inside the vehicle and started the engine. "I don't remember shutting down the engine," she thought to herself.

As she sat in the vehicle, unable to move because she was still trying to put her finger on the day's event, she glanced up again and there he was. This time, he was closer than before. Much closer. It *was* Clarence.

"It couldn't be…he's dead!"

The image appeared closer and closer and it became more apparent that the image was Clarence.

"This can't be," she managed to say aloud.

Suddenly, a multitude of images started flashing across her

eyes. She tried to shake it off, but was unable to. She could no longer see the man that stood in front of her because the monstrous scenes from that troubling night took over her immediate view. Her first image was a fast explosive flash of light that lit up the entire room. She could clearly see an arm extended out holding a silver revolver with a black, almost smokeless explosive breeze weakly moving upward and disappearing into the night air. She could smell the burning of raw meat which practically made her puke. Her gut clenched in a tight knot as the adrenaline rushed through her veins. She pictured the life slip from his eyes as Clarence's head bent backward in a limp motion. She knew he was dead. She shook her head again, "This can't be…what is happening here?" Then, she could clearly hear the annoying sounds as if they were in the car with her tunneling through the car stereo. The air conditioner sang a familiar tone that frightened her senses. Taking her mind back into the house where the terror first began, Evelyn tried to forcibly shake the horrific images that pulsated through her brain like lightening, but nothing worked. The thoughts were too much of a challenge for her fragile soul. The air condition propped in the lower level living room window held up by a two-by-four hummed an unforgettable annoying sound that kept penetrating her ears. It was set as high as it could go but it was still no match for the bloody corpse that lay next to Evelyn. The stench was as thick as a heavily smog field of trees near a river crossing.

Evelyn extended her arms into view, examining her blood covered hands. Her hands dangled loosely as she suspended them in mid-air. Astound by the amount of blood, she panicked—as much as she possibly could panic. Her emotions seemed like an aftermath. Her thoughts were unhurried and her delayed reactions frightened her more. She suddenly realized that she was unable to move her body, except for her arms and head. Feeling the weakness of her mobility, she thought she was paralyzed. Her mind drifted in and out of consciousness as she lay on the living room floor of Clarence's stale, muggy home. "It must be a dream," she desperately thought to herself. "It's got to be dream. Why am I here with him? What happened to me?" Her cries were only a whisper away as she drifts into unconsciousness.

Evelyn finally came back to reality, anxiously scanning her surroundings, searching everywhere for the man that she once saw. Nothing. He was gone and she thought her mind had left too. She turned her wheels cautiously to exit the neighbor's driveway and eased down the road heading toward the club. She was puzzled and frightened by what just occurred. Her mind had wandered off and in an extreme moment, she was engulfed in a flood, about to drown, and gasping for air. Now, the unnerving thoughts that literally took her mind by storm had her wondering what it was all about. Why now? Why was she revisiting these dreadful memories? She had never been nervous to meet a potential member before, so she concluded that the meeting could not be the cause of her nervousness, if she was even nervous at all. Maybe, it was the way Renée explained the circumstances to her about this woman whom she will come to meet? Evelyn pondered these thoughts as she entered into the private security gates of the *MH Women's Club* just on the outskirts of Bloomfield Hills, Michigan, a suburban city outside of Detroit.

Chapter

2

The Present

The Fifth Annual Anniversary Meeting

EVELYN FOUND herself embracing life in a new way. Weeping, although at times invigorating, had long past her system with fully blossomed smiles and considerable hope taking its place. Her lungs no longer choked from the dust and debris of life. Her thoughts were no longer scattered like a pile of broken bones; and her admittance of guilt freed her mind from frustration and suffering, leading to the road of forgiveness. She was, for the first time, a glorious wealthy woman.

As she prepared for an eventful evening with her fellow women, her mind is set at ease with the lavish table cloths that covered the antique tables in the Banquet Hall. Tonight, the Fifth Annual Anniversary Meeting will be well underway at around one P.M. The hand selected gentlemen preparing the hall were many she had used before. Their sleeveless shirts revealed their buffed arms. Their black and white attire consisted of a tightly fitted shirt that covered their torso, with the cut of the sleeve stopping at the shoulders. They wore black tuxedo neck ties that accompanied their white shirts with black buttons leading nowhere—simply there for decoration. Their slightly tight fitted black slacks where custom shaped to each man's physical attributes. These handsome men wore tiny wireless radio earpieces for communicating with each other, due to precise instructions that they were not to speak to be heard and no conversations would be carried on during the meeting. Their job…to bring the food, the drinks and make certain that no woman was left unattended—in need of anything.

The lights are set at a dim, as the clock strikes noon. No time for perfection, Evelyn must rush to one of the SQ Rooms to finish dressing. At five til one, the ladies start to shower in. Evelyn braces herself for the usual speech, at the usual place, but this time, with unusual words. The mercurial events in the last couple of months did not weigh heavily on her shoulder this afternoon, and with the clock showing ten minutes past one, she had now mentally prepared herself for the day. She mingled with the crowd for a moment or two before clutching the microphone, standing at the front of the room, to welcome everyone to another exquisite event. Her voice still held voluptuous depths of compassion and excitement, silencing the crowd with one whisper. Her dazzling eyes traveled across the room by massive force, with the sounds of soft voices gently sweeping the crowd.

On this day, it would be members only with the exception of Melissa. Un-regrettably, she shared her story of her sister to the entire group followed by a long sigh relieving her of a dissipated lifestyle. She shared her grandiose dreams of being the richest woman in the world by diluting her mind from the negative vibes that her soul surrendered to on a daily basis. Life did not seem as insubstantial and distorted as it had before. She went on, seeming especially surprised by the warmth of the crowd, and stated how she had embarked on a journey to bring the suffering of women back to the man, but found herself accepting an entirely different agenda.

When she started the *MH Women's Club*, she had not known the depths of the impact that men imprinted on a woman's soul. She had not known, for certain, what certainty was until she meet Melissa. Evelyn's afflictions had proved to have escorted her down the road to uncertainty. Just when it seemed she had a fighting chance, and she was certain that her grief would subside, she was hit with a wrecking ball. Now, her final blow, would be the deceitful lies of corrupt authorities that tried to dismiss her from society—*all*, by the hands of a man. Her heart falls short of the bitterness she once embraced, and it is now filled with forgiveness. She realized that the only person that she *really* needed to forgive was herself.

Concentrated facial expressions were seen throughout the crowd, eyes glued to Evelyn, as silence crept through the air.

"We ingratiatingly, some unconsciously, by the discussions we engage in and the people we flood ourselves around. Amazingly, if you speak long enough, everyone will soon hear what you are trying to hide. I used all of you to hide my imperfections and it took only five years for them to seep through my veins like a faulty IV, and for that, I am in debt to you. Beneath the old exterior paint, you'll always find a fresh coat waiting to be revealed. Ladies, you are my fresh coat and I am blessed you have revealed yourselves." She raised her voice with her last words and continued, "Thank you all from the bottom of my heart."

Everyone stands to applaud Evelyn, unsuspectingly, she blinked twice and a smile drifted in place. Suddenly, her eyes glared and widen with excitement, as her sister walked through the door of the Banquet Hall with Renée by her side. Evelyn, standing at the front of the room holding the microphone and said, "This is my sister, Veronica Zellman, ladies." She walked to meet her and said, "Can you ever forgive me for being so foolish?"

"I already have. I forgave you the moment I left that night; I just needed to clear my head to confirm the emotions I was feeling." She looked at Evelyn with a serious brow and said, "I once asked Renée a question…I wanted to know: How do I create a better me when this is the only *me* that I know? She suggested that I would find the answer in you. Until the night that I met you, I did not understand what she meant—now, I fully agree. I know that it was not *me* that I was searching for, it was a part of me that had been missing all these years but now I have found it." Stroking the back and palm of Evelyn's right hand, Veronica added, "I had a dream for many years that I had sisters, and since I have found you, I will not waste this time with belligerent arrogance. You are my sister and I want to make things right."

Evelyn grabs her, pulls her into her chest and holds her weightless body in her arms. She held her tight with nearly silent sighs heard clear across the room as all the ladies remained perfectly still and very stagnant. Tears gently dropped from Evelyn's eyes and down Veronica's back. "It will be better, I promise."

"It will be even better if I could breathe," Veronica muffles gasping for a breath in the midst of being engulfed in Evelyn's bosom. Everyone starts to laugh and Evelyn lets her go.

"Oh, I am so sorry. I am trying to kill you already," Evelyn said smiling from ear to ear with her hands wrapped around Veronica's arms.

Veronica smiles and glances at Renée, winks her eye and kisses Evelyn on the cheek. The crowd melted with sentiments. But little did they know this was the kiss of death. Veronica steps back from Evelyn, glance at the tearful crowd and digs in her purse with her eyes glued to Evelyn. Evelyn was concentrated on the moment and did not see what was to come.

One of the members, Erica, watched from a fractured distance as a shiny metal object came into view. Instantaneously as Evelyn pleasingly wailed at the crowd and turned to return to the podium, Melissa walked up to accompany her along the way and with mad force Veronica pulled a knife from her purse. Melissa's face suddenly filled with shock as she tried to reach for the knife and warn Evelyn simultaneously. "No! Evelyn! No!" She cried out.

Most of the crowd jumped to their feet, not quite sure what the commotion was about, and their eyes searched the room for answers.

"Evelyn, watch out!" A neighboring member shouted.

"What the hell?" shouted another.

Melissa made it to Evelyn just in a nick-of-time. She pushed her to the right, opposite of the forceful swing. As Evelyn managed to climb to her feet from the fall, she still had not placed the scene together. She turned to look at Veronica, who was holding a big black handled kitchen knife in her right hand. With a stunned expression, she flickered in disbelief. She did not know what to feel or how to react. Words escaped her, so she stood in the middle of the floor in total fright.

"*Oh my God!*" shouted a member.

Veronica turned her head slightly to see Melissa slumped near a chair holding her side. The blood had dripped onto the floor next to Melissa's body. It was then that Veronica realized that she stabbed Melissa instead of Evelyn. When Evelyn fell on the nearby members that were still seated, she assumed that she hit her target. Veronica became enraged more and looked over at Evelyn and shouted, *"See what you made me do! You always manage to escape."*

Veronica gritted her teeth and charged at Evelyn with the knife raised high above her head in a stabbing motion. Evelyn's eyes got wider and her body became numb. The shock had not worn off and she remained stationary. She could not move. She felt her legs weaken. She couldn't breathe. All she could see was the knife. Not a thought entered her mind.

All of a sudden, a loud piercing blast rang in the air.

POW, POW!

Members scattered for the door, stumbling over chairs and high heel shoes that unknowingly escaped some of the member's feet. The screams were carried throughout the building. The crowd was in an uproar. The gun shot blast lingered through the air for what seemed like forever. The waiters ducked into the hallway, seeking immediate shelter when the violence first occurred. As the shots rang out, they dived on the floor of the hallway, crawling to the kitchen for safety.

Evelyn managed to pull herself together for a moment to see Veronica tunnel to the floor in a swinging motion. Her body hit the floor hard enough to bounce once from the blast. Evelyn gasped for a breath and held her chest in dismay. She faintly turned to see Erica holding the gun in her hand, extended outward, with a blank facial expression. Evelyn's eyes swept across the room and everyone's movements seemed to be in slow motion. Her eyes slowly blinked, her head slowly nodded from side to side, and her movements were restricted by sudden fright. She couldn't believe her eyes.

After the piercing sounds subsided and the frantic members bolted through the doors, Evelyn was at a dilemma. "Who do I go to?" she thought to herself. Melissa lay to her left and Veronica was lying on the floor with a gunshot wound to the chest on her right. She contemplated on this dilemma for a half a second and took one step toward Veronica. She stopped. She looked back at Melissa holding her side with blood spilling over her fragile hands and thought silently, "She saved my life again. What do I do?"

Evelyn turned and headed for Melissa.

"Please, Evelyn, I am alright. Go see about your sister," Melissa stated with struggled words.

"Are you sure you are alright?" Evelyn asked with grave concern as she kneeled to the floor trying to examine Melissa's wound and continued, "I am so confused. I don't know what to do!" The burning sensation in her eyes from the tears that abruptly fell was too much for Evelyn to bear. She collapsed to her knees next to Melissa and slowly dropped her head on Melissa's chest.

"It's okay Evelyn. It is going to be okay. Please don't cry. Go see about your sister, that is what you should do." Melissa tried to guide Evelyn's thoughts, but the excitement had not worn off on her as well. She was only trying to be decisive, although she was just as confused as Evelyn.

Evelyn managed to pull up from her knees and walk over to Veronica. Veronica lay on the floor with the knife loosely sitting in the palm of her right hand. The left side of her chest was oozing with blood which had slowed down with each passing breath that Veronica took. Flashbacks of her father lying on the kitchen floor penetrated Evelyn's mind like a lethal injection. All she could see was the blood. The blood spilling out from underneath Veronica's

12

body seemed to be overflowing, racing quickly across the floor. Evelyn's hands firmly pressed against her chest, trying to stop the bleeding, but it persisted. So much blood. Evelyn's mind became consumed with the site of the blood and she could not control her steady flow of tears.

Then she closed her eyes and raised her head up, facing the ceiling, to release a hefty sigh. She looked down at her hands but there was no blood. She scanned Veronica's body and it was still in the same position. Her mind had gone off track again, taking her back to past events. She wondered if she was losing it.

She watched Veronica's body with a steady eye. Veronica's breaths were at a slow uncontrolled rhythm. Her helpless body twitched once from the shock of the gun shot blast, Evelyn thought. "Why did you do this?" she managed to say.

"I wanted you to suffer just as I have…" Veronica made a fighting effort to respond, paused for a second and continued, *"You left me.* Do…do you know what it feels like to be alone? *Do you know*…what it is like to be scared and realizing that you're all alone? I knew that was you on Renée's mantel. I…knew it was you, my dear sister!" She chocked for a moment on the blood that was running from her mouth. She struggled to continue her words but her life was gradually slipping away.

"I do know what that is like. I have lived with being alone for many years," Evelyn stated with as much certainty as possible.

"You…hide…behind your money. You don't know what it is truly like to be alone because you have all these women here to keep you going. Even before mother died, I was alone. I was trying to fight a battle…I was trying to fight a battle that she no longer…wanted to fight. Because I knew I had to live for her. You a…abandon us! You aban…abandon us!" Evelyn watched her sister as she gasped for her last breath. Veronica's eyes stared straight ahead, as her head slowly limped to the side and her chest rise and fell for the last time.

"*Veronica! Veronica wake up! Don't die on me Veronica,*" Evelyn said frantically. "I didn't abandon you...I abandon...me!" Her words were never heard by Veronica. She was gone. Evelyn kneeled by her sister's side and mutely cried.

The room was silent.

Silence grew stronger and stronger, until the static from the wireless headsets the waiters were wearing could be heard. Evelyn gently swept her hands across Veronica's eyes to close her eyelids. "You rest now," she said to herself.

14

Chapter

3

Meeting Melissa

BLOOMFIELD HILLS, a town of sophisticated charm and wealth with a population of twenty-four thousand residence and the business constituents are very few. Businesses were not the growth of the communities within this town, due to the high price housing, private policing, *paid for by the wealthy of course*, and the women and gentlemen's clubs—all ranging from two million to over forty-eight million dollars. The roads are parallel to each other. The stop signs and light signals are suspended from new birth, and the directive yellow and white lines seemed newly painted, even after the months and years have gone by.

As Evelyn remembers, these streets were not like the grungy streets of Detroit, where directive lines, traffic signals and street names were invisible throughout most neighborhoods. Debris scattered about. Fall leaves remained overwhelming the edge of the walkways and bunched along corner store buildings, *long after the season had passed*, while homeless people and drug addicts mingled about. The neighborhood she grew up in started out with promise and hope but ended in destitute and despair long after her departure. Her neighborhood did not have sociable clubs with perfect lighting. Romantic trees and bushes capturing the earth's beauty with neatly blazed cut grass perfectly trimmed leaving inspiring morning dew that could be seen for miles. Her street, Westminister Street, carried an un-delightful aroma during the early morning hours. The mist in the air was almost ghostly, with visibility being episodic by the hanging branches that sometimes blocked your walking path or the immense roots that barricaded themselves underneath the concrete bringing the sidewalk to a boil.

On her block sat a full row of houses, uninterrupted by vacancies—which occurred on the next block—with partially neatly structured landscaping and mature trees. The homes were not similar in style but of color. Tan and brown paint with reddish brown bricks seem to be the deciding architectural color scheme throughout the block. Homes were small in size, twelve to fourteen hundred square feet. But moderate for the residence, with no comparison to the square footage in Bloomfield Hills where most master suites equaled the size of these homes.

On the next block, vacant homes swallowed up the few slightly livable ones. Occupied by bums and on occasion dead bodies; with the city of Detroit vowing to crack down on the destructive trafficking, but never did. At first, drug trafficking and drug addicts selling their body for drugs –*male and female*– were not blatantly obvious. But as the years moved forward, these activities became more apparent.

As grandmothers passed; mothers washed their aching hands of a Menace-to-Society son that just completed his second stay at Mound Correctional Facility. And the once teenagers become men with more courageous stupidity, insensibilities, and bigger dreadful dreams; the communities are left with hopelessness. But Evelyn departed with the neighborhood before things took a turn for the worse.

As the wheels of Evelyn's BMW strolled through the black seventeen foot security gates, her mind contemplated on the words she would say to another distorted misunderstood woman waiting in the club's MH Meeting Room. She parked in front of the enormously huge French doors attached to the nearly seven thousand square foot building that sat on two and a half acres of enchanting painstakingly fresh cut landscaping. The sign on the building reads, *"The MH Women's Club of Bloomfield Hills"*. At some point Evelyn wanted to open other clubs across Michigan with talk of moving to other parts of the country. Between her busy schedule with managing her businesses and the late night calls from the members of the Women's Club, it didn't leave much time to pursue other goals. Her past success had proved beyond any doubt that she had never been afraid to go after what she wanted. Consequently, all the trials and tribulations that she admits have helped develop her as a person has made her a strong black woman.

Evelyn takes a deep breath, and enters the club. The aroma is one of a proverbial scent—with a mixture of expensive floral scent perfumes, lightly scented chocolate fragrances, and a hint of a soft Clean *Eau De Toilette*. With all the different scents of the women that entered once a month, sometimes once a week, nothing over powered the warm rich enchanting smell of the one hundred year old mahogany wood especially sculptured to form the ceiling to floor pillars on each side of the front entrance. The handcrafted circular desk, made from the same wood with a marble top, stood five feet tall and approximately twelve feet in length. The impressive grand entrance featured twenty-four foot ceilings with a five foot in length chandelier dangling from the ceiling. Custom upholstered Italian Leather Sofa, Loveseat, and Chair surrounded the left side of the lobby as you entered the building.

From the custom drapery to the marble accent floors in the entry way, to the custom craftsmanship of each room throughout the facility; the Women's Club was a warm inviting palace where women came to meet and discuss the encumbrance issues of the world. These meetings included heavy conversations about the charming unsophisticated money grubbing looser existence of men like some of the Detroiters most of the members knew all too well.

The majority of the women that visit the facility were natives of the big city. The newness of the upcoming casinos added value to the growth of Downtown Detroit. And as your senses were pleasantly overwhelmed by the fresh new constructed restaurants, you were delighted to call yourself a Detroiter. Some of the women say they were reluctant to move out of the city realizing the potential. However, the clean-up lasted far too long for them to bear through it. Even though Evelyn moved away from the city to a neighboring city adjacent to Bloomfield Hills, she consciously realized the potential that Detroit had and made several investments to secure her position. But, the seemingly growing potential of the city was yet to be seen within the men of Detroit.

Some men lived their lives with one foot in and one foot out of several different relationships; going from woman to woman deceiving them into thinking that they were the only one. A large number of the Detroit men lay wasting away in prison. Some innocently converted their lives to imprisonment by trying to provide the means to put food on the table. While others embarked on a life of repetitious motion from drug pedaling father to drug pushing son. With the absence of many fathers; due to imprisonment, lack of attendance, or dead-beat dads filling their child's mind with unfulfilled promises—brought criminal mentality to exist in the eyes of the young man growing up, blinding him from seeing other choices made available to him. Boys raised by a young teenage mother, or grandmothers who become overwhelmingly ill or too tired to intervene. Or simply the absence of grandmother's too young to be considered a grandmother—terribly influenced the outcome of learned behavior which born the insensitive, unnoticeably sadden hearts, and reaching out for the attention that escaped them as adolescents. Still, no excuse will be reached in pity for the men of Detroit, because the women had suffered the same living conditions, yet they rose above these obstacles.

Evelyn made her way down the elongated hallway, entering the MH Meeting Room, which was the second door on the right. The atmosphere of the room was similar to a luxurious estate library. With custom bookshelves covering the walls and tall wingback chairs randomly placed throughout the room—all stood on wall-to-wall deep plush tan carpet. In a corner, leaning up against the bookshelf was the woman Evelyn came to meet. The woman embraced Evelyn with a warm subtle smile as she entered the room. She was slow in her movements and Evelyn felt the wretchedness of her circumstances even before she spoke a word.

The woman was dressed aristocratically with navy blue

leather Hermés pumps, carrying a Hermés Bordeaux Crocodile Birkin handbag. A navy blue pinstripe suit looked to be an Armani creation with a white four thousand dollar Gucci under top covered her slim body. Her posture was broken to that of a shy innocent little girl who had just been introduced at a royal family coming out party. Evelyn ached for the misery distributed upon the woman's face.

Her complexion was complemented with a recent tan, but the subtle bags under her eyelids did not go unnoticed. Her adorable short stubby nose was a perfect match for her small head and sharp cheekbones that glowed when she manipulated a smile. Her eyes were normally spaced from each other, with fresh trimmed brows, as the embryonic wrinkles formed faintly along the corners of her eyes making for a youthful appearance. Her long neck was smoother than it should be, given her age—plastic surgery touch-up perhaps, Evelyn thought. Freshly coated powdered makeup denaturalized her beauty or created a flawless appearance that made for a second glance to determine if it were make-up at all. But as you reach the discoloration of her chest, makeup was sure to be present, with delicate light auburn color freckles aimlessly placed across the illuminating part of her chest.

Her comfortable lifestyle was reflected on her left hand, the matrimony finger. Accompany by a magnificent huge six caret yellow cut diamond with four surrounding baguette gems, possibly from *Harry Winston*, pricing at over a quarter of a million dollars. The material appearance did not change the visual adversity observable in her face and gestures. But her graceful demeanor stood out which allowed you to immediately forgive the hardship appearance she tried to methodically displace, covering her emotions with opulence.

Given a closer look as Evelyn approached the woman, she made an unbelievable discovery. Her face was first familiar but soon confirmed remembering seeing photos of the woman standing next to a handsome family of haves and have not's. Standing shoulder-to-shoulder, unhappily gestured with perplexity written across her face, was the lady standing next to the woman—*perhaps the mother*—unsuccessfully trying to conceal her sadness with several coats of makeup. The photo was seen on the cover of *Fortune Magazine*. The featured story cover read, *"Family Riches Runs Deep"* with a huge photograph of the Contour Family and what seem to be the father, holding a graphically designed picture of their estate circled between both hands given the illusion that he was carrying the estate in the palm of his hands.

The father, a handsome sophisticate with a *John Gotti* persona—the smooth slick short black hair with subtle gray that cascaded around the edges, serious eyes, long widen at the tip nose, slightly oval round face with a breathtaking smile, and stylishly dressed. The mother, standing next to Mr. Contour, was delightfully appealing with all the gracefulness of a first lady but with weary eyes. Of course the photo was more than a few years old, but Evelyn holds a fonder memory of the beautiful feigned face of the woman standing next to an obviously love obscured family. According to the article, the family's wealth generated a Number *6* spot on the *Fortune 500* list with an estimated net worth of over twenty billion dollars—which was still unable to capture the smiles of this family, Evelyn thought. Evelyn recalls something about family ties as far as Ireland, with business connections abroad—China, Russia, Japan, and Europe. The details of the article were not as memorable as the woman that stood before her tonight. There was something about the woman that generated a calm sense of peace through Evelyn...she liked her, immediately.

"Hi, I'm Evelyn McKenzie, President of the Man Haters Club." She walked toward the woman with her right arm extended as she positioned her hand to meet the woman's.

The woman slowly stood up, looked at Evelyn with a timid gesture, softly shook Evelyn's hand and said, "My name is Melissa Contour. It is nice to finally meet you." Even in heels her height was average, about five foot seven, three inches under Evelyn.

"Nice to meet you as well. Please, please, have a seat." Evelyn motions her hand for Melissa to have a seat. "So, Renée brought you here today? Where is she? I thought she would be in here with you?" Evelyn looked at Melissa with a slight frown upon her face. She closely studied her gestures as Melissa responded to the questions.

"Yes, she went to the restroom just before you entered the room." Melissa looked toward the door, and then back at Evelyn with her chin vaguely hovered over her chest. Distrusted expressions were not present in the room, which normally followed Melissa, because Evelyn's warmth entered the environment like a lethal gas. Melissa's trust began almost immediately, but a slight reluctance was apparent. Melissa connected eyes with Evelyn and said, "I hear you are the wise one." Feeling awkward as the words spilled from her mouth; given the fact that Melissa noticed that Evelyn did not appear any older than she.

Evelyn chuckled. "I would not necessarily say that I am the *wise one* but I have been places, seen things, and done things that most of us could not fathom. Some people learn things from me and I learn things from them. I believe it's an exchange, like a relationship. Where the wisdom begins is to know what to do in the relationship. Knowing the part you play or should play is the most important first step." Evelyn gets out of her seat, moves swiftly across the floor and pours herself a cup of coffee, black. "May I get you a cup of coffee, some water, some juice?"

"No, I'm fine. Thank you."

A calm silence controlled the room, and then the door to the MH Meeting Room opened quickly and in walks Renée. "Well, hello Miss Evelyn. Nice to see you again. I see you have met Melissa!" She burst in with an inviting smile, hair tossing from side to side as she turns her head to glance at them both.

"Yes, I have. And how are you doing these days, Ms. Renée Castillo?"

"Oh, you know me…same old shit, different day. How about you?"

"Well, I am good," Evelyn said with a wink of an eye and a delightful smile. "You stated that Melissa may be considering counseling and would like to be considered as a possible candidate for membership?" Evelyn turns to look at Melissa, sipping her coffee. There was something about Melissa that captivated her. She sensed that a chilling tale was about to unravel but she could not put her finger on it. She was not sure if it would be Melissa's story or her own. Eyes glued on Melissa, Evelyn felt herself in a daze unable to escape. Finally, she slowly shakes her head as she prepared her lips for another sip of coffee.

Renée turned to look at Melissa, and then she looked at Evelyn. Feeling intensity in the air, appearing to have missed something given the steadiness of the expression that pondered on Evelyn's face, but she did not want to mull over it too long. "Well, Melissa has a story to tell and a situation to get out of…"

Melissa pleasantly interrupts, "My marriage...I want a divorce."

Renée gazed at Melissa through her peripheral vision and continued, "I just thought that you may be able to help her or assist her in finding a way out of the horrible relationship that she is in, if you want to call it a relationship or a marriage or whatever..."

"Okay, okay, Renée. Thank you," Evelyn politely shouted interrupting Renée before colorful language began to emerge from her lips. A brief pause, then she continued, "And I am quite sure that you have more pressing things to tend to. So, you can go and take care of your business and I will talk with Melissa, if that is okay with Mrs. Contour?" Evelyn turns to relax her bottom against the granite countertop, facing Melissa and Renée as she takes another sip of her coffee with her eyes concentrated on Melissa's demeanor.

"Melissa, is that okay with you?" Renée asked, smiling from ear to ear glancing at both Evelyn and Melissa with an antsy look.

"That's fine with me. That's what I came here to do," Melissa stated, glancing up at Evelyn across the room and back at Renée still standing several feet from the door. Melissa held her head in more confidence the moment Renée entered the room. Her chin raised an inch above her chest, her words were not as soft, and her responses were quickly communicated. Her gestures were more powerful than before, not as confident as her appearance, but her words carried more firmness. It was as if she was putting on an act for Renée or for Evelyn for that matter.

"Okay ladies, I will go now and see what trouble I can get into today. It's a Saturday night and my body is screaming for a night out on the town. Time to hit the clubs." Renée motioned her body in a dancing rhythm as she smiled and headed toward the door.

"You're body is always screaming for a night out or a night of something, Renée," Evelyn stated in a sarcastic voice, holding a bright smile.

Renée looked over at Evelyn without surprise and said, "You are right. Maybe I will even get lucky and find me a decent man while I'm out there…or maybe *not!*" Renée laughs and continued toward the door, "Don't you ladies stay up too late. It is ten past seven P.M. now; don't make it an all nighter." Then, Renée quickly exited the room.

Evelyn manipulated a quaint smile and pressed on, "So, where were we before we were interrupted? Oh yes, you were going to tell me a little about yourself."

Silence.

"Or shall I go first?" Evelyn moved over to the table where Melissa was seated, replaced a chair to position it slightly closer to Melissa and sat down, hugging her left leg over the right.

Melissa, feeling to some extent more intimidated, losing all restricted confidence she mustered in Renée's presence and waited for a momentary moment to reply, "I can go first. I have a long story to tell. Actually, it's the story of my life and the other life that I've come to know."

Evelyn silently deliberated for a split second on what that could mean *the other life she's come to know.* The awkward moment in the room seemed protracted, giving Evelyn enough time to think over these words.

Melissa paused for a few moments, and then continued on as her voice drifted softer and softer with each passing word. "You grow up with this wonderful, romantic, enriched picture of life that your parents promised you and your friends pushed you through. Well, you think they're your friends. Assuming life is as you would hope it to be, still you remain numb. Numb to the interpretations that reality has afforded you. Numb to any bad situations, misunderstandings, frustrations, and any other feelings that do not fit the passionate fulfilling image you played over and over again in your mind during your adolescent years. Life has certainly presented a few twisted events that were definitely not a part of any reality I knew. I've walked through life holding a whole host of painful secrets because I had a family name to protect, children to protect, and a husband to stay married to—no matter the cost." She glanced up at Evelyn with a look of perplexity and added, "You know, I don't know if you can help me. I am not sure that anybody can help." Her eyes glared from the semi dim lighting which revealed the hidden tears that slightly engulfed her big light hazel eyes. But...not a tear fell.

Evelyn, never taking her eyes off of Melissa, stretched her arm out to reach her hand in to gently touch Melissa's hand. "Everyone can be helped. The question is, are you ready and willing for someone to help you? The first step is that you came here, which was a bold move and still you made it. Sometimes we just need a listening ear and the help comes from within. We talk ourselves through our own difficulties and know in our mind what we should do but we have to convince our heart to follow. Keep talking and I believe it will come to you." Evelyn softly rubs Melissa's hand and smiles.

Melissa smiles back, feeling a strong relief enter her body and takes a deep breath. But her heart begins to race as the story of her life begins to form inside her head. Her blood seems as if it went into overload. She slowly rotates her right hand inside the left and vise verse. She crossed the right leg over the left and then the left leg over the right. She starts to reposition herself in the seat and frustration encumbered her face. Not knowing where or how to start the horrific story of her life. She was unable to control the impulse movements of her body and managing motion in her lips did not seem that difficult, however, no words escaped. Eyes glance across the room, nervously sweeping the floor. Then she turned to focus on Evelyn, who maintained a consistent calm demeanor and vibes of concerned feelings poured through Evelyn's face.

Evelyn remained silent.

Thoughts plunged forward through Melissa's mind with increasing speed as the seconds past. Horrifying images pierced through her soul like electric shock. She desperately tried to shake the elusions but with little success. She could feel the rapid flickering of her eyelids which remain to be seen by Evelyn. Embarrassment set in, as she tried to calm herself. Still, no success.

"Tell you what!" Evelyn interrupted the silent fidgeting, making a suggestion to ease some of the frustration that was clearly written across Melissa's face.

Melissa's intense eyes glanced up for a split second and back to sweeping the floor. This one look told the wretchedness of her horrific story.

"Melissa, are you okay?" Evelyn asked. Still with no response. Then she continued, "Let's move over to the sofa. You can take off your shoes, grab a pillow and relax. We try to create a relaxing environment here so our members can come to relax and get away from the everyday frustrations of life. That's why I spent so much money on the appearance of this club to help sooth our members mind and body. I wanted it to be like a relaxing spa resort and a home away from home without the children, the husband, and the dog. (Oh, wait a minute, the dog and the husband may be one in the same...I don't know. I get confused.)" They both laugh, and then Evelyn continues on, "We also have, what we call our *Sleeping Quarters – The SQ Rooms*. In the SQ Rooms, you'll find huge king size beds, fabulous vanity settings, three full size baths with double sinks to accompany the six rooms, and plenty of closet space. I sound like I am showing a home for sale." They laugh and Evelyn continues, "Now, we can move to the sofa in here or go to one of the SQ Rooms and maybe you will be more relaxed there. We also have seating areas in all the SQ Rooms as well."

"I'm fine here. We can move to the sofa and maybe I will feel a little more comfortable. Thank you." Melissa rises, feeling her pulsating heart calm to a more normal beat, removes her shoes from her aching feet, and gracefully move over to the sofa. She collapsed in the corner of the sofa surrounding her body with three pillows. One pillow on both sides of her and one pillow placed in her lap as she embraced it in her arms and released a swift sigh.

As her heart rate slowed down, she felt a warm comfort flowing through her body like a hot mug of tea on a cold winter day. She visualized an enchanting evening in the spring time, surrounded by blossoming tulip flowers, with its beautifully lance-shaped leaves inundated in a sea of various colors, and having tea with Uncle William. They sat in the living room setting Garden House. Not an ordinary garden house, but more of an outdoor chapel setting, taking in the cool refreshing breeze that tunneled through their hair, chilling their faces. The small symmetrical garden house hidden behind her family's large estate upheld a perfect view of the neighboring nude baby Angels waterfall. The waterfall illustrated two Angels with water sprouting from their mouths while standing inside an oversized flower pot. With no end near, Melissa and her uncle would sit and talk for hours about family, money, responsibilities, and about not being afraid to follow your passion—all before she reached age eight. Uncle William wanted her to know more than what stood before her. He wanted her to experience life's unique creations. Like the enchanting warmth of the sun; or the amazing caterpillar that blooms into a beautiful butterfly as it matures; or a chance at love and feeling love for herself. Her uncle became her calm before the storm, delivering her a sense of security that was soon washed away with one tide. As a smile brushed across her lips, she said, "I feel much better. I guess I just needed a security blanket." Melissa smiled looking down at the pillow that she was hugging.

Evelyn smiles and asks, "Are you sure you do not want any water or juice?"

"Yes, I am sure. At least not right now. But, thank you."

"Okay, just let me know. If you get cool, let me know and I will get another blanket for you." Both women laugh and Melissa continued her story.

Chapter

4

Everything in Between

GROWING UP with royalty in her blood did not account for the many transgressions Melissa encountered throughout childhood. Her family's wealth began with the Royal Irish Family in the early 19th Century when her ancestors controlled a large majority of the Irish Land in Ireland. She learned that her family contributed to the confiscation of land by law makers which was intended to be dispersed to the Irish tenants, but, somehow her family mysteriously remained the owners of a large portion. Some stories revealed that their ancestry ties go as far back to the Irish King, *Brian Boru*. "I am sure that may be just a tall tale," Melissa thought to herself. Her family affairs grew beyond the deep foggy hills of Ireland, but were frequently seen in Indonesia, Brazil, and with close ties across the Pacific Ocean to New Zealand. The scope of their business was Real Estate but oil and coal were among the popular sources of revenue. Her family owned everything from fourteen hundred square foot residential properties to massive oil refineries; from moderately sized apartment complexes to multi-million dollar condos and lofts. Their businesses owned other businesses that channeled into the world of computer software and hardware, and dabbled in the making of nuclear military missiles.

Her father's secret connections with the underworld of lobbying, police and government official corruption, as well as vanishing members of society that no longer needed to be seen or heard from again, was a tip of the iceberg into the life of The Contour's. His ability to influentially persuade powerful political and ambassadorial connections was a characteristic trait among Irish men. It was said that he lied in bed with the ruthless Irish American gangsters that ruled parts of South *'Southie'* in Boston and *'Hell's Kitchen'* in New York. Charges of illegal activity never reached the Contour's doorstep however. Melissa's father discernible connections, *on paper of course*, with the corrupt showed high-end real estate development transactions and commercial waterfront property, which appeared to be the extent of their correlation. As the lavish stories grew more entertaining than reasonable, it did not dismiss the obvious truth—they were wealthy, extremely.

Even as a child, Melissa learned how manipulative her family could be and that there was a hefty price to pay for some of the privileges that her status afforded her. Yet, with the stories told to her during her youth, she could not fathom what was to come in the future. She could not have expected her life journey to be so complex, so frustrating, so vulgar, and so meaningless. At least, that was how she felt as time glided on.

One would think that the privileges surrounding Melissa would make life easy. Melissa, however, would contest that it was no easier than learning a new language. Because learning a new language was her interpretation of life and every waking hour presented a new challenge; a new language that she had to learn quickly and immediately adapt to, even if she did not want or have the energy to. As an adult, she could recall many times that she wanted to end the tragedy that became her life. At times she felt she had reached the darkest depths of hell and would never return, but eventually, a calm warmth traveled through her body to relax her muscles so she could breathe again. Take away the royalty, the refine clothing, the privilege lifestyle and you'll find an everyday black woman in the mirror staring back at Melissa.

Casually strolling through childhood; she had a team of inconsistent wannabe friends. Merely hanging around to reap the benefits of her enchanting lifestyle and to say…"I was friends with *Melissa Contour*…you know the Contour Family. The daughter of one of the richest men in the country that practically own most of the Real Estate in Detroit, Michigan, you know, *Franklin Contour*." Some muffled around her (identity unknown), just to get a glimpse of her life to have stories to tell—even if some were made up or at best exaggerated. Yes, she had her share of followers, but somehow managed to get one or two true friends out of the bunch that swarmed around her like mesquites.

Her casual stroll eventually led her into the arms of the first man she ever truly loved, her uncle. Admired by the entire family and one of Melissa's favorite relatives; the only relative not dazzled by the superficial elegance of the rich, but emotionally struck by the beauty of life. She learned so much from Uncle William. His mere presence was enough to put a smile on Melissa's face. He taught her how to fight and to stand up for what she believed in; none of that lady-like stuff that bored Melissa. He taught her how to stay true to herself instead of prancing around in a two-thousand dollar dress, *in the 1970's said a lot for a young girl,* with no idea of how to earn a dollar. He spent more time with her than her parents ever did.

Her mother had been too busy trying to keep her father content so he would not have a reason to manifest his anger on her. Her mother, being a petite woman, complimenting figure, an awkward walk, and pleasing looks remained invisible to the man she married. With Melissa's father regretting ever marrying her mother…her mother had her shoes full.

The mistreatment of Melissa's mother from her father started several years after they were married. It was not enough to be Caucasian, he thought. Not being an Irish bred woman or have the blood of the rich was something he thought he could justify. But her father discovered by fortuity through an intimate conversation with Melissa's grandmother that her mother's veins pump the blood of a half breed, Black and Indian. Melissa's mother, though she appeared Caucasian, background lingered on three sides of the nation—a Caucasian and Indian mother and a Caucasian and Black father. This infuriated her father to the point of considering a divorce. He thought that because her mother was raised as a Catholic, a decision solely insisted by her grandfather, that would be proof of her nationality. But he no longer looked at her mother the same and blamed her for entrapment. Melissa wondered what her father ever saw in her mother in the first place that would make him hate her so suddenly now. Did he ever love her or was she supposed to be his trophy wife that backed fired on his plan with her hidden ethnicity? Melissa would never know.

Her father was a mean son-of-a-bitch. He was a big burly man, with a husky scratched voice that carried across a room when excited. A handsomely done up face with concentration spilled across it on a daily basis. In the business world, he was a hard nose businessman, but fair and sentimental with a hint of politeness that could negotiate a stolen pair of underwear, selling it back to its rightful owner without blinking an eye. He was known for his ambitious demeanor, his political connections, and a ruthless cut throat in the underworld. His careful charisma in the public eye was an eluted fantasy of the reality at home. In Melissa's world, he was crude and harsh, with coldness not being his only mannerism behind the cruelty of his behavior. He would shout profound words to her mother and raise his hand to strike with every intension on pounding the words into Melissa's mother's head. Melissa had not seen her father put his hands on her mother, but the vulgar language that soared in the air was painful enough and not suitable for any child, especially an impressible eleven year old.

The words Melissa's father embraced daily were cruel and unnecessary. Most of his anger was aimed at her mother and very few words were spoken to Melissa, except when necessary. Melissa's uncle took her away from all that. He showered her with affection and empowered her brain with knowledge. He was not afraid to live outside the box. Her uncle wanted her to be more than a rich man's wife. He wanted her to be *the* man's wife, if she had to be a wife at all.

~

It was the summer of 1971 and Melissa was just turning thirteen years old. In the long corridor of her family's estate, she collapsed in an antique oversized chair covered in imported Italian silk. She waited patiently for her uncle to arrive. Knowing she would be overwhelmed with unique gifts, hugs and kisses, and spending the entire day with her favorite uncle; playing games and enjoying an afternoon in their favorite spot, the garden house. Melissa sat with a bright smile as she watched the clock planted on the wall several feet high directly across from her move incrementally. She mentally captured a glimpse of her uncle ambling through the double doors of their estate. Huge boxes obstructing his view with one or two empty boxes especially made for a dramatic appearance—while she charged his knees, flourishing them with hugs. Her birthday was not until next week but her uncle promised he would bring her present over a bit early because he had pressing business in Chicago, Illinois the following week.

Watching the clock steadily, a few minutes went by and soon a few hours. Finally, Melissa was hunched over, head positioned on the arm of the chair, slob running from the side of her mouth, hands and arms engulfed in the pink plush dress that covered her tiny body as her legs dangled freely a few inches above the floor.

Melissa was awakened by one of the servants, Ramon. "Ms. Melissa…Ms. Melissa…wake up. Your mother wishes to see you in the dining hall immediately." Ramon gradually removes her from the chair and uses the sleeve of his overly pressed black suit jacket to wipe the residue from her face and dust her dress. She looks at him with indistinct vision, sleepy eyes drifting under like a spell, as she tries to connect her right index finger with her right eye to force a clearer vision. Her body slowly rocks back and forth as if she was going to tumbled back into the chair. He gently forces her direction, leading her to the dining hall where her mother sat in a chair next to a blazing fireplace, with a glass of *Bordeaux'* at her side. Melissa came to realize that the dining hall was her mother's favorite place and most often she would find her next to a burning fire and sipping wine. On rough nights with her father, she would have her share of the hard stuff—Scotch, Whiskey, or any other strong liquor that met her fancy.

"Come, my dear. Come over here," her mother said in a soft spoken remorse voice, but with a firm smile of affection. "Please come and have a seat next to your mother." She directed Melissa to sit down, waving with her gloveless left hand, with the right hand covered in a solid white handcrafted glove with the initials M-C on the sleeve. As a child, Melissa did not fully understand why her mother wore gloves in the middle of the summer, but with age, she understood that it was one of her father's unusual requests. The Contour Estate was an immaculate polished house, inside and out. Her father requested that his servants work overtime, if needed to keep the place tidy, and everyone that came in contact with his food or beverage must wear a fresh pair of white gloves on each occasion. Melissa's mom had just given her father his night cap—a double shot of strong Irish whiskey, straight no ice, and a glass of Crown Royal and coke on the rocks as a chaser.

Melissa paused for a moment when she first entered the room and looked up at Ramon with sleepy sad eyes.

"Go on now, your mother wants you to sit next to her," Ramon said, looking at Melissa with an out of place smile, then looks over at Melissa's mother and added, "I apologize Madam Contour, she has just waken up. I wake her in the corridor."

"That's fine. I had a feeling she would be there waiting on William to arrive," Melissa's mother stated as she took a deep breath and looked up to the ceiling, eyes rolled. Looking in irritation, she beaked for Melissa to regain her senses and come to her at once. Practically shouting, "You and that damn uncle of yours. Come to me at once, enough of this nonsense."

"Where is uncle? I waited and waited, but he did not show. He said he would be here this week, right?" Managing a soft stream of words to leave her mouth, as tears filled her eyes; she walked toward her mother and spoke again, "Mother, was uncle not going to come today?"

"Oh, my dear child, your uncle has been in a terrible accident. He will not be coming today. He will not be coming ever again. Your uncle was killed in a car crash racing over here to get to you." Her words quickly rolled off her tongue in a soft relaxed voice. Her sympathetic nature was not sympathetic at all. Her words raced out of her mouth as if she was telling an enjoyable bedtime story. Melissa no longer embraced the idea that her parents would ever treat her as they loved her and found their indifference to be genuinely absurd. Her mother was not as cruel as her father, but the pathetic nature of her disposition suggest coldness as learned behavior, and agreeability to avoid conflict. Melissa stop longing for love and compassion from her parents many years ago and her mother felt it, but turned the other cheek.

Melissa could not believe what her mother was saying. She watched her mother's graceful demeanor as she spoke those horrible words without batting an eye. She reached for her glass of wine, sophisticatedly took a sip, with little concern to what Melissa was saying. It seemed to have come natural for her. It appeared that she wanted William to die just so Melissa could be alone again and give up the insane ideas that her uncle planted in her head, Melissa thought. "What are you saying, mother?" Melissa finally worked up the courage to say, loudly, as the tears packed her eyes and swallowed up her face. "I don't understand, *Mother.* Where is my uncle?" Melissa shouted with a song to her words, "Where is my Uncle, *Mother*?"

"Your uncle is never coming back and you will need to understand that. Now, go get changed out of that fancy dress and prepare yourself for supper." Melissa's mother looked at her with firm eye contact and handed an order. No remorse ever entered her face. No tear ever fell. No strong drink was ever prepared. What seem to be a remorse feeling when she first entered the room; was not remorse at all, but a piece of resentment of the love Melissa felt for her uncle. With her mother seeming gratified to speak the words to Melissa that her uncle was dead, her feeling of sadness did not sway across her face for the lost of her own brother.

William was her mother's oldest and only brother. Born to a Caucasian and Indian mother and a Caucasian father, put William in a better class than her mother, thought Melissa's mother. His stringy blonde hair, pale white skin, almost alabaster looking, big blue gorgeous eyes, narrow nose, and attractive physique gave him all the attributes of a White Man. And Melissa's mother had a widen nose, full pouty lips, darken skin tone, long thick hair—covered in reddish-brown dye—gave a questionable appearance of a White Woman. Which was questionable to Melissa's father, but he made his own assumption until he stumbled upon the truth. Melissa's grandmother had shared the story of their nationality on impulse, and had been ashamed to admit it before that day, but old age got the best of her and secrets unintentionally surfaced.

Melissa's mother remained in competition with her brother, but with no participation from him. She invented meaningless competitive games raging wars against her brother all through their childhood. She believed he was superior to her and every one admired him because he was *more* White than she. Many years had passed since their times as youths, but Melissa's mother continued to hold bitterness toward her brother, for reasons that would never be known to Melissa.

Melissa ran out of the dining hall and upstairs to her room, crying her eyes out. She heard her father yell, "Pull yourself together. I don't want to see that sob face at supper." She slammed her bedroom door as hard as she could, which could not be heard no more than a few feet with the size of the house, and shouted a song of words that only she could hear, "Forget you, forget both of you. I can't wait until I leave this stupid place. Neither of you even care 'bout me. The only somebody that cared about me is gone." She flopped down on her queen size bed face first and cried herself to sleep.

~

"I guess, when my uncle died, that was my moment of feeling irrelevant. He was the only person in my life that understood me, that catered to my needs (as a child), and that seem to love me. Not even my children love me all that much. Timothy blames me for his father being the way he was. And Kathleen blames me for sticking around too long and letting her father get away with murder, according to her observation. For years I blamed myself for my uncle's death because of the way my mother stated that he died coming to see me." Melissa looked over at Evelyn with a subtle smile. "My life has been smoke and mirrors all the way through. I believe I spiraled out of control after that day. My friends became few. My presence at the dinner table began to vanish. Mother and father could care less one way or the other, showing no signs of compassion or concern for my whereabouts.

ALINA

Our house was big enough to get lost in, and so I did. After a few years had passed, I rarely saw or spoke to my mother or father, except when we had to paint a family portrait to the world at one of dad's public outings, like a story in the Detroit Newspaper or in *US Weekly* or something of that capacity. But—when I turned eighteen, my dad bought me a Porsche'. For the life of me, I never understood why. He just came home one day and told Ramon to find me. As I entered his study, I found him smoking a fancy imported cigar, fireplace roaring, with a complex look upon his face."

Melissa entered the dim lit study with most of the light reflecting from the fire emerged from the custom crafted brick fireplace. Along the walls were rolls of books, neatly placed inside the built-in bookshelf. The books had always intrigued her, but she would not dare to touch them. Portraits of Lady Macbeth, work by an exquisite artist named *Kandinsky*, and a unique unknown artist oil painting of a handsome couple, not known to Melissa, hung orderly on the walls. Her father sat behind an old desk made of fine maple wood with a dark finish, legs crossed and waved for Melissa to sit down. "Come in, have a seat." He glanced at the seat adjacent to him. "You are what, eighteen now?" Her father questioned with a grim look across his face, tapping his cigar ashes in an expensive looking tray; small in diameter—circular, sitting on top of a thick glass with a gold trimmed map of the United States of America underneath, nailed in all four corners of the desk.

"Yes," Reluctant to respond of course, wondering why the hell he was asking.

Still standing.

"I think it is time for you to have your own vehicle. Since I have not been active in your life, I have no idea what you like so I took the liberty of picking out something myself. You will never meet new people being cooped up in this old house."

"He turned to hand me the keys with a smug look on his face and told me to go out with some of my friends and have a good time. The car was smaller than I had imaged from seeing it on TV. The red color shined with the sunlight and with the top down I could fit two, maybe three of my friends comfortably.

I said thank you and left the room. Nothing more was ever said about that day in his study. I found out later that my mom was not aware of the car purchase; I can assume she did not care either way." Melissa repositioned herself in the corner of the sofa and took another deep breath. "Are you bored with my story so far?" she said with smiling eyes and flush cheeks. Melissa appearing slightly exhausted from talking, breathing deeply knowing she has only scratched the surface. Looking at Evelyn, who seemed to be absorbed by her story, resting her right cheek against the fist of her right hand while her elbow was pressed into the back of the sofa. Insomnia had not set in, so Melissa shook her head slowly and waited for a response, which was barely a wait at all.

"I am listening with open ears, nothing bores me. I am actually quite entertained by your mother and father's unloving tenacity toward you. It's quite intriguing how parents with so much to offer give so little and yet they seem to not blink an eye on the monstrous decisions that they made regarding your well being. It always seems to overwhelm my heart with grief for those parents and spouses for that matter that take their relationships for granted. Your father gave you that car to get you out of the house. He had a reputation to uphold and you needed to be married by a

certain timeframe or it would be detrimental to the family name."
Evelyn spoke firmly and with conviction, as her hands swayed
from side to side with her interlocking them as her last word
denounced.

"You know…you are very passionate when you speak."
Evelyn smiled.

"Well, driving my new car did not get me into as much
trouble as you would imagine. Red cars are perfect magnets for the
police, so a few citations were handed out; for reckless driving,
indecent exposure, and speeding. The only *real* trouble that I
encountered was with my so called friends. Hanging out with all
those rich kids who took life for granted was as exhausting as the
story I tell today. They drove around with mommy's and daddy's
car, crashing them, letting their friends drive drunk. It was pathetic.
I will admit, I hung with the wrong crowd in my early teens, which
led me to my lifelong dilemma today, but, I did not try to take
others with me through my journey to hell. I didn't think that I was
above my so-called friends, but I could not understand some of the
things they did. My uncle taught me a lot of things about life that
they had no clue about. They were only concerned with the issues
surrounding them at that time—like deceiving their parents, getting
high, or having sex. I eventually got to a point, when I didn't care. I
had no one to talk to and I felt no one understood me. I suspect in
some way, I had become one of my friends; not caring about what
the effects of my actions would have on another person. I felt I
had nothing to live for, so I inhaled the grass and inebriated myself
to the highest capacity level. Giving my mind and body to the
idiots that did not like me was something that I never thought I
would do. Devouring my soul with horrific temptations reaching a
high that took me away from my inadequacies, ultimately taking me

to another world where I could be happy and my mere presence be meaningful. No such place existed in my world. No such place existed at home with my parents or with my so-called friends.

As I inhaled the drugs, peace began to take over my body, relaxing my muscles as I lay back, on whom ever sofa we happen to be crashed on, with my eyes closed, picturing my uncle walk through the door with a mountain of gifts and smiles. He was my salvation. He was my only hope for a better life and now he was gone. With mixed-up emotions flaring and unworthy feelings knocking at my door, running into the arms of the first man that said I was somebody was inevitable. His name was Steven Bestitch. Steven was a gentle soul…when he wanted to be. He had a wild side, but only activated when provoked by his buddies. He was easily influenced but I didn't care. He showed me the attention I was longing for. Steven was very smart but let his stupidity get in the way of his decisions. Decisions based on getting his friends to think he was the coolest. Decisions based on who can top that and get high the fastest or drink the most without vomiting. Yeah, he was an idiot alright, but he was my idiot. He was the start of my horrendous life."

Chapter

5

MOVING THROUGH the crowd; swaying hips, flat open-toed black Guess sandals (nothing fancy), tight fitting Guess Jeans, with a white tank top. Renée was dressed to fit the atmosphere on this particular Saturday night at Club X in downtown Detroit. Men and women eyes connected with Renée's body. She was what you would call…'built like a brick house.' Renée's ethnicity was Hispanic and Black. Her mother was Hispanic and her father was Black. Her hair was the fierce trait responsible for capturing her beauty. Her black long natural curly hair with subtle blond highlights hung just above her butt. Renée's long neck and back presented a more flattering appeal to her average height. Her light tone skin color glowed with the lighting of the club revealing almost perfectly smooth skin. Her gorgeous gray bedroom eyes melted the souls of men and captured the hatred from most women. Her long pointed nose, spacious eyes, and middling size lips added unique features to her overall look. Her small slightly oval shaped head with an angular shaped jawbone was the added bonus that captivated her attractiveness, making her unforgettable to the poor souls that laid eyes on her. She walked in confidence, but did not like to draw much attention. Most of the attention she received was ignored and shunned off with no regret. Renée went to the clubs to dance and have a good time, mostly with her girls. Most nights, Renée and her girls would dance together all night—no men at all. That's what was so intriguing to men about her; she went through the night without as much as a hello to the men that surrounded her. If approached, she would continue dancing while moving her body closer to a chair or to one of her girls that happen to be on the floor dancing at that time. Not a word would be spoken even when spoken to. But the men never stopped trying. Eventually, she would have to wave her hand, messaging him to go away. Whenever Sydney, Renée's best friend, saw a frowned expression upon Renée's face, Sydney knew to intervene quickly or someone's feelings would get hurt. And, it was not Renée's feelings Sydney was worried about!

Being a thirty-six year old single mother of four, Renée has had her share of charming sweep-you-off-your-feet men. Divorced for three years now, seems like time has accelerated ninety miles per hour. When she was married, some five and a half odd years, time crept on by with never ending days, grueling fights, and relentless lovemaking. Renée's flaw, at least one of them, is that she is foolish. Foolish in believing some of the amazing stories her boyfriends came up with. Still believing the, *"I went to a lingerie store to pick my mother up something,"* stories that men told. We can believe that her foolishness has still convinced her that her knight in shining armor will rise and sweep her off her feet, as soon as he get a job and move out of his mother's house.

The sounds of *50 Cent* cascaded through the club and the crowd roared. Renée got off the bar stool and started moving her hips slowly from side to side. As she rolled her hips and belly like a belly dancer, she waved her hand for Angel to join her on the floor. Angel Martinez was another close girlfriend of Renée's who partied with them often. Angel was Renée's partner on the floor. "Come on girl…this is my jam."

"Okay, okay, let me put down my drink," Angel said, as she hurried to the floor. "Damn, I spilt some on my beautiful blouse."

"Girl, you are shining all over the place." Renée and Angel started laughing while Angel dusts off her blouse. "You are leaving a trail of glitter everywhere. Look at the floor." Renée pointed out as they looked down on the floor and started laughing again.

"Girl, you are not lying. I have glitter everywhere. Damn, I can't hide from anyone with this shirt," Angel said while slowly dancing across the dance floor, smiling. Angel was known for her unique and very sensual attire. Her cleavage was typically revealed and her skirts were usually very short to accentuate her gorgeous legs. With four-inch heels, her height was complimentary to Renée's but she still had to tilt her head up slightly to look up at Renée.

With the song ending and a techno beat gradually moving in, Angel and Renée eased their way back to the bar. Angel grabbed her Amarelle Sour and began sipping again. Before long, she was ordering her third drink and feeling real good by the fifth one, topping off with a Heineken. Angel did not drink often, but when the mood hit her, she took it to the extreme. Being five feet five inches and petite, you would think that after two drinks she would hit the floor. Angel's alcohol consumption could tolerate more than just a few drinks and her appearance remain the same throughout the night—except maybe for her conversation.

"I think I am going to have a drink tonight," Renée said,

out of the blue with a bright smile.

"What…you never drink. What are you going to have?"Almost spilling her drink, Sydney asked and continued, "You don't know what to get!"

"Well, I'll taste yours and then I'll taste Angel's and see which one I want."

"Okay, here, taste mine first," Angel suggested.

"Okay." Renée takes a sip, frown faced and contemplated for a few moments as the wrinkles disappeared that suddenly formed across her forehead. "This is too sour or sweet or something. I don't know, I don't think I like that one."

"Yeah, but they sneak up on you. You never know what hit you," Angel said as she took another drink, nearly devouring the entire drink in one gulp.

"Okay Sydney, lets taste yours. What are you drinking anyway?"

"I'm drinking Long Island Ice Tea."

"Ice Tea…is that an alcoholic beverage or what?" Renée starts to laugh and Sydney looked at her with amazement.

"Girl, Yeah. This drink is a little strong. Here, taste it." Sydney hands her the drink and Renée takes a tiny sip. "Did you even taste it," Sydney shouted, looking at the glass with no visible movement to the liquid substance inside.

Renée frowned as her body shook, moving her head quickly from side to side as if she had the shivers. "You are right, that drink is strong. I just want a drink today; can they water it down or something?"

"Yes, they can. Just go ask the bartender," Angel said, waving a twenty to catch the bartender's attention.

"Yes, what can I get you beautiful ladies?" The bartender

questioned with eyes fixated on Renée as Angel read the order.

"Hey, buddy, did you get that?" Angel shouted, waving her twenty dollar bill closer to his face.

"Yes beautiful, I got it." He turned to wink and smile at Angel.

"Smooth talk will only get you so far and tonight it's not working," Angel added as she handed him the twenty with a grim gaze.

"Ok darling. No need to get your panties in a bunch. I'll bring those drinks right over."

"Thank you," Angel stated in a sarcastic tone.

Angel turns to face Sydney and Renée, eyes rolled, deep breath released. "Fuckin men. So damn pathetic."

"I know, I don't think he heard you because he was mesmerized by Renée," Sydney proclaimed.

"Girl, I didn't notice. I told you I don't pay these men no mind," Renée confirmed, flicking her wrist with a twist of her hand.

"Watch...I bet you he gets the drinks wrong, particularly yours Renée," Angel suggested looking to the other end of the bar as she watched the bartender screw up their order.

~

As the night progressed, the ladies migrated to a booth seat in the far end of the club. From here, they could see the dance floor; watch the door to scope out the fine brothers that walked through; laugh at the desperate women glued to their men or a man in the club; and talk shit amongst each other.

"Owwww, girl, look at that tall drink of water over there! Look how he's moving on the dance floor. Yeah, I bet he can get down in the bedroom," Renée surprisingly stated with Angel and Sydney turning to view.

They look at each other and start laughing.

"Girl, you are a mess," Angel said but totally agreeing. "He looks like our friend, Trenton. The gentleman we use to work with, doesn't he Renée?"Angel recalled.

"Yes he does. Trenton looked like he could get down too." Renée smiles and the others laugh, and then she added, "I wonder do they sit in the club like us and talk about women."

Angel immediately interrupted, "Yes they do! I am quite sure of it." All the ladies start to laugh as they sip their drinks. "See; look at that guy over there with the Down Low expression on his face. I'm not sure if he is checking out the women or the men…hell, maybe both. You know what gets me…how are we suppose to know if he is looking at me or my brother…hell, maybe even my father?"

Renée laughed, spraying Long Island all over Sydney. "Girl, you are nuts! Oh, I'm sorry Sydney, but Angel is crazy."

"Nuts is right. Do we know if he wants the walnuts below or the coconuts up top, I don't know? My coconuts may not be enough for him. Hell, tell me and I may want to share in the fun."Angel stated excitingly, and then added, "Give me a chance, let me know how you feel, maybe we can work it out. You don't have to be on the Down Low (DL). See what it is, it's the excitement of doing something forbidden. It's really not the fact that they prefer men over women, it's the thrill they're after. But, it really proves that men will stick it in any hole available. It's the pleasure of putting it where ever their little heart's desire. Men are dogs, plain and simple. And, just like dogs they like to hump everything with a pulse (hell, a pulse may not need to be included).

I know you've gone to your friend's house or aunt's house and the dogs were glued to your leg, humping away."

Everyone begins to laugh hysterically. Angel smiled but her facial expression remained the same and she continued, "Come on ladies, you know what I mean. I think just about every man has the potential to have sex with another man. All men have a feminine side, and that's fine, but others venture off and like to explore their feministic qualities and develop them into something more. You know, I think they all have a little sugar in their tank. *Ladies*, we haven't got a fighting chance." With everyone still laughing, and Angel managing to get in a chuckle or two, she starts on another subject. "Now, lets get back to the men who *do* want to have sex with women *only*, that may be few and far in between, but what the hell. Can they work with what they got? *Not!* Girl, I don't know how many times I had to walk away dissatisfied because he thought he was doing it up right. It's my own fault, I should have stopped him and told him that he was horrible....don't you think? I mean, why can't we be honest with men? Why can't we say, in a polite non-criticizing sort of way, you *suck*. You stroke like you're running to catch a boat that is departing to leave you behind on a deserted island. I mean really, why can't we say that? They are quick to tell us about something that they do not like or would like for us to do. We so kindly become admissive to their needs, even when it is not our reality. We should be able to admit any truth to men and have an adult discussion without it being about their ego. Yes, you have those few who want to be told that he is not awakening the tiger inside you. But, how can you tell who is for real and who is playing the part. Most of them beg to be told how to please a woman, but very few act on the advice."

"Oh man, Angel has gotten loose," Renée stated the

obvious as she took another tiny sip of her Long Island. She repositioned herself in her seat and listened attentively.

"I know, I'm drunk. But that's okay." Angel turned her head away from the dance floor and smiled at Renée and Sydney.

Soon, a stranger joined them at their booth. She stated that she heard the laughter and wanted to see what the excitement was about, "I know it's not the men in here," she quickly intervened, glancing around the room. Everyone chuckled and welcomed The Stranger. After all, Sydney and Angel were feeling pretty good and Renée didn't care one way or the other, as long as she did not sit next to her. Renée had a thing about people touching or sitting close to her. The Stranger added, "Are you guys like dogging men over here or what?"

"Probably a bit of both," Angel replied. Everyone hysterically laughed, including The Stranger.

"Oh, so you're the one that has this section live," The Stranger shouted, trying to be heard over the loud music while stroking her dark long wavy hair pushing it to the back. She could have stood in the category with Renée, but she was not a threat. She was pretty, slightly sleazy but not too bad. The Stranger seemed to know when to compose herself and when to let loose. Yeah, Angel liked her, Sydney thought she was cool; Renée didn't seem to mind her presence, but from a distance.

Angel gulped the remainder of her drink in one swallow, slams the glass on the table and said, "I want another drink, but I don't need one." Sydney agreed. "What the hell, I'll have one more and call it quits. Someone fetch me the tender. That tender guy over there. Well, don't know how tender he is, maybe we should ask him. Why are we so afraid to ask these men questions? Like; what's your name, where were you born, have you ever had sex

51

with another man, can you 'F' or are your moves on the dance floor misleading? That thing I saw jumping in your pants, what size might that be? We should not be afraid to ask such questions."

"Man, you are drunk…but I couldn't agree with you more. We should be able to ask those questions," The Stranger stated, appearing to be shocked by the comments, but in a good way.

"Take that tall drink of *Absolute* over there for instance. It appears he may be hiding something special in the air." All the women laughed and Angel continued, "It's got to be at least eight inches. Don't you think?"

"I need at least eight or nine," Renée said.

"Well, my husband is certainly fully packaged in that department but lacks the motion in the ocean," said Sydney.

Everyone sighed harmoniously, "*OH NO!*" And they laughed uncontrollably, gasping for a breath as the tears created by the laughter slowly ran down their faces.

"But, he's a sweetheart, isn't he? He has other qualities that make you say *yes*, Right?" Angel shouted over the laughter.

"You got it. That's my baby," Sydney proclaimed with true feelings.

"Now, would he still love you if it were you who were lacking something, or go and find himself another?"Angel replied, searching for a truthful response.

Everyone looked at Angel, including Sydney, and said, "Probably find another." The ladies practically fell from their seats in the midst of laughter.

~

Renée gazed across the club, slightly tipsy from the one drink. "Okay ladies, I guess it is time for us to go. Maybe on my way out I can find someone to go home with me tonight." All the ladies started to laugh.

The Stranger smiled with gleam and glanced around the room and added, "I could go home with you. It would be better than selecting one of these *'I'll call you tomorrow'* and you wishing he wouldn't guys." The laughter continued and Renée accepted her proposal.

"I think you're right. Come on, you can come with me." Renée slowly stood from her seat, slightly rocked back and forth, and motioned for The Stranger to follow.

Angel was drunk, Sydney was next in line and no one should have been driving home that night. Angel went to her car and Renée handed her keys to The Stranger and demanded that she drive. "You look the least blasted out of us, here, you drive! Wait, can you drive?"

"Yes, I can drive. I had one beer tonight."

"How did you get here?" Sydney asked The Stranger with wonder in her eyes.

"My friends and I got here about ten-thirty and most of them left at twelve-forty five or so. I just live up the street here. See those apartments across the street...I live there so I could walk home," The Stranger responded as she tried to place the car keys back in Renée's hand.

"Oh...I don't care one way or the other, I was just wondering," Sydney explained as she flopped her bottom in the front passenger seat of Renée's Cadillac Escalade. Taking another glance at the apartments across the street, Sydney added, "Wait a minute, you stay at the Lofts across the street?"

The Stranger, standing next to the passenger side of the truck, responded, "Yes...."

Before she could say another word, Renée quickly interrupted, "Look, we can have this discussion on the road. Get in the damn car and drive. We are going to take Sydney home first. She lives on the East Side. Do you know how to get to Sixteen Mile and Gratiot?"

"Yeah, I know where that is. I have a cousin that stays over there," The Stranger confirmed.

"Good, then let's go!" Renée barked while climbing into the back seat of the truck.

The Stranger starts the truck and straps on her seat beat. She looks over at Sydney who was positioning herself quite comfortably in the front passenger seat but without her seat belt. The Stranger waited for a while and stated, "Sydney, can you put your seat belt on?"

"Look, just drive the damn car. She'll put it on when she gets ready," Renée shouted from the back seat.

"Then maybe you should drive. We are going too far for her to relax in the front seat without a seat belt." The firmness in The Stranger's voice was surprising to Renée. Although surprise should not have been a reaction since she did not know The Stranger at all. Renée's eyes widen, her head jerk back and her neck bent toward the right side of her body.

Sydney sat up in the seat and agreed, "She's right Renée. I am putting it on now. Please, just drive so she can shut up. She's okay. Her bark is worse than her bite." Sydney smiled at The Stranger while buckling her seat belt. "Hey, you never answered my question. So you live in the Lofts downtown?"

"I sure do."

"Those apartments are what…thirteen-hundred a month?" Sydney delicately frowned, sweeping her eyes across The Stranger's clothing with one glance. The Stranger was wearing a black glitter halter top, a mini skirt with an inch split in the front on the right side and four inch red heels that strapped up to her calf. Her choice of clothing was tasteless, but she carried a Burberry handbag, red. Stella wondered if it was a knock-off.

"Try fourteen-hundred and fifty. I got it for a deal because the unit typically goes for nineteen-hundred a month."

"*What!* How big is your unit?" Sydney questioned with inquisitive ears.

"My loft is about sixteen-hundred square feet." The Stranger answered.

"Ohh, where do you work?" Sydney said looking moderately surprised.

The Stranger softly laughed, and then answered, "I'm a hair stylist. I run a salon on West Seven Mile Road, right off Evergreen Road."

"I know where that is. Right next to the Arapaho Market!" Sydney gesturing her hands in the direction of Seven Mile. Then she added, "You make that kind of money that you can stay there?"

"Well, I do make good money but I don't use my money to pay my rent. One of my friend *boys* picks up the tab. My loft is paid up for eight more months," The Stranger insisted with a smile across her face.

"Oh, you got a sugar daddy with a wife!" Sydney started to laugh and Renée joined in.

"No, she's got a drug dealer with a generous wallet," Renée added in a sarcastic tone.

"You are correct. He has two baby momma's, a long term relationship of fifteen years, and another girlfriend on the side, not including me," The Stranger stated with sureness.

"Aren't you bothered by that at all?" Sydney asked.

"No, it doesn't bother me because I know where I stand. I don't need to compete with his other women because they know about me too and his interests in each of us are uniquely different. We are all in this together, so-to-speak. He established the communication from the start. As far as I know, he has been honest with me regarding his other relationships from day one. I have been involved with him for over five years and we have a good time together. Some women could not handle this type of relationship, but for me, this is all I know. Most of my relationships resulted in me being the other woman and that's fine as long as the other woman or women know about me. I draw the line at being someone's mistress or being the cheating spouse's girlfriend. I don't want to have that label hanging over my head."

"Wow, I would never have looked at it like that. I didn't think those kind of relationships existed. You hear some people say that the spouse or girlfriend knew about the other woman and you think to yourself, yeah right. If she knew about the other women she would have left his ass so fast. I see now that is not always true. This is a good example of how effective communication is and what some women will tolerate."

"Well, you've got to be a fair participant. I never looked at it as something that I am tolerating from him because I get what I want. I have my boy associates, *as I like to call them*, too. Although he would freak if he knew to what extent." She laughed, and then continued, "If you are the jealous type or you like to bleach your man's clothes over petty shit, then you could not be in this kind of relationship. One of my girlfriends bleached her man's clothing when she caught him with another woman. I made her aware of the fact that she bought the clothes she had destroyed. She laughed about it and agreed that it was a stupid thing to do. But—, she didn't regret doing it. She stated that she wanted to prove a point to him, but I beg to differ. I wanted to know what point was being made from watching a man's clothes burn in the middle of the street. It was to let him know that she knew about the relationship and that she was upset, she stated. And I told her I understood her being upset but could not see how her reaction proved her point. I mean, what do you gain by lashing out at your man? For me, it just proves how immature and insane you are and that you allowed his actions to take your mind to another level. Some women do not understand or know themselves enough to trust the actions that they say they would not do. They think they can handle it but later they find out that they can't. This goes for some men too, especially in thinking that they can handle a sexual relationship with a woman without getting deeply involved and later he finds out that he is not able to control himself." The Stranger's intellectual tone captured her audience's attention.

Reminiscing on a chapter in her past when she became sexually involved with one of her ex's, Carlos. Carlos was a charming, sophisticated gentleman, but let him tell it, he was a plain ordinary guy. His two hundred and ten pound frame was muscular and proportionate in all areas, including his ass, she recalled. His butt was one of his better features for The Stranger. She loved his big hands that held her bottom tight. He was her sex slave. When she needed it, he was there to give it to her—day or night. She established in the beginning that their relationship would be *strictly sexual* and he was more than understanding. Their no-holds bare sex was only restricted by their imagination. There was nothing that The Stranger would not do, aside from whips and chains.

As time went on and the intensity began to thicken, Carlos started to develop feelings for her that was not part of the bargain, so she decided to call it quits. The Stranger could not take the multiple phone calls and crude manipulative messages saying, "Oh, so you don't want to answer my calls. Are you with another guy or something? Call me if you're not too busy? So, what's up, you don't want to talk to me anymore?" It became overwhelmingly pathetic. After a month of persistent phone calls, she decided to meet with him one last time…

Before she could finish her thought, she came back to reality. As the memory exited her mind, she gazed onto the road for a moment.

"Are you okay?" Sydney said, noticing the intense disposition.

It took a moment for The Stranger to respond and then she said, "I am fine, just thinking about a time in my past. It was nothing." She was still slightly gazed, thinking how awful she felt after having sex with Carlos that night. It was not like one of the magical nights she had before, it was almost repulse. That was the last time she would ever see him again.

Renée sat in the back seat, directly behind The Stranger observing the entire conversation as The Stranger drove across town. Renée thought she may have misjudged The Stranger. Realizing that she never got her name, still, she didn't bother with asking. Renée thought, just as Sydney did, that The Stranger at first glance may be a little trashy but in a subtle way. During the long ride to Sydney's house, Renée came to the conclusion that The Stranger was only ghetto in her appearance but intellectually confident in her expressions. She was not some club girl who was simply looking for a good time from one of the useless men at the club; it seemed that she had another agenda in mind. Renée would not have guessed in a million years that The Stranger was a business owner. Long before the business owner announcement, Renée immediately become very trusting of The Stranger—another one of her familiar flaws. Renée tends to trust on impulse without thinking things through. She had no genuine information to go on regarding The Stranger's fascinating story, yet she believed her.

Renée has trusted her life and the life of her children in the hands of strangers on more than several occasions. A time in particular would be when Tony, a man she had known for only a month, was invited to live with her and her children. Tony tried to make it obvious that he was interested in pursuing a deeper relationship with Renée, which she believed to be true until the stream of women started parading back and forth throughout her back yard. Tony claimed to be down on his luck and needed a place to stay because he did not want to be another grown ass man living at home with mom, so he decided to live off women instead. She offered to help him out for a few months until he got back on his feet. By month four, Renée had had enough of Tony.

There were several experiences like this one that Renée seemed to be drawn to. Yet she continues with the spontaneity of her actions that resulted in tonight's decision to welcome The Stranger into her palace.

Approaching Sydney's house, The Stranger asked Renée where she lived. Renée smiled and stated that she lived a lot further than this and she would direct her once Sydney made it out of the car and safely into the house. They approached a nice white framed house, with a well maintained lawn and a kid's tricycle standing on the small porch. The porch was practically engulfed by the flourished bushes on either side. A shadow of a body greeted Sydney at the door. With a vague view, The Stranger could only assume that the person at the door was Sydney's husband. Sydney said her goodbyes as she exited the vehicle. A few minutes later, Renée swiftly crawled from the back seat to the front passenger seat and fastened her seat belt. She looked over at The Stranger and smiled. The Stranger smiled back and put the car in drive.

"So, where to now?"

"I stay right off Thirty-Two Mile Road." Renée glanced at The Stranger to see her reaction. She was astounded that the statement hardly had any bearing on her demeanor. Believe it or not, Renée was a little shocked and impressed. She unambiguously thought that the stunned reaction would probably come when they approached the house.

Entering *The Willow Bend Estates* with the relaxing enchanting clear sky, the tall palm like trees that sheltered the lawns and the glow from the moonlight made it more appealing than ever before. The neighboring houses were huge and all looked to be very pricy, The Stranger thought. She was directed to continue driving down Paul Drive and make a right on Michael Street, then drive down to the end of the block to a cul-de-sac. It was apparent that The Stranger tried to hide her reactions, but a hint gleamed through her pours. Renée smiled inside as she glanced at The Stranger trying to conceal her emotions. As they approached the house, shock stood in and The Stranger blurted out, "I hope your husband isn't home!" She could not think of anything else to say aside from revealing that she was extremely mesmerized by the sight of Renée's home, but the *"Wow"* thoughts remained in her head. The Stranger had to say something to try and justify the expression on her face.

Renée's house practically covered the entire cul-de-sac lot. The lot was three fourth of an acre with mature trees and a tall slim bush on opposite sides of the entrance pressed closely against the front of the house. You could estimate the height of the ceilings from the chandelier that descended from the ceiling reflecting a romantic mood setting from the front window in the foyer. The triangular shaped entrance of the house was crafted in stone and the surrounding structure was designed with a mixture of brown and reddish brown Acme bricks. The front glass door had dark stained Burch wood trimming, a thin crafty floral design outlined in gold, and a light smog appearance cast throughout the glass, added a charming view as you approached the house. The curb appeal was breathtaking. With the outside of the home's beauty reflecting inside the house, it could market for no less than three quarters of a million dollars, The Stranger thought.

"Come on in, my kids are with grandma tonight."

"And your husband?" The Stranger asked to keep with the theme from a moment ago.

Renée laughed and said, "I don't have a husband...divorced, for three years now. I believe it was the best move that I ever made. My life has been better since. Most people are faced with agony, frustration, financial difficulty and the like during and after their divorce, but not me. I was liberated when I got my divorce. I am not saying divorce is a good thing, but it was for me. My husband was a two timing nothing. He forgets that he has children and he forgets to sign the damn check every month too. Sometimes, I have to send him reminders—you know, like a court date for not staying in compliance."

The Stranger starts to laugh as she shuffles across the front living room, admiring the size and the art work mirrored on the walls hinting at suggestions of Renée's culture and background, she thought. "My mom loved art work. She used to paint these magnificent portraits of life. They were amazing," The Stranger recalled while releasing a soft comfortable sigh.

"Do you have any hanging in your place?"

"No, my stepfather destroyed everything after my mom died."

"Oh, I am sorry to hear that, how did she die?" Renée asked with hesitant concern.

"It's a long story and I am not inclined to tell it just yet." The Stranger turned to smile at Renée but sensed that she was not amused by her response. "I just…well…"

"It's okay; it was just an inquisitive question. You can talk about it when you are ready."

Looking intently across the room trying to transition to a more common subject, "Are those your children?" She asked, glancing at a photograph with four children, a younger Renée, and a man of whom The Stranger suspected was her ex-husband.

"Yes. Those are my little darlings. Well, big darlings I should say. The three girls are Darianna age fifteen, McKenzie age eleven, and Lolita age eight. My son's name is Alan and he is thirteen years old."

"So, how long were you married?" The Stranger continued her questions as she positioned herself on the sofa, crossing her legs.

Renée placed her body right beside The Stranger and said with a long sigh, "About five or so long years. My ex-husband and I were together for thirteen years. I met him when Darianna was two years old. Darianna's father was more of a jerk than my ex-husband. He hasn't visited or called her in over eight years. My ex-husband adopted her when we were married—a lot of good that did. But, he spends more time with her than her biological father ever did. I figure, you can't have your cake and eat it too. My Ex doesn't see the kids as much as I think he should but he is still present in their lives. Between the overwhelming demand from his job as Vice-President of AtlantaSoft Technologies and swinging with the ladies, he manages to get in a day or two every other week."

"Why can't you have your cake and eat it too?" The Stranger asked with aggression.

"What!" Renée smiles and add, "I can't complain too much. My babies are healthy, they have a lavish roof over their heads, and he is still in their lives. Even if it is for an hour or two."

"That's the problem with us women, no matter which way the stick swings, we always get the short end. We seem to settle for just a little, when we deserve so much more. Your children deserve more. If half of the men stand up and be diligent fathers, juvenile delinquency would not be such a high factor in this country. I am not trying to preach or take this to another level, but why must the woman burden herself with all the challenges of raising children and the daddy's keep their nice cushy lifestyle?" The Stranger turns slightly to face Renée and gently grabs her hand. "I know you are probably doing great with your children, but wouldn't it make you and the kids feel better if he was more active in the growth of your children. Wouldn't it be wonderful if you could say, 'hell, it didn't work with us but look how he's doing with the kids'? I know, deep down in our hearts we don't like to settle but why do we give up so soon and utter the words, *'it's okay, he's doing his best'* or *'I expected this behavior from him'*. I believe that teaches our children that it is okay to settle for a dysfunctional parent. It's teaching our girls to be passive and accept the excuses of men to delay an altercation. That's what my mom did. She settled. She was too afraid to speak her mind and it cost her—her life."

Renée appearing grim at first but now calmer and the pieces to the puzzle connected as The Stranger's last words spilled out. Renée knew The Stranger seemed preoccupied when the question about her mother arose, trying to deviate from the subject. But no matter how many curves, turns, and bumps we dodge through, we find ourselves back at the same starting point but with less time than before, she thought. "I don't think I settled, and I do speak my mind most often, but I am sort of passive. I tend to let things slide when I shouldn't. I don't ask enough questions sometimes and I take people at face value. For instance, I welcomed you into my home on an impulse because you seemed trustworthy. Some of my decisions or choices have not been great but I learn from them or I learn to adapt. One of the things that women have been blessed with is the ability to adapt to the many changes of life. I believe the burden was put on women to raise the children because we can handle the different dilemmas that arise as our children's needs grow. Yes, most of us are forced into this way of life—being a single mother—but sometimes, for the sake of our children, we have to roll with the punches and move on. Occasionally, when we are married, we are still acting as a single parent because we absorb all the responsibilities. Even when we are tired, at our wits end, or exhausted from thinking about tomorrow, we still keep moving. Now, do you really think your mother settled or was she doing what she knew to keep you safe, fed and a roof over your head? I don't believe that I settled, I just couldn't afford to worry my head over the things that I could not change."

Puzzled for a moment…thinking, "I still believe she settled to a certain extent. My mother moved from the hands of the man who beat her to the point of no return, to the hands of the man who finally killed her. My father was an abusive man. I don't remember much about him because my mother worked up enough courage to leave him when I was five years old. I believe my memory may be hazy because of the circumstances surrounding the tragic events displayed to my eyes on a daily basis has forced me to temporarily forget the past. I do remember visiting my mom in the hospital when I was four. My father had beaten the energy out of her. I stood next to her bed as she was covered in head bandages, an arm cast, and her right leg suspended in the air in a sling. I thought—who could be this cruel and harsh. Her eyes were blackened by the mighty blows from his powerful fist. And the bruises I could not see were buried inside her chest—cracked ribs and a broken heart, I presumed. The doctors called it head trauma. I called it suicide. My mother endured five long arduous years with that man. After she was patched up and sent home, he cried on her shoulder for a week and vowed to never hurt her again. I went to my room and prayed for me to be bigger so I could kill him." The Stranger laughed and continued her story, "I blamed him for years for everything that he put my mother through, but as I got older I realized that she allowed herself to be in that position. Maybe that was all she knew but I wanted one question answered… 'Why did she think that was enough for her'?

I still ponder over the details and try to rationalize her thoughts while fighting with my own stubborn frame of mind. Finally, something overwhelmed my mother and she packed a few of our things in the middle of the night and tip-toed out into the mid November chilly air with no shoes, one bag, and my favorite

Barbie doll. I did not feel the cold air that hit my amateur face, nor the cold moistness from the ground. I was smiling from ear to ear; glad to see the distance between me and the *house of cruelty*. That's what I named the house. To bear through some of the events, I pretended that I was escaping from *The House of Cruelty*. I would put on different shows where I would escape, get bigger and come back as a giant and squash my father. Oh, the imagination of a child."

Renée agreeing, "Yes, children are delightful creatures. You seem to turn out fine, what happened? They say girls that witness abuse as a child grow up to think that it is okay. Like me, my mother was passive in her early years. I heard stories of my mother getting beat by my father when she was younger, just a teenager herself, fifteen, and he was in his late twenties. But growing up, I remember my mom slapping him around a few times with a boyfriend in one room and my father living in another room. I don't know what that set-up was about, but it was understood that he was not to put his hands on her ever again. We've taken some mess off the men in our lives. It may have taken us a while to catch on to the bull but when we did your ass was history." They both laugh.

As quickly as The Stranger laughed, it ended abruptly as she looked deep into Renée's eyes with untainted anger.

"I was not taking that shit! *Not off any man*. If my father would come to me now and try to put his hands on me, I would be in someone's prison after leaving the hospital because the doctors would have to surgically remove my foot from his ass. I told myself early on that I would be in charge of my own destiny, as much as we can be in charge. I was not going to let a man decide my fate. This brings me to the current relationship, along with past ones, where I feel like I am in control. This way, I can still enjoy the comfort of a man's presence without getting too close. I admit that I have fears about being hurt by a man, but I prayed that it would not be physical abuse."

"But, do you think that you are in control? I am sure you see him when it is convenient for him, not for you. Is the control you have really different from the control your mother had? You've changed the scenery but not the situation. See, the situation boils down to determining what is best for you and what you can live with. Abuse is a horrific act but she probably felt like she could handle it if it meant a roof over your head. She may have felt that she could not do it alone or would bear that pain so she would not be alone. I can only speculate how your mother felt but you have her inside you. You don't want to be alone, so you choose to be in this unstable relationship, no matter how stable you think it is. Sometimes we do all that is necessary to be in the comforting arms of a man, *why?* Because it feels good. We bend over backwards, we *settle*, we take the beatings, we beat our own heads against the wall *(even if he doesn't)* just to get a good whiff of his masculine fragrance. There is a very thin line between love and hate and the problem is finding where the love line ends and the hatred begin.

We search for ourselves inside another, most often a man. We define ourselves through our worldly relationships instead of searching within ourselves to determine who we are. I am guilty of the male factor myself. Most of us act out vigorously because of the relationships we are in: being a target for aggression, allowing men to take precedence over us; women who are willing to fight another woman over a man's decision; women who specially search high and low for the best husband, at any cost; the woman who degrades a man and scorches him for the next woman. The

ALINA

list goes on and on."

"You make very good points, but I don't understand how my decision is in the same ball park as my mother's," The Stranger said with a melancholy facial expression. She wanted Renée to shed some light on the subject. Deep inside she knew Renée was on the right track but she needed to hear it from someone else. For years she was bewildered by the actions or inactions of her mother, blaming her for her own transgressions. But being in her current relationship has made her realize that that may have been all that her mother knew to be.

"Your mother, for reasons unknown to me, stayed in that abusive relationship because of something she wanted, not something he wanted. It was about her needs. Her needs could have been to be sure you had a roof over your head or food to eat. Her motives could have been directed by guilt. She could have been more self-absorbed and just wanted to be in the arms of a man, even if it meant her life. Your mother was probably a sweet warmhearted lady who would give the shirt off her back for anyone but would not give herself the one thing *she* needed, the benefit of the doubt. She believed that was what she needed to do to get what she wanted.

By the same token, you are just the same. You are in this relationship to benefit you. Hell, most people are! If you do not benefit from the relationship, why enter into it. But, what sets both of you in the same direction is the reasoning behind the action. You both felt that the situations you encountered were the best for you. To be with a man, she risked her life. To be with a man, you risk yours. Your life may not be at risk with physical abuse but your abuse lies elsewhere, emotionally and spiritually. Your risk lies in the hands of the other women that he is messing around with too. With all the diseases that are out there, we need to be more careful of our sexual partners. Although, I must admit that I am guilty of that as well. Like I said before, I am too trusting. But, I think your biggest risk is the emotional damage that you are doing to yourself, even if you may not see it. Now…do you think you will be able to handle that?"

The Stranger slowly drops her chin and Renée witnessed a tear drop fall onto her right knee. She was bemused by the comments Renée presented but felt the truth emerge from her aching heart. She realized that she was hiding behind an act as thick as the make belief plays she put on as a child. The Stranger's mission tonight was to obtain a sense of direction, yet she didn't understand it. She thought by coming out tonight, she would be able to ease her mind and reconstruct her way of thinking, yet she was puzzled by how. Be careful what you wish for, she thought.

Renée moves in closer to The Stranger and stretches her arm out to wipe the tears from The Stranger's face. She placed her hand across her cheek gracing her hand slowly across her face. Renée moved The Stranger's chin up toward her with her right index finger and her thumb. The Stranger glanced up at Renée and smiled with frantic tears rolling off her face. Renée used the bottom half of her shirt to wipe away the tears. Her shirt was eventually drenched from the flow of tears but she didn't care. Renée moved The Stranger's head closer and positioned it in her lap. She stroked her hair as she whispered, "Shhhh. It's okay, it's okay. I bet you haven't cried like this in a long while." Both of the ladies start to laugh uncontrollably.

"No, I haven't cried this hard since my mother died and that was about ten years ago." As Renée continued to run her fingers through The Stranger's hair; The Stranger felt a calm cool breeze skate across her face and arms, chilling her body. She shivered slightly and whispered her story. "I was raised by the streets and grandma. I was destined not to be like my mother, so I shunned from boyfriend-girlfriend relationships all throughout high school and most of my late teenage-early twenty years. That's how I started doing hair. I needed to make money, stay out of trouble and away from boys, so I learned to do hair. My grandmother taught me the basics to earn some pocket money and I went to cosmetology school to learn the rest. During the late 50's, my grandmother use to do hair for the women in the neighborhood and that was how she made her living. She worked in a half-way house running numbers for the owner. Not the half-way house you would think but a sort of juke joint. She fried chicken, cooked coon and roasted turkeys; whatever the special was for that night. They loved my grandmother and to this day, the few people who remain alive, still love her. She pride herself on not working for the White Man, she called it. She did hair, sold dinners, and did some house gambling. I love my grandmother. She gave me hope just when I thought it was gone.

But when my mother died, I wanted to die too. Being in and out of the hospital often, she had not taught me the necessities of being a woman. Some of the things I had to learn the hard and embarrassing way. Like my period. I didn't know what tampons or maxi-pads were. When Mister Red arrived, I was flabbergasted. I had no idea what to do and was too ashamed to ask my grandmother. My mother was in the hospital, as usual, so I had to be creative. I remember taking a face towel, folding it the long way twice so it would fit inside my panties. I must have used about ten damn towels before it stopped. Then, after being embarrassed at school, I learned from a teacher as to what I should buy and that it would happen once a month—I was sick with worry."

Long sigh.

"So…when she married my stepfather I was thrilled. I thought he was different. I did not realize, however, that he was beating her in the dark. His bruises remained unseen until two years after they were married. One day, I jokingly tapped my mother on the shoulder, I forget why, but she almost jumped out of her skin. Before I could ask what the matter was, I noticed her facial expression. It was a very familiar face of shame and grief. I was blown away and the urge to hit her myself took control of my hand.

From that day forward, I never looked at my stepfather the same and pitied my mother. Still, through the years, I blamed my father for forcing her into that lifestyle. I blamed a sister that I use to have that left me there to rot in that hell-hole. I blamed my sister's father for starting the trend. But, most of all, I blamed my mother for allowing this to happen." The Stranger silenced a moment and looked up at Renée. Her heartfelt expression was all that Renée could bear as she released a tear from her pressure penetrated eyes. The Stranger's words slowly poured out of her mouth with confused sadness. "It was the mighty blow of a Paul Masson bottle that submitted the fatal blow to my mother's brain. The doctors stated that years of abuse would not allow her to recover from this head trauma. She had many head traumas before and I had heard those words so often, I could not determine what the problem was. I was only fourteen, what did I know. I shouted, 'just fix her so we can go home', but they were not able to patch her up this time. I remember staring into the glass window of her hospital room in disbelief. I felt like I was just hit by a bus that knocked the breath out of my frail little body. My eyes roamed around the room in frames. Soon my body collapsed and I hit the hospital floor. A nurse came rushing to my aid but her words were muffled and I was not able to focus my eyes to follow her instructions."

Weeping. Uncontrollable laughter followed by more weeping.

Renée wiped the tears from her own eyes and was puzzled at first as to why The Stranger started laughing. Then, she remembered that Evelyn once told her that everyone deals with tragedy in a different way. Some laugh to grieve while others cry in sorrow.

The Stranger pulled herself together and continued, "It was a bumpy ride but I made it through with some dignity left. I have moved passed my anger with her, and now, because of you I think I may know how to move pass my anger toward my father and my stepfather. But I still need to know how do I search within to find myself? How do I create a better me when this is the only *me* that I know?"

Renée looked at The Stranger as if a light bulb just went off inside her head. "I know what you need. I am a member of this woman's club and you need to attend one of our networking affairs. We will have another event on the nineteenth of this month and you can go with me. A lot of brilliant minds will be there. Tragic stories, sad stories, stories that will anger you, and happy endings. My mentor, the President, Miss Evelyn McKenzie will be hosting our annual anniversary meeting on the thirteenth of September. You should come to that as well and she'll know the answer to that question or help you find it." Renée embraced The Stranger with a warm smile. She could clearly remember the day when she first stepped into the MH Women's Club. She had just filed for divorce from her husband and the custody of the children was left hanging in the balance. Renée was hysterically impatient and could not rest. Her eyes were puffy and red from lack of sleep by the time she met Evelyn. Evelyn welcomed her and assured her that everything would be fine and that she had been beating herself up for nothing for the last two days. Renée knew that her ex-husband did not want custody of the children, but it was the mere fact that the option was available that set her off. Through it all, she recalled how supportive and understanding Evelyn was and she would hold that dear to her heart forever.

"A woman's club...I never been to a woman's club before. The night club, but that's it." Both start to laugh and The Stranger rolled her face slightly upward so that she was facing Renée and she could look into Renée's beautiful eyes. "You have the most beautiful bedroom eyes I've ever seen. What color are they?"

"Girl, you are crazy...they are gray, well, sometimes greenish." Renée looked down at The Stranger and for a moment, they shared an uncomfortable intense silence. Renée jerked in a panic, "Do you want something to drink—water, pop, juice? I know you are probably hungry and all that crying should have made you thirsty."

"Yes, please, anything is fine."

Renée went to the kitchen to fetch beverages and food to share with her guest. While in the kitchen, The Stranger gradually moved her eyes across the room feeling engulfed by the size of the living room. She had not noticed before that the ceilings were enormously high with the second floor hallway opened to the living room. The staircase was one out of a magazine, she thought. The house had to be at least twenty-one hundred square feet, but what did she know. The Stranger yelled leaning her body in an upright position slightly bent over the edge of the sofa, toward the right side, "Do you need any help in there?"

"No...I'm fine. I am warming up some food I cooked yesterday. I hope you like Fettuccine with shrimp and vegetables."

"Damn...sounds good. I thought you were warming up hotdogs or something. I feel important," The Stranger stated humorously.

Renée shouts from the kitchen "Don't!" They both laugh and Renée calls The Stranger into the kitchen. "You can come on back here and we can eat in here."

"Okay." The Stranger agreed and headed toward the kitchen. "Can this house get any bigger?" She said with much enthusiasm.

Renée starts to laugh and said, "Yeah, it is pretty big. It has five bedrooms and four baths."

"How big is this house, if you don't mind me asking?" Reaching for the glass of pop Renée handed her.

"It is a little over three thousand square feet."

The Stranger suddenly had a whole in her mouth, spilling her pop on the floor where she stood. While wiping the wetness from her mouth, she said, "Wow! I wanted to say that when I first drove up to the place but I did not want to seem like a dork. But, your home is quite lovely."

"Thank you. I think so too." The ladies smile at each other and toast there glasses. "Now, look over there in the broom closet and you'll find a mop so you can clean up that damn mess you've made."

The Stranger smiled, located the mop, and cleaned the mess.

After enjoying a hearty meal, Renée and The Stranger

retired upstairs to Renée's bedroom. Giving The Stranger a quick tour of the house, Renée pointed out areas of importance like the bathrooms. Renée and The Stranger talked a little longer in the seating section of the master bedroom before falling onto the bed, both sighed from an exhausting night. The Stranger turned to face Renée and said she needed a nightgown or something to put on. Before Renée could move from the bed, The Stranger softly grabbed her arm and pulled Renée toward her as she moved in for a kiss. Their lips interlocked for what seemed like forever to Renée, but it only lasted a few moments. Being with a woman had entered her curiosity but she was not ready to give up on men just yet. Renée felt uneasy, but she did not pull away.

Chapter

6

MOST OF the parties Melissa attended were Raves. Parties held in huge old abandon warehouse buildings, in the middle of nowhere which should have been torn down years prior, housing more than a thousand underage drinkers. With ages ranging from thirteen to twenty-four, maybe older, these parties became a central haven for young teenagers. Melissa was eighteen. She was old enough to be out late, but too young to drink and smoke grass. Melissa attended these parties before they were quite popular among high school drop-outs; unpopular kids destined to be popular; the uneasy kids that everyone called freaks; and kids who just lived for getting high. It was the late seventies and coke was in full swing, with some of Melissa's friends insisting it illuminated their high, making them feel like birds in the wind that could soar any and every where. Melissa chose to stay away from that high.

Outside the party on a scorching hot August summer day, stood some abandon railroad train carts. Leaning against one of the carts were two intertwined lips locked together in a fighting kiss.

"Get off me, damnit. Sometimes I can't stand you. Why must you do everything they tell you to do? Don't you have a mind of your own?" Melissa shouted while slowly pushing Steven away from her in a girlish sort of way. She gave him a subtle smile and said, "I hate you."

Steven kissed her lips again and responded, "No you don't." He smiled then continued, "Of course I have a mind of my own. And I don't do everything they tell me to do. I don't care what they think, I am my own man and I call the shots...*You Got That!*" He barked the last comment in her ear and pushed her forehead with his index finger and walked away.

"Punk!" Melissa yelled. "Those sorry ass friends of yours are going to get you in trouble. Don't you freakin walk away from me!" Melissa was shouting amongst herself because Steven was long gone. She leaned her thin body against another cart and it moved. It startled her for a moment. She turned around to face the cart with curious wonder and slowly slid the door ajar...then, a little more. The door was heavier than Melissa imagined when first trying to open it, not to mention, she was a little drunk and high from smoking marijuana. She stumbled as she tried to open the door some more. She stepped back with puzzling curiosity, looked at the door, and laughed. Her eyes traveled from the small door opening to the top of the cart to the bottom of the cart and back to the door. She thought, "This is ludicrous, I am undeniably drunk." She staggered back toward the Rave.

At the top of the cart, standing in full form, was one of Steven's friends. A pretentious, know-it-all jerk named Bull. Everyone called him Bull because he was full of it, but no one messed with him because he was just one of those guys everyone feared for one reason or another. He did not care about the nickname, everyone assumed he knew he was full of bullshit and maybe he adopted it on purpose to make a name for himself. Who knows and certainly no one cared. Bull heard Steven and Melissa's argument and presented a repugnant look on his face with vulgar thoughts going through his mind. Bull jumps down from the cart and heads back to the party.

Melissa located her prized boyfriend inside the Rave huddled in a corner with his body pressed against the wall. Music blasted, blue-greenish, red and yellow spots within white dim search lights were the only light reflected throughout the building. Circled reams of light bounced off the paint pilling and crumbled brick walls, flickering rapidly throughout the party. With visibility reacting to the drunkenness of the party goers, it was almost invisible. Doctor facial masks used to hold in the smoke they inhaled covered some of their faces. Melissa stumbled over to Steven and kicked him as he lay on the floor in the corner. "You are too high," Melissa shouted. "You need to take your ass home." She paused for a moment—no responsive movement. "Do you hear me Steven?"

"Yeah, *Yeah*, I hear you. I hear you all the damn time. Would you get out of my ear? You need to take your high ass home, I'm fine," Steven finally responded with hostility in his voice. Still, no body movement except for his eyes which remained closed with motion underneath his eyelids.

"Then come and dance with me." Melissa tugged on his clothing, motioning for him to get up.

"You are really blowing my high." Steven slowly bounces to his feet and moves toward the dance floor. "Come on, let's dance." The dance floor really consisted of any where you wanted to dance. A big open space in the middle of the warehouse ultimately became the dance floor. Steven and Melissa moved to the center of the room and danced for a few songs, and then

Melissa directed Steven to go and get her a drink. "What type of drink do you want?" He shouted over the loud rock music.

"I'll have a beer. It doesn't matter what kind just something to drink, my high is coming down," Melissa shouted in his ear waving her hands toward the bar area.

"Do you want some more grass?"

"No, I just want a beer or something for my throat. It's dry now from smoking all that grass."

"Okay, I'll be right back." Steven strolled over to the homemade bar with busted windows which used to be the offices of the head foreman and the warehouse manager. All that remained was the wood trimmings that left the impression of a window. "Let me get a beer man."

"Sure dude, that's two dollars," The bartender demanded.

"Whatever man," Steven said as he tossed the bartender a ten dollar bill and said to keep the change. As Steven started to walk away, Bull approached.

"What's up man? Where's your big mouth girl?" Bull said with a wide smile across his face and sarcasm in his eyes.

"She's on the dance floor, getting on my last nerve."

"Man…I would not take that shit from her," Bull implied, trying to provoke Steven.

"Whatever man. Let me take her this beer before her mouth starts again." Steven laughed and walked to the dance floor. Bull followed.

"And how can we help you?" Melissa exasperated by the site of Bull, stated with sarcasm.

"Girl ain't nobody talkin' to you. I am here with Steven. Dude, give her that drink so I can show you somethin'."

"Whatever you need to show him, you can show me too,"

Melissa said with a firm voice and hands propped loosely on her side.

"Don't nobody want you to come, damn!" Bull shouted with irritation in his tone.

"I don't care if you want me to come or not. Steven, you better tell your friend something." Melissa focused her attention on Steven. Waiting for him to side with her and send Bull away.

Bull walked away and beckon for Steven to follow. Steven followed and Melissa followed behind Steven.

Bull stopped just before reaching a non functioning emergency exit door in the rear of the old building. "I just wanted to get away from the crowd," Bull whispered while reaching into his front right jean pocket. "Look at this dude," he said with excitement.

"Hey, what is it?" Steven asked curiously.

"It's the coolest pill ever. It supposed to be the ultimate high." Bull bucked his eyes and smiled, showing practically all thirty-two teeth. Looking suspiciously, Bull handed the drugs to Steven. "Wait, I better give you just one. They are potent."

"You don't need to give him any. What the hell is that anyway?" Melissa angrily stated, trying to reach around Steven to snatch the drugs from Bull's hand.

"Dude, you really need to do something with her. Are you the *man* or what? Get rid of her, *Now*," Bull shouted, confronting Steven.

Steven grabbed Melissa by the arm and pulled her to the side. "Look, I can take care of this myself, okay. Please, just go to the dance floor and I will be there in a minute, *Okay*."

"Look, Steven...look...do you really trust this guy. I don't like it. Don't take that mess." She tried to instill a little compassion in her tone of voice. She did not want to argue with Steven because her attention was focused on Bull. With her high settling down, she could see more clearly that Bull was up to something. "Steven, promise me."

"Look Melissa…."

Melissa interrupted, "Promise me that you will not take that stuff."

"Okay, just go. I will be with you in a moment…*Go!*" Steven yelled as he looked into her eyes and for a moment he realized that she seemed a little frighten. He briefly felt her concern but he had no intentions of leaving Bull's side. He reached out to touch her face with a pleasant sweep of his hand and added, "Go, I'll be there in a minute…go now. Please!"

Before Melissa could walk away, a classmate from school showed up. "Hey Bull, do you have any more of those pills," she insisted while she held out her hand.

"Yeah, that will be twenty-five dollars. For you Jackie, only twenty-five dollars," he said with a smile.

"You are such an ass. I can pay whatever, but I can't believe you are charging me. You act like you are some kind of drug dealer now. Give me a break…whatever!" She looks at him in disbelief, shakes her head, and simultaneously hands him the cash and snatches several pills.

"Hey, dude, you took more than one." He tried to be heard over the laughter as Jackie took off running toward the crowd. He didn't care, he was on another mission.

"One of your entourages," Melissa said with cynicism.

"I thought you were leaving?" Bull demanded, appearing irritated.

"I will leave when I am ready," she said with fury.

"Please, baby, go. I will be on the dance floor in a minute. I want to talk to Bull for a minute. *Go!*" Steven insisted.

Melissa walked away and headed for the bar to grab another drink. She gulped the beer Steven bought and took a big swallow of beer the bartender handed her with a wink. She smiled and leaned against the paint chipped wall next to the opening of the homemade bar. Glancing around the room, searching for a familiar face, Melissa spotted one of her so-called friends.

"Hey girl," Melissa said to Jackie, a friend from high school that she only associated with when there was no one else. Melissa had to admit that she did not recognize Jackie a moment ago. Her mind was solely concentrated on what Bull was up to. Melissa felt compelled to speak to Jackie after she practically ignored her when she came over to get some drugs from Bull. Melissa only frequents the Raves because of the high and her boyfriend but Jackie lived for them. Pushing twenty, Jackie was a wild one. Never graduated from high school, but another friend told Melissa that she got her GED a few months ago. Rumor has it that she was in good company with Bull some time ago as well, but Melissa never saw them together. Melissa thought she could talk to Jackie until Steven came to his senses and perhaps retrieve some information from her about these new found pills that Bull had in his possession.

"Hey, Melissa. You're just drinking beer? Here, hit this?" Jackie passes her a joint.

"Na...no thanks. I am high enough, trying to ease my high before I head home."

"Okay, more for us." Jackie inhaled a long puff and blew it into her companion's mouth. Melissa had never seen the dude Jackie was dancing with but then again, she didn't care. There were a lot of faces at those parties that were unfamiliar to Melissa.

"So, what's up with these pills?" Melissa asked while searching across the floor for Steven.

"They are the coolest. Bull wants to act like he is high and mighty—that little shit. I can't believe he was really charging me for them. But they are worth it. I am so high right now, I could float," she said with a delicate smile—as delicate as her tired worn face could possibly get. Jackie looked like she was pushing thirty, with wrinkles around her eyes and mouth. Her skin complexion was pale, almost powdery and the white-pink powder foundation did not help any. The blue eye shadow was thicker than the triple coated mascara that she placed on top of the artificial eye lashes. Her hair was a neatly shaped afro with two skinny long braids resting on her breast and back. Melissa wondered how a white woman managed to get her hair in an afro, but she didn't care enough to dwell over it for too long.

"What are they, some kind of miracle high?" she inquisitively questioned with a smile.

"They just might be," Jackie slowly answered, kissing her dance partner while they shared smoke inhalation. "You ought to try one," she suggested.

"Na...I will have to pass." She stopped for a moment and said, "Is that Steven? Na, it's not him. So, what's up with Bull? Why is he such an asshole sometimes?"

Appearing offended by the comment, Jackie turned to Melissa with much attention and said, "I don't think he's an asshole. I wouldn't put it like that. He can get on your nerves sometimes. Why? Why do you care?"

Melissa viewing the hostility written across Jackie's face and added, "He's an asshole to me. He needs to stay out of our business."

83

"What business?" Jackie asked.

"Me and Steven."

"No honey, Steven just needs to be a man and stand up for himself. He doesn't need some girlfriend telling him how to act."

"What you mean by that?" Melissa said with much interest.

"Nothing...he needs to grow a backbone, that's all I am saying."

"Bull just needs to mind his own damn business and leave our relationship to us. Why are you defending Bull?"

"I'm not defending him, I am just saying."

"You're just saying what?"

"Nothin', Melissa. You are blowing my high talking about this shit. Anyway, do you want one or not?" she regrettably stated trying to wing off the subject.

"Do I want one of what?"

"One of these pills." Jackie pulls two pills out of her pocket and said, "Here, it will calm your nerves."

Melissa raised her beer and confirmed, "This is all I will drink and I am headed home." She turned for a moment searching desperately for Steven.

"Okay, suit yourself. Tell you what, no hard feelings okay," Jackie added with a smile.

"No hard feelings about what? We are just having a conversation. I don't let things get under my skin. It's whatever!" Melissa stated with very little concern.

"Okay, Okay. Let me at least buy you another drink."

"I told you, this is the last one."

"Oh, come on. Don't be a drag. You know Steven is not coming around for a while. When Bull and Steven get together, it is impossible to tear them apart."

Melissa agreed, smiled and approved the drink. Jackie walked over to the bar and purchased another Budweiser for Melissa. Melissa chatted with Jackie for a little while longer then spotted Steven.

"Hey, there's Steven. I'll talk to you later girl. Oh, and thanks again for the drink."

"Yeah, okay. It's cool."

Melissa walked away and headed in the direction of the bar. She thought she saw Steven buying another drink. As Melissa walked away, Jackie whispered to her dance partner, "I can't stand that arrogant bitch." Jackie flared her nostrils, placed her left hand on her hip and took another drag of the grass she was smoking.

Melissa was displaced after waiting by the bar for Steven for over twenty minutes, so she had decided to head home. Before she headed to the car, she decided to finish her beer. Melissa made her way back to the train carts and leaned her back up against the center one. Beer in hand, she started taking small sips looking at the party. The flashing lights from inside the party were dimming. The manual flood lights outside the building were brighter but blurred. She shook her head slowly and looked at her drink. She was holding a Budweiser beer bottle, with nothing out of the ordinary. She moved her head and held out her hand holding the beer bottle back and forth, moving it from side to side to correct her focus. No matter what she did she could not see clearly. She started to walk back toward the party but her legs buckled and suddenly she collapsed on the grass a few steps away from the carts. She heard a voice in the distance. Words "are you alright" were muttered, but her response was not apparent. Suddenly voices formed around her and her heart raced further. The motion in legs were undetected, the movement in her lips were ignored, as her mind grasp for thoughts. Then, she felt her body lifting into the air. Focusing on the life forms that surrounded her, she tried to grab onto the arm of the person pressed beside her.

After a split second, she felt a hard cool surface beneath her back with darkness behind her. She slowly moved her head in disbelief and her legs squirmed in discomfort. Words managed to escape into the night mist, "What is going on? Can you help me? I don't know what is happening."

Voices from a near distance laughed and said, "We'll help you. You will be alright." More laughter filled the air.

With Melissa lying on her back partially inside the opened center train cart, a group of boys hovered around her helpless body, smiling and laughing. As she twists and turned rapidly but slowly with distorted vision, her assailants smiled and rubbed their drunken hands all over her body. The first assailant appeared more intoxicated than the rest. He blinked his eyes twice to regain a clearer focus on the girl. He slowly caressed his hands across her thighs rising up between her legs. The more he rubbed the more excited he became. His movements gradually flowed faster and faster, rougher and rougher. He grabbed the seam of her jeans and tried to rip them off. The other assailant shouted, "hey wait…those are jeans dude. You can't just rip those." Everyone overwhelmed themselves in laughter. It enraged the first assailant even more. "I'll get these damn jeans off…forget you assholes." He pulled and tugged and pulled and ripped until her pink panties surfaced. He managed to rip a hole near the zipper of the jeans. Pulling her panties off was not an easy task. Melissa rolled and moved with more mobility than they had hoped. A voice from the crowd shouted, "are you sure the drug will work for a while?" Another voice from a further distance, observing the performance said, "It will work for a while. If lover boy will get on with the show, maybe someone else can get a taste before she comes to."

The first assailant, being more agitated, unbuckled his belt and lowered his pants. With his penis not quite erected, he tried to place it inside her. His unsuccessful efforts raised more laughter from his peers. In more of a rage, he pulled Melissa closer to him with her back lying inside the cart and her butt pressed against the edge of the outside of the cart while her legs dangled mercifully. Grabbing her butt while forcing his way inside her, the other assailants grabbed her legs and stretched them as far as their minds would go, practically ripping her in half. Giggles and laughter overcrowded the air, with chanting words of encouragement being shouted from afar. "Get her, dude. Get her. You finally got you some. Get her. Yeah, you can do it." The first assailant pushed and pushed until he ejaculated inside her. Ripped flesh was smothered in blood from the assailant's nails being embedded in her butt. There were bruises forming across her butt cheeks from the edge of the cart being pressed against it. The cart left discolored black and blue marks with rust and dirt particles sticking to her moist body.

With the first assailant meeting his accomplished goal, the next one took his position. Grabbing her by the breast to pull her closer, he roughly shoves his way inside her and pushed hard. His thrusts caused her body to jump as the others lost hold of her legs. Her legs fell abruptly and her right leg hit a steel pole attached to the cart, prompting a gash on the back of her foot. He pushed her legs up with both his hands forcing them above her head with her feet practically touching the inside of the cart as he thrust harder and harder, ripping all the innocence she once possessed. Before he could really force all the emotional life out of her a voice was heard from a distance.

"Hey, what are you guys doing?" A man walking casually toward the scene smoking a cigarette with his right hand neatly tucked inside his jean pocket asked.

"Nothing, dude. Just having a little fun," one of the assailants said, showing all teeth.

"Maybe I can join you. Even supposing, I thought the party was inside," he said with a smile across his face as he approached the scene.

"We are having our own party out her too," a bystander added, anxiously awaiting his turn.

The man walked up to the cart and shock settled in his eyes. *"What the Hell!"*

"Pretty freakin cool, huh dude," another bystander implied.

"Get your asses out of here. All of you! You sick son-of-a-bitches! Are you guys raping her? *Are you nuts? Get the hell out of here…All of you!"* The man pushed the assailants away. Every one flees and runs back toward the party—some jump into their daddy's car and sped away; others were too cocky to leave the party, so they bolted inside. No one stood up to the man, although he was not a big guy, about five nine weighing only one hundred and fifty pounds and appeared to be drunk too. A select few of the assailants had the distinct pleasure of meeting his acquaintance on a dark afternoon and it was not a pleasant affair. Let's not mention those same few knew his father or at least heard the rumors.

He looked at her fatigued body; legs lifeless, pants and shoes scattered about and felt enormous anger. He picked her pants and shoes off the grass and rescued her body inside his arms. He said with a horse throat, almost in tears, "You son-of-a-bitches. This is really sick," he whispered to himself as he carried her to shelter.

He recognized her as the woman that came over and spoke to him and Jackie. He did not care about the comment Jackie made earlier, but his mind began to puzzle trying to put the pieces together. He figured Jackie may have been ignorant enough to send those boys to attack her. He had not really known Jackie all that well, but her disposition suggested that she would be the kind of girl to orchestrate something as heinous as this. He remembered Jackie saying something about the lady owning a Porsche and thinking she was high and mighty. So, thankfully, there was only one Porsche parked in the grass so he placed the woman inside. His eyes searched quickly around the area of the car for a purse or tote bag of some sort—there wasn't one. He wondered where her keys could be; then, he heard something jingle as he positioned her legs inside the car—the keys were still in the ignition. He considered whether or not to take her to the hospital but his mind was set against it. He was only nineteen and he was stoned himself. He did not want to have to answer questions about the Rave or what he saw. Being a witness in his family was not a good thing. Being Italian with a highly attention attraction father did not give him an option of being a rat. No matter what they did, he was not the one to tell the story.

The man placed her inside, locked and closed the door, and walked away. He laid her down as far as he could so her body would not be visible to the passerby's. The man did not feel right leaving her there alone, so he sat on a stack of steel rods in the rear of the building and watched her vehicle all night. He was usually out all night with some bimbo anyway, so he knew his family would not worry.

~

"**I** awoke, sitting in my car covered in rust particles, debris, embarrassment and blood seeping from underneath me. It was morning. When I moved to boost myself up, an unbearable pain went through my abdomen like lightning. It was like menstrual cramps times three or four. My thoughts were still obscured and my arms were weak. My head and my eyelids were very heavy. It took a moment to gain focus. When I finally managed to sit up, I looked outside my window and saw miles of empty grass on opposite sides of me. Looking through my rearview mirror revealed the abandon building—deserted. I looked down in my lap and inhaled a short gasp of limited air. My mind went into shock looking at my naked body with blood accompanying my legs in the seat. I started to weep while I searched in the car for my pants. Panic started to settle in and my eyes became overwhelmed with tears. I was frightened at first to get out of the car, but my car was so small I could not put my pants on sitting inside—especially in my condition.

With all of the energy I had left, I opened the car door and forced my body in motion. I leaned toward the door and stuck my left leg out. As I turned to position myself to get out of the car, another pain exploded through my abdomen like a rocket on full blast. When I tried to stand up outside of the car, my legs collapsed from under me. That's when I noticed the gash in my foot. It was not pretty. I looked up with tear filled eyes asking the Lord *why me*. How was I going to explain this night to my parents? Moreover, was I going to the hospital? I had to, something could have been seriously wrong with me. It was evident that I was raped but I did not think I should have been bleeding like that, even taking into consideration that I was a virgin. With all those thoughts running through my head, that's when I saw him. The man that saved my life, I suspected. I looked over and noticed a man lying near the back of the building. He appeared to be sleeping. But, when my vision regrouped, I saw him looking right at me. My first reaction was fear. But something came over me, a sudden calmness put my mind at ease and I immediately knew. I knew he was the one that carried me to the car. I felt his warm body against my chest as he carried me to safety. Yet, in my comatose state, I still was able to capture the warmness of his heart. I didn't see my hero again—until years later, coincidentally."

Evelyn was surprised by the outcome of the story. She would not have guessed that this happened to Melissa. She allowed herself to set judgment before Melissa's story was exposed. Hearing so many horrific stories, Evelyn was not easily shocked but for the first time, she was overwhelmed with silence. Hearing Melissa's story allowed her to remember her own. It was a time that Evelyn thought she had swept those problems under the rug and nailed it to the floor. Time has healed her wounds, but nothing would allow her to forget.

"Evelyn, are you okay?" Melissa asked as she wiped the tears from her eyes.

"Yes, Dear. I am overwhelmed by your ordeal. Did you ever find out who raped you? Did you go to the hospital?"

"Yes and Yes. When I mustered enough energy to drive, I drove myself to the hospital. It was not an easy decision. I wondered how lengthy the questions would be from the hospital, the doctors and nurses, and the police. I pondered what I would say and decided against it and rethought it again. I was hurting, I was confused, and I could not remember my way to the nearest hospital, but somehow I made it without realizing.

Pulling up to the emergency room door—I got out of my car, left it running and slowly limped inside holding the bottom of my stomach. My clothing was torn and since my zipper was some how broken, my pink panties were revealed, although they were torn too. Eyes were glued to me as I entered through the sliding doors of Birmingham General Hospital. Unexpectedly, the nurse from behind the desk rushed over to my aide and placed my altered body inside a wheelchair. I held my head inside my hands, trying to mentally embrace what would happen next. The first question was, *'are you okay, child?'* Next, *'what happened to you?'* My mind drew a blank for the first thirty seconds or so, and then I answered. *'I was attacked'*, I managed to say. The nurse rushed me to the back, shouting words I could no longer hear. I had tuned her out with strong concentration on the excruciating pain entering in and out of my abdomen piercing my vagina. Before I knew it, I was on an examination table, doctors and nurses swarmed over me like flies, asking questions, poking places on my body, flashing light in my eyes, and reviewing my torn clothing.

'Dear…do you know where you are? What happened? Can you tell us your name?' a woman wearing a nurse's uniform asked, with her face held close to mine while she held my hand.

My eyes were dazed and I felt myself going in and out of consciousness. I believe the long drive to the hospital with the ordeal and loss of blood made me slightly faintish. I made them aware that I knew I was in a hospital and told them I was raped, but I hesitated to tell them where. I had gotten the directions from a classmate and I was drunk when I arrived at the party, so I did not know *exactly* where the warehouse was located. I simply skipped over that question and answered the many others that were thrown at me.

'What's your name?' one of the nurses asked again.

'Melissa…Melissa Contour,' I struggled to say. I heard one of the voices in the distance say, 'do you think she is *thee* Melissa Contour, as in the billionaire *Contour*?'

'It is quite possible. But we need to concentrate on trying to examine her, because she doesn't look too good,' one of the other nurses addressed.

'My name is Melissa. I was attacked. I don't know by whom. I…don't… know…I…don't. I don't…know…by…who.' I struggled even harder to say, while passing out. And, when I opened my eyes, I was greeted by a nurse with a warm smile.

'Hello, Dear. You have had quite an ordeal,' she stated.

I tried to sit up and move, but she was against it.

'No, please, Dear. Don't strain yourself. You just rest now. Do you have a purse or handbag of some sort that will have your identification inside?' she asked.

'Yes…it is in my car.'

'Where is your car?'

'I drove it here…it should be out…it should be outside at the door.'

'We thought that was your car, so we had one of the hospital attendants move it to a parking spot, but we did not want to check inside without your permission,' she stated very clearly.

Her bedside manners were quite impressive and she made me feel much more relaxed. I advised her that they would find my *Louis Vuttion* handbag under the seat toward the back of the car. There, they would find ID and a phone book with my parents contact numbers. You would think I would know them without guessing, but for some odd reason, I could not remember them. I suppose since my parents and I have not really had a decent conversation with each other in years, there was no need to call them.

The nurse informed me after she called my parents. I looked at her with anticipation, wondering what they had to say.

'I called your mother Dear. She was very shocked and said very little. I asked if she would come to take you home and she said call her back once you were ready to be discharged.'

'Did she say if she was coming down sooner? When will I be discharged?' I asked with a frog in my throat, trying to hold back the tears that crowded my vision.

'She didn't say. I thought that was odd. But, you may be able to go home today. We normally do not need to keep you more than one day, but your blood pressure was elevated, so the doctor wants you to be monitored for a few more hours. Now, try and get some rest, you've had a long day,' she insisted. Then, she got up from the chair beside my bed and proceeded to walk out the door, stopped and said, 'Oh, the police are here to speak with you. I advised them that they can talk to you when you were ready, but they need some further information from you. Okay, dear?' She waited for a few minutes for my response, but I never gave one.

I was hurt that my mother did not say more or stated if she would come down or not, but I expected it. I guess you never stop hoping – even though, I thought I did long ago. With a tragedy like this, you look for your parents to be there and for one moment, all I wanted was to snuggle up to my mother. A few hours had past after I spoke with the police and still no sign of my mother. I knew, deep in my heart, that she would not come but I was wishing that she did."

"**D**id you get discharged that same day and did your mother ever make it to the hospital?" Evelyn asked, interrupting the still gaze in Melissa's eyes as she looked straight ahead.

"No, I did not and no she did not. I received a thorough examination—fourteen stitches were needed to sew my vagina up, a head bandage *(for whatever reason)*, and seven stitches and crutches for a fractured foot—and yet, she did not bother to come see how I was. I remained there for a week, autonomously of course. They wanted to release me the same day, but I convinced them that I was detrimental to my own health."

"Were you?"

"I wasn't sure. Before I was attacked, I really believed I wanted to die. I wanted the pain to go away. The mental anguish I suffered after my uncle died was unbearable, I thought. A good dose of reality woke me up and advised me that I really had no idea what pain was. Life really showed me that when you thought it was bad, it could get worse and so it did. The brutal attack I suffered through was a hint of more to come."

Evelyn looked at Melissa with befuddled eyes. She thought she needed a cigarette and she didn't smoke. Evelyn needed to stretch for a moment and get a grip on her thoughts. She asked, "Do you want something to drink. You must be thirsty now after sharing that story. Let me get you some water, at least." Evelyn rose from the sofa and went to the icebox to fetch a bottled water for Melissa and some air for herself. Evelyn needed to redeploy her thoughts and prepare herself for the next session. She was not prepared for the magnitude of this story on this day. When Renée stated that she had a rich friend that needed her help with divorcing her husband, Evelyn did not dream that she would need deep emotional comfort. She did not want to judge, but the

ALINA

judgment was already handed down. She felt as if she was facing Melissa's agony with her, as she pictured her own horrific tragedy. She imagined sharing a few stories to break the ice, but eventually, with a firm hand, shouting for her to just simply divorce him. No, this was not an ordinary woman with an ordinary situation. This was no rich royal white woman with gee *'what am I going to have for supper today'*—she was real, with real problems, in the real world. Many sad emotional wrecks had entered Evelyn's door, but no one like her. She was distinctive. Although a good number of her members had been forced into sexual intercourse, Melissa sparked a flurry of passionate wonder of what was to come. Evelyn didn't marvel or indulge the repulse behavior of the uncompassionate men that entered her innocence unannounced, but she was besieged by the narration of those events and the gracefulness of Melissa's disposition. It was just something about Melissa. She couldn't put her finger on it just yet.

Melissa took a sip of water, not realizing how thirsty she was—she took another. Then she noticed that she continued a long drink until her breath weakened. "Thank you. I guess I needed that," she said while releasing a deep inhaled breath.

"I figured you would." Both of the ladies smiled at one another and Melissa continued.

"Well, as you very well may have guessed, my father was livid. He never made it to the hospital and my mom graced me with her presence upon my release. While in the hospital, I was contending with a lie and reality. Although the truth was impossible to fathom, I decided on the truth. I took their unloving response as a sign—a deliverance that motivated me into action. My plan was to move out into a place of my own. The details had yet to be worked out but that was my goal. I did not know how I

96

would make a living, but I had made up my mind that it would be best if I seek a residence of my own.

I tried to put the pieces back together after I was released from the hospital, but it became more difficult for me to function. I had nightmares almost every single night and would awake in a sweat, with my clothing and sheets drenched. I could still smell their heavy alcohol breathes when I awoke—even months after the incident. I could still feel the hard thrust and the pounding of my body hitting against the train carts. Sometimes, I would wake-up with bruises across my arms and wrist, assuming that I must have inflected them during the nightmare. The abdominal pain continued for months, with more excruciating pain to come. Suddenly a sickness took over my body that landed me in the emergency room, yet again. Several months after the incident, I was told by a nurse practitioner that I was about nine to eleven weeks pregnant. Of course this news trickled through my heart like sharp pins. I was a wreck. I did not think it could get any worse.

Telling my mother the news was not difficult but my father was another predicament all together. My mother handled bad news rather well, but with silence. She would press her hand up against her chest and utter the words, 'my goodness...this can't be happening' while blindly reaching for a seat. It was her look that chilled my heart. Her look of disappointment and embarrassment, all at the same time, told what she was feeling. It was not a caring look for my well being, it was a look of what people will think. Now, my father would be more difficult, more verbal, more vulgar, and more insensitive. Revealing the facts to him was more challenging than making the decision to go to the hospital after I was raped. Finally, after deep deliberation, I handed my father the news on a silver platter. I literally wrote him a note and advised

Ramon to deliver it to him in his study. Profanity filled the room with one crash against the wall and a piercing rotation noise danced across the floor until silence landed. After the fuse was over, he called me into his study."

Melissa entered her father's study with tear filled eyes, moving hunched over as if she was sick to her stomach. Silence seemed deader than before with the delicate squeak from the study room door being the only sound. Melissa felt naked as if being stripped all over again. The knot in her throat congregated enough for her to manage a swallow. But her nerves in her body did not go unnoticed.

"Well, what a sticky situation you've gotten yourself in, not to mention the reputation of this family. What are we suppose to do now? Please, entertain me with your suggestions. I'm eager to hear them. Please elucidate on how you plan to fix this damn *Mess.*" Her father's exigent words melted within her soul and snatch the life right out of her.

Melissa made a sad dumbfounded expression and said with little conviction, "I don't know, dad. You act as if I asked for this. I didn't ask to be in this situation. I didn't ask to be here." She softly answered and sniffed as she wiped her nose then added, "Are you trying to say this was my fault? I did nothing different than I normally do. I know…but everything is always my fault. Like uncles death, right. That was my fault too."

"Is this what this little charade is about, that *Damn Uncle* of yours? He is dead missy and you need to get over it." He aggressively stated in a high tone of voice but still remained calm. "Your uncle should have been more careful. His ignorance was not going to be the downfall of this family. I will not tolerate that."

"No this is not about him damnit. It's about me. Don't you get it? You and mom never really cared about me. You didn't care enough to come to the hospital to make sure I wasn't dying. You didn't care," Melissa shouted cogently as she slowly pasted the floor of his study. "And what do you mean that my uncle's ignorance was not going to be the downfall of this family? What the hell does that suppose to mean, father?" She demanded with little regard to who she was speaking to, then added, "You are my father. You don't get to choose your children or your parents or your situations. Now, I need you to be a parent and help me through this. You talk about, *'that damn uncle'*, but had he not taught me to be strong and independent, I would have died a long time ago. Especially in this place! Of course, that may have been right in the ball park of your hopes."

"I see you have a mouth on you," he ostentatiously stated. "Since I feel compelled to help you I will do just that. Give me a few days to figure out what we need to do." He looked at Melissa's surprised face and added, "What about that boyfriend of yours? What does he have to say about all this?"

"I've only spoken to him once within the last month and he expressed his sorrow and wanted to come over to be sure I was okay. I declined his visit."

"Why?" her father said angrily.

"Father…I am having trouble looking at you. I don't think I could look at another man right now. Especially one that wants to comfort me by wrapping me within his arms," she shared with sarcasm.

"Leave me. I don't know where this egalitarianism comes from but I suppose it was the cause for your afflictions. Maybe you ought to be glad the young man considers seeing you again. With the vagrant like behavior you've presented, it amazes me that anyone could look at you. You hold your head down because of shame. And shame you shall, but just know that I will not share in your reprehensible misfortune. I will determine what should be done but only because of my obligation to this family's name. You are not to speak to anyone about this situation. It wasn't enough that I had to clean up your damn mess when you got out the hospital the first time, now I have to clean up this one too. I thought it was clear that we do not speak to the police, *under no circumstances*, without consulting *me* first," he shouted unmercifully, hitting his hand against the desk in aggravation.

Melissa's body jerked from the sound, but she said nothing. He waved his hand dismissing her, so she turned around and walked out. Melissa happily strolled out of her father's study and went back to her room. As she strolled back to her bedroom, a light bulb went off in her head that her father never answered her question about her uncle. What he meant by that, she thought. But her mind became more consumed with her own pain to contemplate another. Several minutes later she reached her bedroom, slipped inside, and fastened the door shut. There, she slept for two days with frequent trips in-between to the bathroom, primarily to vomit on occasion.

"I received a surprise visit from my diligently proficient stalker boyfriend. He was totally not giving up on seeing me. Ramon welcomed him in and my father directed him to my room. I can assume it was my father, because I heard him talking near the bedroom door and soon after, Steven entered without a knock. I was a mess. He didn't care. He entered my room chatting about events that meant nothing to me and then he proposed, right between what he ate for dinner and what speech his father gave the night before. I was too sick to release the shock I felt but I uttered the words, 'why?' He really never stated his reasons but he strongly concentrated on the notion that he wanted to take me away from that place. With those words brimming around in the air in billow form, to light to grasp, I searched for an unrestricted response. Excited to hear those words about *getting away from my parents* was enough for me to say yes.

I announced my engagement to my father, understanding that he would be happy to finally remove me from his home and possibly his life. On the contrary, he asked more questions than I presumed. 'How will you two make a living, with a baby on the way? Do you think this is the answer to your problems? Does he have any idea where you two will live?' I must admit, those were questions that I had not reached because I was beset with the thought of leaving my parents house. Then, as if my father could not get any more shocking, he offered my boyfriend a job with one of his companies. I was astounded."

"So the old man finally expressed a hint of compassion!" Evelyn asked in wonder.

Melissa looked with regret and said, "Not really, he was quite ambivalent but the mere fact that my foolish announcement was an answer to his question—how to get rid of me, quietly—was satisfying enough to get a compassionate twitch out of him."

Evelyn looked at Melissa with intensity in her eyes and sensed more to this grueling story. She shifted her body in the sofa to acquire a more comfortable position and focused her attention back on Melissa.

"I really could not determine where my father would position Steven. Steven was a handsome guy, twenty—well, at that time—and a little immature to hold a heavy title. But, I didn't care at the time. I briefly deliberated on the thought of where we would live, but with bewilderment still settling in I had no time to give it a constructive thought. Ironically, Steven found us a place in Grosse Pointe. A nice home with three bedrooms, two baths with a lakefront view, downsized from what I was accustom too, but as long as I was far from my parents, it did not matter. The fully furnished house belonged to a friend of Steven's father. Steven's father was a Michigan State Representative with more friends than enemies. With his clout, he pulled strings not even my father could believe possible. He was a good man who believed in changing the world one state at a time. I don't understand how those values missed Steven.

The home, being moderate in size and style to me, it was just over three thousand square feet with inadequate style furnishing; but with no money, complicated circumstances, and pressed for time it was the best we could do. Not to sound unappreciative but my parent's home in Oxford, was over nine thousand square feet, I believe, with over twelve bedrooms and eight baths. The house had a family room, two dining areas, my father's study, a family library, and an entertaining room. We also had a guest house, approximately three thousand square feet, were Ramon and several other employees resided. It was only my parents and I that occupied our home but from time to time we would have the privilege of having overnight guest with extended stays, sometimes for months at a time. Some were family members and some were not. I was taught as early as seven years old not to ask many questions. It's almost like we lived separate lives, my parents and I."

"I presume you and Steven were married right away?"

Evelyn said confidently, sipping her water.

"Yes. We got married at the Justice of the Peace in downtown Mount Clemons. My father did not attend the ceremony. But my mother appeared, hidden behind an oversized black hat with black sheer that covered her face which lapsed over the top of the hat. Her little black dress indicated that she was perhaps attending a funeral. My family's amazing performance left nothing to the imagination. It was blatantly obvious that the shame beleaguered them and they considered my actions atrocious. It was my entire fault in their minds. This situation happened to them, not to me. Not compassionate to my suffering, they concentrated on their own embarrassment setting my feelings to the side for they were of no importance. My dad held meetings with the press to share his concern for his troubled daughter, with my pathetic mother by his side with flowing tears. He advised them that my stay at the hospital was an outburst, simply seeking the attention of others. He had somehow suppressed my hospital records and nothing more was ever revealed, not even today. But, our wedding ceremony went on and so we began our lives together." Melissa takes a profound breath and silenced for a moment.

"Do you want to take a break, Melissa?" Evelyn asked with much concern, gently touching Melissa's hands that were locked together resting on the pillow between her arms.

"No, I'm fine."

"Do you want something to eat?"

"No, I'm fine." She smiles and glances around the room. "So, what exactly do you do here? What is the women's club all about?" she asked with strong curiosity in her voice.

Evelyn smiled and said, "We network here. When I first started this club, I was a bitter woman whose heart and soul had

ALINA

been scorn by the lack of sensitivity in men. And the ones that were sensitive were a little *too* sensitive, if you understand my meaning." Both women laugh and Evelyn continued, "Oh, the stories I could tell." She slowly shook her head from side to side slightly bent to the right. "I have a few stories myself, but tonight is all about you. We need to determine how I or we can help you. I have seen many women trample through those doors with crushed hearts and perplexed minds. I do not pretend to be a healer, or a counselor, or a fix all, but I can offer you a listening ear. I can offer you a comfortable surrounding and a place to escape to reconnect with yourself. I can share my experiences in hopes to gain trust that I understand yours. We conduct meetings here, in this very room, on a weekly or monthly basis, depending on what life brought us. We host networking parties for members and non-members to come and share their experiences, their achievements, and opinions. Our networking parties also allow our members to share our atmosphere with other friends who may not want to be a part of a club but wish to share their experience simply to have someone who is willing to listen. Some come and find out that they are not alone, especially if you've been in a relationship with a man."

Melissa politely interrupted, "Do you practice hating men or shall I say, do the members here hate men and this is where they get out their frustrations?"

"This is where they can release frustrations, but no, we do not hate men. The Man Hater's Club name came to me out of heartfelt anger, but after a long while, I decided that the name was straight to the point and perfect for what we were trying to accomplish here. It was just as it should be because *'hatred'* is what we feel when we are first betrayed or abused. It is what we feel

104

when our hearts are first broken and flat lined by our trusted partner. The name of the club was not intended to depict an image that we were a group of man hating women that practice bomb fire rituals in the backyard over roaring heart pounding songs; it was meant to express our anger and what we must focus *on* in order to move *on*.

Although there is a very thin line between love and hate, some women come here to discover just that. Sometimes we give our love so strongly that we hate *him* for it. Other times, we wish he could be more attentive, less arrogant, less overbearing, and more empathetic, and the list goes on. We reflect the emotions that we want our men to give but do we tell them? They can't read our minds. Or can they? The problem that most concerns me is the lack of sensitivity. I say that to mean that men are so nonchalant with their demeanor and their behavior. The only thing of importance to them is what is good for them, but only for that moment. Some men are more benevolent with the events of a sports game than with the affairs of their woman. You have some men who will wear the sensitive mask for a while to silence their spouse just to relieve *their* agony, but this does not correct the situation.

What beseeches me to differ from saying that boys will be boys is that they can turn on the sincere charming sympathetic role when they want to, possibly when they feel that there is a threat to their domain. His disposition changes when he feels his woman is considering vacating the premises or may be giving her love to another. Instead, most of the women feel the *true love* affect after they have left their man. He suddenly realized that she was the best thing that ever happened to him. I find this hard to swallow.

What men don't realize and had never considered is when

the woman returns, it is because of her own necessity and the fact that she still feels love for him. Once she has no more love to give, she will walk away and there is nothing he can say or do to compel her to stay. I can recall a past relationship, where my ex suddenly discovered that I would make a perfect wife. We dated for seven months before I questioned our relationship. I didn't bring it up to him; he announced it during a casual conversation we embarked on about past relationships. He stated to me that he could not handle a serious relationship at this time and that he has given up on having a woman in his life. This came clear out of the blue, without me ever bringing the words *'serious relationship'* or *'being his woman'* to the table. It had not entered my mind at that time but it sprung a leak, as all kind of thoughts trickled through my brain. I stated to him that I was sick and tired of having un-meaningful sexual relationships that were going nowhere and I told him to lose my number. Of course he played the macho roll and he didn't call for a week. After a while, my phone was exploding with messages of pleas for me to reconsider. He suddenly realized that I was a good catch. He continued to call me well after three months, but I stood my ground and I never saw him again.

You have to think, what if the woman behaved as the man? She unexpectedly started to stay out late, and she moved about the house in a nonchalant fashion. Or she didn't return his phone calls for numerous days. How long would it take before he confronted her? How long would it be before he started to track her every step? How long would he suffer this kind of mistreatment? I guarantee you, not for long—at least, not as long as a woman would. We tend to stay too long. In some incurable way, we believe he will come around. We provide all the excuses…'he's under a lot of pressure; I know he loves me; he just can't express his feelings;

he's too tired from work to make love to me tonight and for the last three months; he better be lucky I love his ass or I would leave; or I don't have anywhere else to go.' But, we don't stay for him, we stay for us. Either we are frightened by the world outside of our relationship or we lack the discipline to handle the sacrifices we must make when we decide to capture of glimpse of life.

Do we hate men? No! It is their ways that are not highly favored. I think we make understanding the male species much more complicated than they really are. Men are not any more difficult than women, if you want to believe that. It is the willingness to take the time to get to know each other, instead of shunning off the things that we do not understand and defining them to be complex simply because we don't care to understand. I guess it is our human nature to have some kind of complexity in our lives."

Both of the ladies smiled and silenced for a moment.

"My situation reflects most of the challenges you mentioned. I stayed too long for the sake of my children, my family name, and my parents. I stayed in the beginning because I was led to believe my choices were limited. I stayed thirty years too long. Now, my children are grown and I feel I have no other ties holding me to this relationship. When I married my husband, comprehending the events to come was not something that one would imagine. When I look back at all that I have been through, my lungs collapse and I find myself gasping. I can no longer make the excuses you mentioned. I can no longer think with my heart, I must think with my mind. Forget about love, because it was never. Forget about peace, because it has passed. Forget about saving my soul, because it has vanished." Her head gently falls to the top backing of the sofa. She places her feet inside the plush sofa with knees bent to her chest and arms stretched around her legs with fingers entwined. Hopelessness smeared across her face assisting the light bags under her beautifully widen eyes.

"My great grandmother on my father's side, we called her Madea, had a distinctive way of reasoning with suffering. She would say that a life without trials and tribulations is not a life at all but resembles a perfect world which does not exist. What happened after you were married?" Evelyn causally intervenes trying to create a more positive spin, assuming that marriage life was a little better for Melissa in the beginning.

Melissa's sad puppy dog face looked up at Evelyn with a tear trapped within the right corner of her left eye. She gently licked her dry lips which did not assist much because her mouth was just as dry. She felt her words stall in her abraded throat as she tried to speak. Her first words escaped muffled, "My husband and…"

"Take your time. If you do not want to talk about it now, that's fine," Evelyn insisted, leaning in toward Melissa to try and comfort her.

"It's fine. I want to talk about it…"

Before Melissa could complete her sentence, Evelyn's cell phone rang. "Excuse me Melissa, I truly apologize. I thought my phone was off. I truly apologize for the interruption." Evelyn reached for her cell phone hidden inside her purse tossed on the glass antique coffee table positioned in front of the sofa. "It's…I don't know who this is," she said with little concern. Suddenly, the phone rings again. "It's an emergency. One of my members has text me 911! Oh my goodness, I need to find out what has happened." Evelyn shifts to a more frantic reaction, but still remaining as calm as she possibly could.

"It's not Renée is it?" Melissa asked with trepidation.

"No, it's not her. It's another one of our members. It's the sister of one of our members. Leah Sallad. Leah has been one of our members since the day we opened. She has been my long term friend as well. I look to her as one of my sisters, not in the same respect, but in a better one." Evelyn leans her head down, staring motionless at the cell phone. "My sisters and I have not always seen eye to eye. Their decisions in life have hindered them from getting the most out of life. And with choosing those decisions, they have taken many people down their destructive paths out of spite and jealousy, me included. I had to put it in the Lord's hands so I could wash mine and move on with my life. But, Leah, she is an exceptional one."

"Is she okay?" Melissa asked with grave concern.

"We shall see. We shall see," Evelyn stated with sadness in her eyes in a low tone, continuing to stare blankly at the cell phone.

Chapter

7

LOOKING FOR security, a man with a job and a car, and defining herself through the eyes of her man was Leah's perfect view of life and the pursuit of happiness. A huge luxurious mansion with a perfect view of the stars was not her idea of contentment. Accepting the complexities of life and hoping to gain clarity wrapped in the arms of her man while continuing to challenge his love for her was all she could wish for. Her decisions were made around his responsiveness. Her capabilities were centered on his love and affection. But, do not misunderstand her strength. It was his love and devotion that kept her happy, but it was her self-preservation and strength that kept her alive and moving. At times, she could be very demanding with impossibilities and still he loved her. Putting all her energy into loving, understanding, and being responsive to the men in her life was a life in itself for her. Leah set the rest of her family aside ten years prior to the communion of her immediate family—her live-in spouse, Martin and her two sons, Trevor and Lamont.

Martin was one of the exceptions to the average man rule. He was compassionate and understanding. Functioning as the man of the house did not automatically ensure that his decisions were final, because he knew the final answer rolled off the tongue of his woman, Leah. He cooked, he cleaned, he debated, and he loved her body, heart, and soul. He had the sensibility that some women thrived but very few received. Having her bath water warm and ready when she returned home from a hard day's work was his specialty beside the full course meal he placed in her lap as she rested in bed from having her bath. Because he worked midnights, he would only have three to four hours with her, so he vowed to make the most of them. If her exhaustion was too much to bear, he would comb her hair until she fell into a deep sleep before he left for work.

On some occasions, he would send the children to his sister's home and prepare the house with the luxuries of a five star hotel suite with rose petals tracking from the door to the bath tub, from the bath tub to the bed. He would reset the lighting in the kitchen and bedroom to dimmers before she arrived home. As she walked through the door, he led her to the bedroom and removed her clothing. He placed her in the hot bath to thoroughly wash her body while he caressed her neck with kisses, whispering romantic gestures in her ear. Continuously conveying to her how much he loved her and how much he needed her in his life. Wrapping the towel around her body and escorting her to the bedroom, where he laid out a lingerie outfit, slipping her body into it after he massaged her with motion oil. He prepared a candlelight meal to nourish her body before they made love for the next hour and a half. He kissed her on the forehead before he left for work as she lay helplessly on her back, wearing the fatigue across her face.

With a match made for the big screen, it was hard to believe that after eleven years of devotion, they are no longer together. It was her infatuation with the *'Plan'* of life that became too persistent for Martin to bear, he said. It was her concerns with marriage and planning for their future that drove him to depart. Martin had gotten comfortable in the eleven year arrangement, so much so, that he believed marriage was a useless step. They did not need a piece of paper to define their love, he said. Leah insisted, frequently, on a daily basis for the last year before their final separation. Stating final separation identifies that they've separated once before.

After nine years together, they decided to split up for a while and go their separate ways. Feelings seemed to shift, at that time, toward a more negative light. They held their compassion for love making together but their day activities became overpowering for both Leah and Martin. Martin moved back in with his parents for two months and then he was back at Leah's doorstep, on one knee, with a ring and begging to be in her presence again. But the happiness lasted for a brief moment and back to the relentless fighting over the big question, *"when are we going to get married."*

Working as a banquet host catering to the rich of the rich fundraising and festival parties was Leah's job but not her way of life. She prided herself on living a normal life and being married would be the icing on the cake. Leah could not comprehend why confusion lived within Martin's heart. His efforts confirmed his love for her but his restricted behavior over the marriage life was unexplainable. Leah began to question him being *in-love* with her; as she announced her feelings to him, stating that she believed he loved her but he was no longer in-love with her. She questioned his motives and stated that there must be another woman that he was in-love with. Of course he denied the accusations, but his words were still not to her satisfaction. She believed he contradicted himself when he placed the ring on her finger and that was the basis of her argument during the last year of their relationship. With their relationship taking so much energy out of her, she had to take a leave of absence from work. During her stay at home, their debates sprung into full swing and Leah gave Martin an ultimatum, marry me or leave now. Martin chose to leave, but the relationship was beyond reconciliation, he said.

After Martin left, Leah was a mess for a few days. She was never the kind of woman to reflect weakness in her appearance, talk, or her walk, but this took a toll on her emotionally. One would not know if she was in need or unhappy by a simple conversation; you would need to dig a lot deeper to capture a glimpse of her disturbance. She pulled herself together and prepared a 'Plan' for the rest of her life without Martin. It was difficult and for a long while she did not give up the hope that he would return. She would frequent his sister and mother's house with the idea that she may run into Martin. She called with trivial request for the children, without making her motives known to him. Her desperate actions went undetected and Martin would come to her beck and call, no matter what time of night she phoned. Even being separated, he was still drawn to answer her every need except one—marriage. Leah took it for what it was worth and did not capitalize the circumstances; she just continued with the flow. Her last attempt, which soon became obvious to Martin, was when she lured him over to the house for what would be their last rendezvous.

With Martin's male ego and testosterone taking hold of him, still he tried to resist her gestures. "I thought you needed me to fix the kitchen pipes?" he said with a wide smile across his face.

"I do, but I thought we could have a little fun first," Leah

ALINA

said with a bigger smile on her face noticing the bulge in his pants. She sat in one of the kitchen chairs wearing a deep plum color short silk robe, which was his favorite color on her. She crossed her seamlessly long gorgeous legs revealing a hint of her butt cheek, with bare feet.

He leaned in toward her and whispered softly, "You are so wrong for this. You know I love it when you are in this robe with bare feet, wearing that beautiful ass smile." Then, he kissed her right cheek, then her left one.

"Does this mean that I can have what I want?" she asked firmly in a low voice.

"You can have whatever you want tonight," he conceded, gently kissing her lips. Positioning his hands under her arms and slowly moving her body out of the seat and up toward him for a face to face view. She stood five feet nine inches, just three inches under him.

Speaking in a soft delicate voice, eyes linked directly to his with her left arm droopily positioned around his neck and the right arm snuggled around his waist pulling his body closer, she whispered, "I want you. I want you to make hard love to me like never before."

"I think that can be arranged."

He calmly motions her body toward the living room sofa. Penetrating his body against her coke bottle shaped body, in a slow circular rotation pleasing all anxious nerves throughout her body. Back pressed against the sofa cushion, Leah releases her slim arms over her head as Martin slowly unties her robe exposing her b-cup breast. He captured a glimpse of her beautiful widen dark brown eyes roll to the ceiling, eyelids slowly opening and closing, soon resting in a closed position. Leah, feeling the temperature rise throughout her body, her breath releases soft whispered moans of satisfaction while he swallowed her breast inside his mouth. His hands stroked up and down her thighs, roughly gripping her perfectly round shaped butt as he moves up her body placing his erected nature between her legs. With a soft slow steady scream, Leah felt him enter inside her and her heart melted. His love pulsated inside her reiterating on a relationship so beautiful. Watching his smooth rapid motions and his sexy facial expressions turned her on even more. She embraced his chest with her lips while easing their bodies off the sofa onto the floor. She slowly guided their bodies around as she took over the motion. Hands resting on his buffed masculine chest gripping his breast while crowding his neck with passionate kisses. Feeling the pressure deeper inside her as she swiftly rocked back and forth, up and down, around and around on top of him. Ungraceful breath, moving faster and faster, he cringed and moaned for her to stop, but she continued with more passion than before. With feelings exploding inside each other, they both completed with long steady sighs.

"With the simplicity of love, why does it seem so complex to stay in love?" Leah softly said as her body collapsed in the middle of the living room floor.

"I don't know. Maybe we event more because we think it should be more to it. Sometimes, simplicity can be complicated, at least with us. When we try to analyze everything, we have a propensity to over emphasize on areas that were okay to begin with."

"What's wrong with having a plan?"

"Nothing. It is when you develop a fascination on perfecting the plan is when it becomes a problem. When we realize that all things cannot be perfect, then we can live a more gleefully fulfilled life. I think we use our relationships to fill a void in our hearts, instead of understanding that a relationship is an added bonus to the pursuit of happiness. I think all men need women and women need men, but we need to understand and be true to ourselves first."

"So you think that I need you to fill a void? What void am I trying to fill?" she asked with slight hostility.

"We are all guilty of trying to fill a void. Not being loved enough as a child. Trying to make up for the lost love of relatives, and the list is endless. In the case of you and me, I thought that we could make it work, but there was something missing."

"Something missing, like what?"

"I don't know, that's the problem. I have loved you for many years, still do, but for some reason we are growing further and further apart."

"You don't know...well that's a sorry ass excuse. Did we outgrow our love for each other or what?"

"Possibly so! But neither one of us will be the hero to admit to that, I'm sure," he stated with a restrained smile.

"I guess we are two stubborn fools with one fool still in-love," she said as she smiled and reached for her robe. "Well, it is time for you to be going."

"I see, just put a brother out. Use him up and kick him out."

"Yep, you are correct about that. Seriously, you need to go because I need to get some sleep for tomorrow."

"What's going on tomorrow?" he asked with wonder in his eyes.

"Now you are all in my business. I have a few errands to

run, that's all you need to know. Oh, look at that pipe before you leave. It's working on my nerves with that faint drip. Oh, and leave me two hundred dollars, I have some things I need to get," she barked while adjusting the water to the shower, closing the bathroom door, and jumping into the tub.

Martin studied the pipes under the kitchen sink exhaustingly, and discovered that a washer would do the trick, but he would need to buy one and return in the morning to replace it. He advised Leah, placed two hundred and fifteen dollars, all of what he had in his pocket, on the kitchen table and left out the side door.

~

The office smelled of Ben gay and ethyl alcohol. The furniture in the room was as old as Leah's oldest boy Lamont, thirteen years old. She thought perhaps a few years older. The equipment was out dated and the flooring was scarred with scuff marks representing a well used facility. Leah had not really thought about today, but that she was coming in to get the results from a routine test. As she sat in the examination room waiting patiently for her well used doctor to enter, she reminisced on the event from the night before. A smile glowed across her face revealing her almost perfect teeth. In the middle of her recap, the doctor entered the room.

"Good morning Ms. Sallad. How are you this morning?" The doctor greeted her with a puzzled look and slow movements.

"Good morning Dr. Winchestinowski," she replied, watching him slowly move around the tiny room searching for the doctor stool.

"Well, let's see. I wanted to discuss the results of some

testing done on the fifth of April, about two months ago."

Leah was starting to get impatient with the length of time Dr. Winchestinowski took to deliver the results. His lazy dragging voice and pretentious demeanor was too familiar to Leah. She thought to herself, "Please hurry so I can take care of some business today."

"Some of the test came back questionable," he finally managed to blurt out.

"What do you mean questionable? Is there anything wrong?" she asked with a mystified look upon her face.

"Nothing I think you should be alarmed about but we want to take every necessary precaution. We want to do a biopsy on your breast to determine if the tumors we see are cancerous tumors or malignant tumors…"

Leah interrupted, "What do you mean nothing I should worry about? You are talking cancer here! What did you see? How many? You said *Lumps* as in plural," she said infuriatingly.

"I don't think you will need to be concerned, this is just a routine and it may not be cancerous. I will have Martha schedule you for the biopsy and we will discuss the results the following week. Okay, Ms. Sallad? It will be okay. We just need to check to rule out all possibilities," he tried to reassure her that everything would be alright.

"Okay, that's fine. Just schedule me as soon as possible, please," she said releasing a long sigh.

A couple of weeks later, Leah got the news that her tumors were indeed cancerous. So much for reassurance, she thought. Leah was diagnosed with Stage I Breast Cancer, though treatable, it was critical for her to move right away to Chemotherapy to shrink the size of the tumors and time was a luxury that she could no longer afford. With time against her, Leah stalled on the therapy and demanded a second opinion. Three months lapsed before she consulted another physician to only receive the same results, but worse. Dr. Willington's opinion concurred with her doctor's opinion and he also noted that she was in Stage II of IV, with Stage IV being fatal. The reality had not set into Leah's mind and she went on with life as usual for the next two weeks. Under Dr. Winchestinowski's advice, she took her time and researched the pros and cons of chemotherapy and with an Internet flooded with information about breast cancer; she had a lot to review. While feeding her mind with information her body was being fed by the toxic poison inside her, stripping the life from underneath.

Undergoing chemotherapy was challenging for Leah, primarily because she tried to conceal her diagnosis from the rest of the world, especially her family. She believed that she could overcome the disease with great willpower and strength from inside her, without the assistance from outside help. It became demanding to obscure the hair lost, the lack of energy, and the dark subtle shadows around her eyes as if she hadn't slept in days. She wore oversized clothing to hide her rapid weight lost. A thin moderate wool cap covered her small head with a scarf tied around her head to capture the appearance of hair underneath. Oversized clothing, wool cap, and scarf being worn in the middle of the summer raised eyebrows and floating rumors.

Eventually, she told Martin's family the news and reassured them that all was under control and not to worry. Martin's mother suggested that she tell her sisters, but she was not ready to consult them. She was not ready for the lack of concern questions, but of inquisitiveness merely to have a topic of discussion during one of their drunken sessions. Her mother's side of the family consisted of three aunts, two uncles, both heavily into the use of drugs, three sisters on a spiraling path to destruction, twenty-eight first cousins, twelve nieces and nephews, and a brother that she had not seen in over twenty years. The family plot thickens with the absence of her father, which occurred over twenty years ago and a mother too bitter for anyone to stay by her side long enough to discover that her heart was not cold, but empty. A great-grandmother that drank like a fish and could not keep a place of residence to save her life. Leah, she would be the middle child of the bunch, thirty-five, ambitious, and high on life's energy. She never looked at herself as being better than her family but her life achievements outweighed most and her search for a more normal *white picket fence* life could not be done in the company of her inexorable good for nothing back-stabbing family members. Oh, there were a few family members that were different from the rest, but very few. Leah's oldest sister was the worst of them all. She drank, cursed her children daily, and insisted on concocting another money grabbing scheme that would destroy someone else's life and fill her pockets with a hundred or so dollars. Too ignorant to elaborate on a more enriching scheme, she settled for the peanut robberies that fed her for one day instead of a lifetime. The corruption within the family was far more than Leah could bear, so she chose to stay away, albeit it hurt her heart to see them ruin one another this way. Leah could not turn to her family for any moral support. Although she intended to tell the few that she could trust, this would not be the time. Instead, she turned to her dear friend, Evelyn.

Chapter

8

EXITING OFF Interstate Ninety-Six onto the Grand River ramp, heading toward *one* of the roughest sectors of the big city, Evelyn's eyes were narrowed imperceptibly in the bright sun. Between the drug addicts, the prostitution, and the drug dealers, sat a small neighborhood of family and friends. Surrounding Cascade Street, several streets up and several streets back, everyone knew one another—being family or knew someone within the family. A close net neighborhood where no one outside the family circle dared to enter and as you drove down the streets, you were under tight security watch by the residence and friends of the residence. This was by no means a homeowner's association block; it was the *stay off my block* association. The families within this square owned the respecting streets. In a city with a ring of corrupt cops and crooked lawyers, the members of Cascade wrote their own laws and delivered their own justice.

Right in the middle of it all was Evelyn's ninety-three year old great-grandmother on her father's side of the family. Her great-grandmother, Elise, was a stubborn old bird that refused to leave the neighborhood. No matter how bad the conditions were, she insisted she would stay. Elise would contest that she was a proud homeowner and it took her thirty-five years to pay off her home and she would not allow the punks in the neighborhood to run her off. Elise, being six foot two, over two hundred fifty pounds, it was no wonder none of the crooks in the neighborhood would try to tackle her, not to mention the reputation her grandson carried.

Except for a time when she was sixty-two and a man tried to snatch her purse from her shoulder after she had cashed her work check. As she walked out the door of Butch's Liquor Store, a man in his late twenties approached Elise and demanded her purse. She refused and the robber punched her, grazing her across the face with his fist. And almost, in a simultaneous motion, she hit him back. He started to tug on her purse, but he was unable to remove it from her shoulder. While she continued to fight off the assailant, a stranger drove-up and startled the robber. The assailant turned in the opposite direction and fled the scene. The gentleman asked Elise if she was okay and with little concern for what just occurred, she insisted that she was unharmed and okay to walk home.

He said to her, "Ma'am, maybe I can take you home or call for someone to come and get you."

She refused.

"You shouldn't have been fighting him like that," he said as he smiled with gleam and seemed impressed by the elder woman.

She looked at him with a surprised gesture of *'are you crazy written over her face'* and said, "I just cashed my check…he was not gettin' my pocketbook. No Sir. I worked too hard for my money to let some thug take it in five seconds."

"Well, I suppose he was not." The gentleman smiled, and

then continued, "Are you sure you are okay to walk home."

"Yes, I Am," she said with pride then added, "I am not worried about those pitiful crooks…tryin' to take my check…he bopped me so I bopped him back. Yes Sir, I can take care of myself."

And so she did for the next thirty years or so. Now, at ninety-three years old, her posture was slightly worn down, her turtle movements were to be expected, yet her mind was as sharp as a razor. Her dark complexion skin was as smooth as a baby, and the bags under her eyelids did not come until she reached seventy-five which were hidden behind her enormously thick bifocals, so they remained unseen. Elise was as healthy as an ox, with Bayer aspirin being her only dose of daily medication.

"Doctors say it will stop me from having a heart attack," Elise said with a smile.

"Yeah, I suppose Madea," Evelyn stated with uncertainty.

"How is my baby doing today?"

"Fine. How are *you* doing?"

"I could not be better. Just got this pain in my belly that will not go away, but I keep on movin'," Elise said, patting her stomach with her right hand and holding a lit cigarette in the other. "Baby," she said as slow as she could muster, "go to the front closet and get me another pack of cigarettes. I am on my last pack and that damn nephew of mine has taken 'bout five from this pack."

"I don't know why you deal with him, Madea."

"Because they are my nephews. To tell you the truth, baby, I have grown tired of their nonsense. I only keep 'em here because as long as people see 'em running in and out of this house they will not enter. Plus, most of anybody that will want to rob me or attack me is their damn friends. So, keeping them around is good for me and I suspect better for *them*."

"I guess so. You really need to move from here and come and stay with me," Evelyn convincingly hinted.

"No I *do not!*" she replied in a firm voice, looking at Evelyn through the top of her bifocals. Unintentionally, she positioned her glasses to the edge of her nose and slightly tilted her head down to get a good look at Evelyn. "While you are talkin' 'bout me, you look like you gain some weight."

"I may have, Madea."

"Umm umm…you better pull away from the table next time." She gave her a quick scan and smiled.

"Madea, you say that every time I see you," Evelyn noted, with no offense taken. If you were more than a hundred pounds, Madea considered you to be overweight, and if you were under that, she would say that you needed to eat. She was your typical grandmother—wanting to feed you if they thought you were *too* thin and still fed you, even if they thought you were *too* fat, and made strong comments on the subject.

"You keep messin' around and you will be as big as *me*," she chuckled.

"Madea, you are a mess," Evelyn said.

"My baby…I am glad you came to see me." She smiled and leaned back in her favorite recliner. That was where she sat every day. Elise's recliner was ten years or more old with torn seat cushions, stripped fabric arms, with the reclining knob on the right side of the chair broken. She covered the chair with old dust dresses from many moons ago. The sleeves of the chair were sophisticatedly patched up with duct tape, re-padded with old cushion from an outdated chair she got rid of back in 1981, and

124

wrapped with a piece of fabric from a thirty year old table cloth. She gracefully rocked back and forth, patting her stomach.

"You said you have some pain in your stomach? Your belly looks more swollen than usual, are you sure you are okay?" Evelyn said, sitting up from the sofa to the right of the recliner, while reaching over to touch Elise's stomach to make a determination for herself.

"Yes, I am alright. I have endured pain for more than fifty years. I will not let a little stomach pain bother me, no ma'am. And I will not go to the hospital. Paul asked me that question yesterday," she said with certainty.

"Yesterday! That means you are in more pain than usual. If Paul noticed you were in pain, if he notices anything besides where he would find his next fix, then you may need to go to the hospital. Madea, don't sit here in pain when you do not need to."

"I am okay, I tell you. Now, let me be and we will need to not discuss this any further," she said with frustration. "Now, turn to channel four for me so I can watch *Jeopardy*."

"Yes ma'am." Evelyn gets up to turn the TV to channel four. Turning the knob twice on the 1986 TV was all that was needed to complete the task. Elise's TV could only receive four stations and she watched only two, channel four and channel sixty-two.

"You got here so late I wanted you to cash my check today."

"I will come tomorrow and cash it. Do you want me to take you to the supermarket as well?"

"If that won't be any trouble?"

"Madea, you know it will not be any trouble. I can be here around eleven. Have one of your sorry nephews to accompany us

125

so they can carry the groceries."

"Willie said he would go. I told him yesterday."

"That's fine." Evelyn rested her body in the sheet covered sofa, stooped down with her fingers locked inside each other neatly placed in her lap. A moment passed and then the door bell rang.

Yelling through the door like an anxious mad man was her nephew Paul. "Hey, Evelyn, alright, open the door," he barked overly excited. He had rung the door bell again, as if Evelyn could possibly be far from the door. Elise's home was engulfed by a huge country porch with oversized windows throughout. Her house was one of the few largest homes in the area, standing with three stories and approximately twenty-one hundred square feet, including the upper level which was converted to another unit all together. Her living room was about nine by ten with the front door overpowering the entrance. Sliding by the TV stand and the end of the sofa planted comfortably against the window, Evelyn made it to the door in two steps and opened it.

"Hey Paul," she said with a sour tone.

"Hey there, cous', it's good to see you and feeling good out here too." Exaggeratedly energized, as Evelyn opened the door, he reached in for a hug. "Yeah, it is good to see you. How you doin'?"

"I'm fine. Looks like you are doing fine as well," she said with sarcasm. Looking over his malnourished body, which was not a surprising appearance. His short height brought his face just above Evelyn's bosom and his thin body was lost in her arms. His fiery eyes conquered the whiteness around his pupils, leaving no mystery behind his midnight affairs. Exhausted eyes, a missing front tooth, and foam forming in the cracked corners of his mouth revealed his troubling lifestyle.

The remark never appealed Paul's attention, because his

mind was dancing to its own tune. His behavior spoke loud and clear and the fidgeting confirmed her suspicions. He raced past Evelyn to the back of the house to his bedroom, and returned with his shirt off and a fresh lit cigarette in hand. "Boy, it is good to see you. Aintie was given me a hard time about her going to see the doctor...please tell her." He laughed when no joke had emerged. Unable to stand in one spot, he pasted the floor back and forth between Elise and Evelyn. "Tell her she needs to go," he noted again, looking for confirmation from Evelyn.

"If she is hurting that bad she does need to go."

"Yeah...yeah...that's what I said."

"Quit talking about me like I'm not here. I will go when I get ready to go. I have never been to a hospital in all ninety-three years and I don't plan to start now. Now, you two just let me be."

"Okay aintie. But you really need to go," he said in a more serious tone.

"Just watch her, Paul. I will be back tomorrow to check on you Madea."

"Okay dear, it was nice of you to come by. I will see you tomorrow."

"Oh...you going so soon cous'? But I just got here...stay for a spell."

"I've been here for three hours or so and I must head back to complete some work."

"Ms. Businesswoman, always on the go." He laughs colorfully, covering his mouth with his left hand while gripping Evelyn's shoulder bone with the other. He was not afraid of touching, it was how he expressed himself, but Evelyn was not fawn of his behavior.

"Yeah, you ought to try it sometimes," she said

sarcastically. "I will see you tomorrow, Madea."

"Okay baby, be careful out there this time of night."

"I will."

"Wait, let me walk you to the car…hold on a minute let me get my shirt." He beckoned for Evelyn to wait a moment.

"See, Madea, he is high or on his way," she calmly whispered to Elise.

"What he does is his business. If everyone mined their own business, then the world would be a better place. He's got a few problems, but so do you."

"I don't pretend I don't have problems, but he is a crack-head."

"Crack-head or not, he is my nephew, and he is destroying himself baby, not you or me. Himself!"

"I guess you are right, but, I don't trust him around you."

"Yeah, I see how much, you're leaving. But, I don't fault you for that, just as you should not fault him for what he do. We all have our lives to live baby and yours is no exception. You say you do not trust him here but still you have work to do and you must go. Your life or what you need to do is important to you, just as what he is doing is important to him. He may not be able to help himself."

"Yeah, they say that about all men. Men will be men, I suppose," she said in a whispered anger.

"Yes, men will be men. We make the man more complicated that he really is. Just 'cause we do not agree with his choices does not mean he is less important than you or me. 'Cause he does not behave in a particular manner that is appropriate for you doesn't make him any less of a man than you think he should be. We are all human, baby, and that's all we need to remember.

Sometimes men are assholes but sometimes we are too. Sometimes men are confused and challenged, but adversity lies on our backs harder than theirs because the Lord knew who to give it to. We need to accept that men will be men and that they will not always understand us 'cause they don't understand themselves and most of the time, neither do we."

"Okay grandma. You are right, but he does not need to be high around you. He could have stayed where he was."

"Baby, he did the right thing comin' home. Whatever you do or goin' to do that will jeopardize your health, always make your way home first, if possible." Both of them laughed and Paul entered the room.

"What's so funny? You ladies are a trip. I suppose you are male-bashing again?"

"Of course we are that's what we do. No, seriously, I will see you tomorrow Madea."

"Be careful and remember what I said. What you do is important to you, not necessarily everyone else," she shouted while Evelyn stood outside the front door, listening from the veranda.

"Aintie crazy."

"Look, you know I don't bite my tongue…"

Paul interrupted her, "I know, I know. Look, you know I have been trying really hard to stay clean but this monkey will not get off my back."

"I cannot point fingers, as a wise old woman once told me, but you need to stay on track tonight. I don't like how her stomach felt and she refuses to go to the hospital. Being Friday night and all, we will not be able to take her to the doctor in the morning. Will you do that for me?" She pleaded with him to stay abstemious, at least for tonight.

"I will. I will keep my eye on her tonight. You know I usually go out on Friday nights but I did not like the way she was lookin' today. She was sleep in that damn chair until about seven in the morning. You know she usually hit the kitchen, getting her ingredients together for dinner, around five in the morning. I know 'cause I was getting ready for work at six-thirty and she was still asleep. I had to call her name about three times before she answered. Normally, when I start up in the morning, she calls my name and say, *is that you rustling around back their Paul,* as if it would be anyone else that time of morning. She knows my schedule better than me," he said with a smile but with serious concern.

"Really," Evelyn studied with absolute concern and continued, "I will call tonight to see how she is doing. You have my number, right?"

"Yeah, I got it somewhere. But, aintie got it on a scratch pad on the table behind her chair."

"Good. Be sure to contact me if her condition worsens."

"See ya cous'. Be careful." Paul quickly swept his eyes across her car and said, "Boy you better be lucky the neighborhood knows your old man, 'cause you would have been jacked for this ride a long time ago. Man, you really have some nice wheels here," he sharply stated, laughing with enormous thrill.

"Yeah…that I do know." She opens the driver door, tossed her purse in the passenger seat, placed her right foot on the rim of the car, partially inside the vehicle. Her hands were planted firmly on top of the roof with keys in hand as she swiftly glanced around the area. "This neighborhood has gone to the dogs. I've been trying to get her to move, but she is more stubborn than I and it's like pulling teeth. She refuses to budge."

"This neighborhood has gotten bad, but we know

everybody here. Aint nobody gone bother her, the neighborhood would not allow it. Just like you. Your daddy grew up in this neighborhood and everyone is still afraid of him and he's dead. That's why you can walk these streets and get the same respect he did."

"I feel privileged," she said with mockery.

"Okay cous'. See you tomorrow and be careful."

Memories of her father channeled her mind. She could perceive the sound of the boyhood stories of her father's reputation whistling in her ear, even tonight. The neighborhood, as she remembered it, was nice and pleasant but with frivolous crimes of petty theft to drunken fights—much to the dismay she feels today. Homes were manicured with great appreciation from grandmothers and grandfathers who sold their blood to keep their homes in immaculate condition and a roof over their heads. But the street had become destitute and worn down. Simplified, it was practically unlivable.

Evelyn's father was a man of many faces. To his grandmother, he was a stubborn but gentle man who cared for his family. To his mother, he was a cruel man, who cared only for himself. And, to his wife, Evelyn's mother, he was her everything. From his striking head to his ferocious feet, she loved every inch of him. Even in the late hours, when his precious soul unraveled to a cruel beast, she loved him still. A wolf in sheep's clothing was how neighboring streets would describe her father. He left a penetrating fear in the air when he walked by, and his prey would be desperately clinching their bodies to a well lit porch of witnesses, breaking free from vulnerability and out of his reach. He did not wander the streets seeking trouble, yet, he was known to have done so. His six foot eight, three hundred and ten pound body was fairly intimidating to people in the neighborhood. Although his fierce reputation left a cold impression on the neighboring streets, he was still a respectful man with a thoughtful heart, who seemed isolated at times. It was Evelyn's mother that made him feel he had a place in life. In her arms, he did not feel insignificant, confused, and troubled. But, this heartfelt feeling challenged his mind and created a different person all together. He never learned how to deal with his emotions, so he took his disturbance out on Evelyn's mother.

~

Four o'clock in the morning on an exceedingly hot summer day in the middle of July, the phone rang. Five rings had passed before Evelyn realized that she was not dreaming. Visibility in her master suite was nearly zero, but feeling for the phone was something she had mastered from numerous middle-of-the-night phone calls from several of her club members. She reluctantly answered, "Hello." The words managed to escape her lips while dismissing a deep breath at the same time.

"Evelyn...man...its Paul," he said hesitantly.

"Paul...what's the matter. Where is Madea?" The words poured out like lightning.

"We had to call the E.M.S. She was not doing so good. Her stomach had swelled up like a balloon and she said her side and back was hurting really bad. She looked weak...and...I just called emergency. They are taking her out the door now and she will go to Grace Hospital off West McNichols. Do you know where that is?"

"Of course I do. I will meet you guys there. Thank you Paul. Thank you for looking out for her. I will not forget this."

"No need to thank me...she is my aintie...well, she's all I got." Despondency intervene his voice crushing his words. Then, Evelyn hung up.

When Evelyn arrived at the hospital, the nurse directed her to the fourth floor. "She's got a room already," she thought to herself. Evelyn took the elevator to the fourth floor and was welcomed by a grumpy receptionist.

"Can I help you?" The woman with the blond hair piece, tracks showing, revealing the true black color of her seemingly wool hair said as Evelyn approached the desk.

"My great-grandmother, Elise Tidy, was brought here with pain in her stomach. The nurse at the nurses' station directed me to this floor."

"Let me see," her lips smacked apart loudly, mouth partially opened while she unmercifully chewed a piece of gum—head faintly hidden behind a clipboard holding a mountain of papers, and continued her rude tone, "she's in room two forty-eight, through these doors, down the hall, to the right."

"Thank you."

Evelyn followed the instructions, passing another nurse's station and entered the room. Paul was seated in the chair next to the bed, head in hand, and sleep was wearing his face like a wet suit. To Evelyn's surprise, locked straps covered Elise's wrist and ankles. Her eyes bucked and furry settled in her stomach. *"What the hell is this?"* she chaotically stated to Paul.

"Oh...Hey cous'...I told them not to do that, but they said she was a risk to her health 'cause she keep trying to get out of the bed. Aintie is really strong. It took four of them to hold her down and a doctor came in to examine her and aintie knocked the chart out of her hand. Aintie keep saying that she wants to go home, but they said she is really sick. What are we going to do?" Paul stated, looking Evelyn directly in the eye with grave concern.

Evelyn glanced at Elise; she was finally asleep, at least for a moment. She looked at Paul and said, "Come with me." She exited the room and went to the nearby nurses' station. "Hi, I am Elise Tidy's great-granddaughter and I wish to speak to the individual in-charge at once, please."

The only nurse present at the station looked at Evelyn with irrelevant concern. "You need to wait. All the head nurses are at lunch or in another patient's room," she uncouthly stated.

"No, what you need to do is call for someone to assist me, *now*, or it will be a misunderstanding in this damn lobby." Evelyn bent her face in toward the nurses' face with fire in her eyes and resentment in her voice, "I can't believe that you call yourself a professional…that tone of voice along with that unprofessional response was totally uncalled-for."

"Well, everyone is assisting other patients."

"Someone needs to get here in a few minutes that is all I will say," she blurted with certainty.

The nurse picked up the phone and beckoned for a head nurse to come to the nurses' station immediately. Evelyn waited for several minutes before a heavy-set nurse with uncontrollable labored breathing and appeared exhausted from the short walk from the nearby room, approached her. She greeted Evelyn with a warm smile and said, "How can I help you?"

"I am Elise Tidy's great-granddaughter and I have a few questions along with a request."

"Okay, we will handle the request first, if possible—request tend to be of a more primary nature." She smiled and winked an eye.

Evelyn felt she was trying to ease the situation but her gestures were not invited with open arms. Evelyn was too infuriated and the mere fact that her great-grandmother was in restraints was appalling. "I would like the restraints removed from my great-grandmother's wrist and ankles. That has got to be inhuman."

"She has restraints, but why?" She turned to the rude nurse at the desk, who seemed to have tuned out the entire conversation and drifted into a world of her own. "Nurse Walters, why does this young lady's grandmother have restraints?"

"She is a strong old lady and we were not able to control her. She was trying to get out of bed."

"Oh, that's ridiculous. We will remove them right away. I do apologize." The head nurse immediately glanced back at the rude nurse with disappointing eyes and a look of; *this is causes for an immediate review.*

"Thank you. Now, I wish to speak with a doctor regarding her condition. How did she get a room so fast? She came in through the emergency, did she not?"

"Let me take a look at her chart and I may be able to answer that question." The nurse, Paul and Evelyn walked back to Elise's room, where she was still napping. The nurse grabbed the chart out of the basket attached to the wall. "Let's see what's going on with your grandmother," a steady pause from the nurse and she continued, "it looks like her doctor was called and he advised the nurses in the emergency room that she was on the way and to have a room available."

"Who called her doctor?" Evelyn stated with a puzzled expression.

"I did. His number is on the refrigerator. Willie said that

when she went to the doctor last month, he asked us to call him if she got worse, so I called him after I called E.M.S," Paul admitted.

"If she got worse! You mean to tell me that her doctor was concerned last month and no one told me?" she said with deep concern and disappointment.

"Aintie did not want to worry you so she told us not to say anything. Sorry cous'." He wailed with a true apology.

"Your grandmother is really sick. I will send in the doctor to confirm her diagnosis," The head nurse stated, quickly exiting the room.

Elise's doctor entered the room and confirmed that Elise would only have thirteen days to live. Evelyn thought, "How could he be so exact?" Elise had suffered from kidney failure and the doctor was quite surprised that she lived this long without being hospitalized sooner. Evelyn's heart dropped in her stomach and anguish emerged over her face. Paul had a dumbfounded expression deposited across his face as he stared into the air. Both collapsed in the chairs next to the bed staring at the floor. Evelyn had not imagined life without her great-grandmother, even with her age she had never considered living without her. She was the woman that kept her head afloat. She was her backbone when hers gave out. For the first time, Evelyn did not know what to do next.

~

The funeral home smelled of embalming fluid, multiple scents of flowers—some not favorable—and musty smelly socks all rolled up into one inside the old, in desperate need of repairs, building. The third class funeral home was one that Evelyn's great-grandmother had selected over twenty years ago. She was pleased with the great home sending of her husband that she pre-arranged her services, *paid in full*. Evelyn was not pleased with the likes of the funeral home but she was too upset to complain.

She visited the funeral home several days before to confirm the arrangements her great-grandmother had made many years prior. The professional secretary behind the desk, wearing small frame glasses riding the tip of her nose, with sleepy eyelids agreed that her great-grandmother's arrangements were on their books as *Paid*. Although Evelyn was not pleased with the look of the building, she was more than pleased with the service. The caring humbleness of the staff was a breath of fresh air. Dealing with unprofessional, careless people over the last two weeks, it was refreshing to be in the company of true professionals. Her great-grandmother taught her not to judge a book by its cover and Evelyn found that she was doing it more than usual. She wondered if her manners died with her great-grandmother. Evelyn wiped her eyes and erased the complaining thoughts from her mind.

On the day of the funeral, Evelyn strolled in much slower than before. A black *A'zhaEriq* dress covered her body, black Gucci heels covered her feet, and grief covered her heart. Welcoming her heartache, she balled her body around a chair in the back corner of a small restroom that could only fit one and a half people inside at a time. The antique painting on the restroom door disturbed by rust filled in the corners of the door screws and spots screaming through the old paint were not noticed by Evelyn, at least, not at that time. She felt that she had died with Madea. Her strength was ripped from her body and her soul diminished. She had never felt the agony she felt on this day, not even when her mother passed. She was overwhelmed with grief the day her mother passed but the passing of her *Madea* was too much for her to bear. Evelyn felt hopelessly fragile. On this day, July 23, 2004, she buried the most important person in her life. And on this day, her dear friend Leah expressed her warm remorse for the passing of Madea, while delivering the news that she was diagnosed with breast cancer. Evelyn felt the pulsating irregular rhythm in her heart and her breath collapsed, leaving her heart grief stricken and her body trembled with weakness. Evelyn did not think she would make it to the morning— and so she did, with the thought that her dear friend needed her now, more than ever. She gathered her thoughts, dust off her clothes and pulled herself together. She held her head up high, looking at her reflection through the stained crookedly hanged mirror, and said to herself, "I will miss you. I know you had a wonderful life here and hopefully you are with your husband, where you ought to be. Just know that I will always love you because you were the best thing in my life and I live for the day I would see you again. Your words will hold dear to my heart and your memory will be with me forever."

The funeral service was dignified and short. Many distinguished faces surrendered their busy schedules to grace the family with their presence. Out-of-towners were scattered about, soft mutters filled the chapel with an enchanting twine, while one glorified her grief in a frantic display. Aunt Carolyn Ann was a drama queen who appreciated her fifteen minutes of fame whenever possible. She hovered over the casket, sobbing hysterically, overstated trembling hands and persistent efforts to get attention. Her emotions went over the top when her voice carried at a high tone, "Not my Madea…not my Madea. I loved you Madea. Why must you go so soon?" Her impractical behavior was surprising to some, but expected to others who knew her well, including Evelyn. A cluster of unknowns surrounded her collapsed body and provided the attention she was seeking, and helped her to her seat. Evelyn, watching from a far, but only for a moment, was too self-absorbed to concentrate on Aunt Carolyn's fiasco. Especially since the family, *let alone Madea*, had not seen or heard from her in over a year. Beside the family reunion five years ago, no one had any *real* contact with Aunt Carolyn for several years. Her life reeked of troubling behavior; erratically, she lived in the fast lane. At age fifty-two, she still homelessly wandered the streets, living from house to house with pathetic boyfriends and disturbed women friends. But none of this was a concern to Evelyn.

An hour after the service, Evelyn sat at her great-grandmother's house unconsciously ignoring the guest, as she stumbled on fine memories of her Madea. She reminisced on the stories Madea shared about her deceased husband. She expressed her deep love for him and the exasperating countless hours of torment during his final day. Evelyn pictured her great-grandfather, lying in the hospital bed, smiling from Madea's extraordinary sense of humor, nearly choking from laughter. After his passing, she was devastated with grief, but she wore a smile. She told how she went into their bedroom and pulled out old sentiments and flourished on each story with a dilate smile. She told Evelyn how she would place each one of her sophisticated hats on her head and each told a different story. She told how they would dance the night away at the neighboring juke joints in the south. She smiled with gleam when she described his freshly tailored suit that captured his charisma and dazzled the ladies. Evelyn smiled as she remembered these stories. She had not concerned herself with the other people in the room, but consumed her thoughts with pleasantries of a great-grandmother that she would surely miss.

~

ALINA

Driving to the MH Women's Club was one of the longest trips she had ever taken. Anticipating what her friend was going to say became more aggravating than the trip itself. The news that Leah had cancer was overwhelming and Evelyn was fervent to find out what stage she was in, what treatment she was undergoing, and so many other questions of concern. She had buried one of the most important people in her life and she did not want to bury another.

Chapter

9

ENTERING THE club, Evelyn walked impatiently to the SQ room on the south end of the building in the back corner. She opened the door of the SQ room and Leah was nowhere in sight. In the background, she heard a grunt coming from one of the bathrooms. She walked to the master quarters that contained its own private bathroom and found Leah hovering over the toilet.

Leah slowly motioned her head up for a fleeting moment with tiredness in her eyes and said, "Oh hey, sister. I'll be out in a min…" she manipulated a smile and paused with sudden jerks of her body and the vomiting continued.

Evelyn went a few steps back into the master quarters and waited on one of the king size beds for Leah to finish. Evelyn took a mental note of Leah's appearance. It was the middle of the summer and Leah was wearing a wool cap. Clothing that swallowed her thin body and a long length jacket stretched across the master bed. Thoughts of final stage came to mind, but knowing Leah, all this was only to conceal her illness.

"I hate that. That medication has me throwing up every time I take it. I really wonder if it works. If I am vomiting it up within thirty minutes of taking it, who's to say it is really working or am I disposing of it in one setting? Or, maybe it's the poison in my body that it is discharging. Who knows? I am happy to see you sister." Leah walks over to Evelyn and gives her a big long steady hug, with the feeling of not wanting to let go.

"And so am I. How are you feeling?" Evelyn tries to suppress her concern, though unsuccessful.

"Well, I am not doing so well. I thought I could handle this on my own. I thought it would go away," she laughed hysterically. Totally inappropriate given the circumstances, but laughter was her only form of salvation.

"How far are you?"

"I am currently at Stage II and climbing," she confirmed with an unimpressive smile. Trying to turn light on a gloomy subject, she added, "Well, now I can smoke weed and it will be perfectly legal." Both of the women began to laugh uncontrollably.

Evelyn managed to intervene, "Our heartache has guided us into major laughter. Oh what obstacles life delivers!"

"You can say that again!"

"How long have you known? Because if I know you, you have known since day one and you have been too stubborn and independent to let anyone know."

"Since I was in Stage I, about a year ago," she looked with mild shame, chin to chest.

"A year ago! My goodness *Leah*. What were you thinking? Why didn't you come to me sooner? I can't believe you were dealing with this on your own. And the children—how are they?"

"Poor Lamont has gotten the worse end of it. It's getting to the point, sometimes he has to carry me inside the house after therapy. Trevor hangs by my side every waking hour. He never wants to go to school because he said he is afraid that he will come home and I will be gone. He said he would blame himself for not being there to assist me if something should happen. Can you believe that? Can you imagine an eight year old concerned with more than himself, especially a boy?"

"Trevor is a sweetheart, always have been. What about Martin? He is probably heartbroken."

Leah glanced at Evelyn and turned her head quickly in discomfort. "I have not told Martin."

With a hint of rage in her voice, she said, *"Why Not?"*

"We are not together anymore," Leah said hastily.

"You can't be serious, what happened?"

"Indifference."

"Indifference my ass. What happened, Leah?" she said in disbelief.

"He was trapped with the decision whether or not he should marry me, so I gave him a push."

"You did not give him an ultimatum?"

"Yes I did," she said with sureness.

"Now you know that ultimatums are not good for men. It does one of two things; turn them away, in-which it may have been the best thing, or makes them stay, which is most often not a good thing. Giving them an ultimatum is your way of saying I am willing to keep you, even if you don't want to be kept. It only suggests that you are hopelessly in-love with them and you are willing to make sacrifices and change your life—willing to disregard their past behavior as insignificant. We are showing them that we will put up with their trash in the name of love."

"I know…I know. See, he refuse to contribute to the plan of our life and I told him to contribute or leave."

"Maybe his plan was to leave," she stated with opinion.

"Just four months after we were separated, he was engaged to be married to another woman," she added with very little interest.

You could see the pressure building in Evelyn's pores, sweat glands bursting with moisture. "He did *what*? What the hell was he thinking? When is the wedding?"

"I don't know what he was thinking. It took me a few days but I'm over it now. I have more pressing business to tend to, like survival." She paused with an awkward smile. "To answer your question, he is already married. A commitment he made to another woman but found it diffidently impossible to fathom with me. What are the odds of that happening?" She smiled, rested her head on one of the oversized pillows decorating the master bed.

"That bastard. I would not have thought that Martin would do something like that. He loved you to death."

"Well, it looks like he will get his wish since death is tapping at my door." Leah was always wild with her sense of humor. Evelyn believed that nothing could get her down, but she could clearly see that her separation from Martin took its toll on her and yet she remained in good spirits. "I am over it. I have moved on. I will tell him when it is over and the disease has taken me by storm."

"Why would you wait so long?"

"Because he doesn't need to know. This is my life, my body, and I will decide when he should know."

"You still sound bitter to me. And you have every right to be." Evelyn looked at Leah, searching for a response but Leah remained silent, so she continued, "If you've known for a year that means that you guys separated about a year ago. Which would explain why I have not seen your face at the club in a while? Would it be fair to say that?"

"Yes, we broke-up a year and three months ago."

"Can count it right down to the wire?" Evelyn allowed a curious smile to take form of her face.

"Yeah, I was diagnosed the day after our last rendezvous. I know that timeframe all too well I'm afraid." She inhaled an immense breath and released a subtle sigh and closed her eyes with no thoughts in particular just in an effort to rest them.

"So, enough of that asshole; what's the prognosis? How is the cancer doing?"

"They say I have a fighting chance but the cancer is moving too rapidly. I went from Stage I to Stage II in a matter of months. My body is not accepting the chemo like they believe it should. But there is a small window of hope in the vast of darkness, which is a hope and a prayer." In what seemed like slow motion, Leah graced her head across the pillow to face Evelyn directly and said, "Do you think God will forgive us for what we have done?"

"He already has. Believe me, he already has."

"It's funny how certain thoughts just enter your mind and you can't explain why," Leah said. Not searching for a particular response, just blurting a thought.

Evelyn believed more was to be read into this story, but she remained silent. It was hard for her to watch her friend shrivel away from the world. Hiding behind locked doors, baggy clothes, and wool caps with non-matching scarves underneath, was not an effective way to deal with the cancer. She wondered just how much weight had she lost. If she could see, it would unassumingly reveal the truth. Evelyn felt she was hiding behind her own fears. Who could blame her, she thought. Losing the man that meant so much and facing the loss of her life that means so much more, especially to her children, who could blame her. Earlier, Evelyn was vanishing deep inside from the passing of her great-grandmother and now her feelings seem trivial in comparison to Leah's dilemma. Evelyn still had not reached the right words to say, if any were apposite but it would only be a matter of time.

~

Evelyn never appreciated the aroma of hospitals and yet she was making a second trip within a month's time. The dull depressing appearance did not help her displacement. She walked down the elongated widen hallways of Providence Memorial Hospital in Troy, MI. She had heard wonderful things about the hospital, but so far, she was not impressed. The staff was not as helpful as one would think, being one of the top ranked hospitals in the Detroit Metropolitan Area. Urine reeked from a few of the patient rooms as Evelyn strolled down the hallways in search of Leah's room. Surgical tape held up a number of postings located on several doors throughout the third floor of the hospital. Evelyn traveled, for what seemed like forever, to reach Leah's room—room 3-2-5-6. She takes an anticipatory breath of relief when she stumbles upon Leah's room. "Here it is, finally," she thought to herself. She entered the room and found Leah sleeping. She did not feel the need to wake her, so she searched the room for an empty chair. Evelyn sat in the chair beside the bed and watched TV until Leah awakened thirty minutes later.

"Hey sister...you should have woke me up," Leah uttered with drowsy medicated eyes.

"It's fine. I just got here several minutes ago." Evelyn did not feel the need to provide a drawn-out story that would only produce more questions. Leah was always suspicious of whispers around her and did not like ever feeling left out, even when there was nothing to tell. So, if she had discovered that Evelyn arrived thirty minutes before she had awakened her mind would be filled with wonder. She would wonder if Evelyn was secretly communicating with her doctor, in which he may have conveyed information to Evelyn that was not told to her. Her fragile mind would be in a frenzy, so Evelyn felt it to be best if she managed a small white lie.

"My dingy doctor will come in at four o'clock and let me know what we need to do from here."

"What do you mean?" Evelyn stated while noticing the time, three fifty-six, showed on the wall clock near the TV.

"I don't know. Getting information out of him is the same as pulling a dogs tooth. Men! He is an idiot. I think I am doing worse than he wants me to believe," she said with all the energy she could muster.

"That's not fair or ethical. He knows you have children, I'm sure? He can't be afraid to tell you the full story, it's not just your life hanging in the balance; it's the life of your children too." She turned to monitor the door—nothing. "It's four o'clock now, where is he?"

"Oh, he's probably at the nurses' station dilly-dallying around. He is an exceptional procrastinator."

"He can't be a procrastinator when it comes to his patient's health. He should have become an artist if he's seeking time and creativity. This is not a unique contest, this is your life. There is no special unique way to say what he needs to say…he needs to just say it with all the truth he can congregate," she said unwaveringly.

Leah nodded her head agreeably. "I don't know what his problem is. I know I can be stubborn and refuse some of the treatment but he has not convinced me that he knows what is best for me."

"Have you considered finding a new doctor?"

"Yeah, I got a second opinion and it was some of the same."

"Have you talked to anyone at the Cancer Treatment Centers?"

"No, I am a member of a cancer chat room group and with their helpful insight, it turns out that Doc may know what he is doing, but my stubbornness insists on questioning his options. I don't fully trust him, but I have never been one to trust easily."

"Yes, that is true," she smiled at Leah as both their heads swung toward the door as it opened.

The doctor quickly entered the room. Leah's nerves jumped through her skin because she had never seen him move this quick before now. His walk was a swagger similar to the nerd from the 1950 or 1960 *Nutty Professor* movie, "I forget what year," she thought to herself. A strange looking character; tall, goofy expression upon his face, thinning hair on top of his head, which was exposed when he sat in the chair on the opposite side of the bed, while his eyes were glued to Leah's chart. He crossed his legs, leaned back in the chair and managed to assemble a few syllables. "The new test ran on…" He paused for a moment and flipped through the pages in the chart.

"Look, we don't care about the day the test were administered. Just get to the results." Leah looks over at Evelyn with abhorrence. "He makes me sick when he does this. Just get to the damn point."

"My apologies Ms. Sallad," he said calmly. Her words did not seem to alter his behavior. "Your cancer is spreading. The chemotherapy treatment has been unsuccessful. It is spreading too rapidly…"

"So what are my options?"

"We can do radiation. This will attack the tumors directly and may be more effective."

"And if the radiation doesn't work?"

"Then…we can…we'll look into…"

"See…see what I mean? Spit it out," Leah said nauseatingly.

"We may need to look into other options, at that time."

"At that time, what do you mean at that time? I need you to look into the other options *now*. I may not have '*at that time*' to consider.

"Dr…"

"Dr. Winchestinowski," he said, completing Evelyn's response.

"Well, Dr. Winchestinowski, what are some of the other treatment options that may be discussed if the radiation is not effective as it needs to be?"

"Her condition is not good."

"What other options, Doctor?" Evelyn said exhibiting mild frustration.

"We may need to do a unique surgery that will allow the radiation to get to the brain a lot faster than other treatments," he managed a complete sentence, very calmly with little assurance.

"The brain! Has the cancer spread to her brain?"

"The treatment will be more effective when administered through the brain."

Leah looked at Evelyn, astound by what she was hearing. Her eyes were troubled and the agony left her breathless. Her emotions had remained stable up until now. Suddenly, she felt a thick layer of fear building up within her thin body. She had spent so much time being angry at Dr. Winchestinowski, perhaps hiding from the fear that bottled inside her, that she had not seriously considered the fact that she may die.

"Dr. Winchestinowski, you are avoiding the question—has the cancer spread to the brain or not?"

"I am afraid so," he unwillingly responded as he placed his pen inside his jacket pocket—hands unnoticeably shaking. He looked directly at Leah and then at Evelyn. He saw the disappointment written on Leah's face and he felt as if he had failed her. At this point, the waiting game had come to a screeching halt and it was time for him to be more boldly direct and advise her that he had no other options to consider. His eyes burned with moisture, he shook his head and said, "I am sorry, Leah. The cancer has spread to your brain, lungs and your bones. I was really hoping that we could catch some of it. The treatment was the highest dose we were able to administer and it was not working. The cancer was simply moving too fast." His cracked voice became almost a whisper—soft and powered with feelings of guilt and betrayal. He really wanted to save her. He told her everything in moderation, being confirmatory, when he should have been truly honest from the start. He thought he was giving Leah hope but he gave her more pain. She believed she was fighting her cancer head on and this spell of sickness would last for a moment, and then pass. But she did not realize that the end was near and that he allowed her to waste so much time with anger, hostility, and repugnant behavior.

Leah had four months, give or take a few, to live. She suffered through the brain surgery, but no other treatment worked. Her family was made aware of her illness the last two months before she passed. It was just as Leah thought. They were grabbing for information, furniture, money, and looking forward to more drama within their sick circle of life. Leah spent her last days in a hospice care facility, where they tended to her every need. Thanks to her good friend Evelyn, she was admitted to one of the top care facilities in Michigan.

~

Evelyn received the voicemail messages on her cell phone to go to the care facility immediately. Leah's sister had left a couple of messages, all nonchalant, but expressing urgency through her selection of words. "I must go. I don't mean to run out on you Melissa, but I need to check on my friend."

"That's okay. Would you like for me to go with you? You know, to keep you company, I am sure it is a long drive."

"No, I put her in a facility near my house. I am surprised that her sister was there this late or that she managed to get a ride. The facility is on Twenty-Three Mile Road near Woodward Avenue. Did you drive here or did Renée bring you?"

"I drove. I followed Renée here. My car is parked outside. Do you need me to drive? I will drive you there."

"No, I will manage. Maybe you should go home or go lay down in one of the SQ rooms. Does your husband know where you are or if you will be returning? Or do you care?" she said, marshaling a smile, while swiftly moving about the room to gather her belongings.

"No and No. I would like to accompany you, if you do not

mind." She looked with puppy dog eyes and Evelyn could not resist.

"It would be fine. Come now, we must go promptly."

Evelyn and Melissa entered the care facility and were greeted by a round-the-clock receptionist. "Good evening ladies, how may I be of service to you this evening?"

"Hello! We are here to see Leah Sallad. She's in Care Suite 1-2-7."

"Yes, Ms. Sallad. Come with me, I will escort you to her suite," The receptionist said in a compassionate tone, moving away from the desk and kindly demanding them to follow.

They reached Leah's room in a matter of minutes—a splendid quiet retreat with an artificial five foot plant greeting you at the door in the corner to the left. Dim lights absorbed the concentrated mood as Evelyn's heart started to race a mile a minute as she approached the bed. Her expression of grief soaked her face as the fears weighed down her movement. Evelyn continued to wait for the words to come, but they never did. The smog within her heart clouded her thinking. The knot in her stomach made her face cringe. And the sickeningly nauseous feeling in her throat traveled to the pit of her stomach. She peeked around the partially drawn curtain and placed a reluctant smile on her face. Clearing her thoughts, she said, "Hey lady. This will not put you in the clear." Leah and Evelyn released restrained laughs. Evelyn gestured a wave of her right hand, not visible to Leah, to suggest Melissa have a seat on the other side of the curtain. "How are they treating you in here?" Knowing the response—Evelyn needed something of less awkwardness to address.

Leah slowly motions her body and tried to sit-up. She

flaccidly stretched out her arm requesting Evelyn to assist. Evelyn gently grabbed Leah's hand and positioned her arm under Leah's underarm to place her upright in the bed. Between the both of them, they were able to move Leah two-thirds of an inch—not much, but they tried. The tangle resulted in laughter among the women and smiles that lit up the room. "Oh, we are a pair," Leah said while clearing her throat. "It's the end of the road for me now. Although I am only thirty-six, I feel that I have lived a full life. I did not know that my stay in this world would be so brief, but here it is," she slowly stated with earnestness in her voice, capitalizing on all the good things in her life. "I think I was truly blessed, you know that?"

"Yes, I would have to agree. You are among very few and far in between and I would not have it any other way. You say you were blessed—I say that everyone else, myself included, were the blessed ones to be graced with your presence." She smiled at Leah, placing her right hand over Leah's fragile shrunken hands that lay in her lap.

"You have always moved me with your words of encouragement and assiduousness of the truth. You have been the best friend—the sister—that a woman could ever have. With all the things that you have been through, one would suspect that you would be bitter, evil, and contaminated. But no matter what, your heart has always remained reasonable and caring." She managed another smile and continued, "When you first started the Woman's Club, I was against it, remember that?"

"How could I forget? You told me that I was behaving like a bitter old woman who needed to let it go and move forward with my life. You told me that I was fishing for other bitter women because misery loves company," she recalled.

The women laughed and shook their heads agreeing with the recap. "I said that because I was perfectly happy. I did not share your pain at the time. They say that no one truly understands your pain until they have walked a mile in your shoes. I believe that to be true now. I knew you were a good person, and yet I felt that men scalded your heart forever. I did not know nor understand, at the time, that you were expressing a greater concern—healing. It took me to lose the one that was dearest to me, beside my boys, to totally comprehend what your bitterness was about. I take my hat off to you Miss Evelyn McKenzie. You are one of the most humble, warm, captivating women that I have ever known and your concerns are always in the right place at the right time. I would like to thank you for everything that you have done for me. I would like to thank you and simultaneously apologize for my tenacity," she said slowly with warm feeling, trying to hold back the tears.

"No apology necessary. But you were correct about one thing; I was a bitter old woman. My first thought when I started the club was to gather woman to bash men, then something came over me. I sat myself down on the vanity in my bedroom at home, looked into the mirror and did not like what I was becoming. Male bashing was not me. Yes, I was bitter, but it did not account for my unscrupulous actions toward *all* men. I discovered, in that little pep talk with myself, that it was not about them, it was about me. It was about *us* women, and the things that we allowed men to do to us. As the stories flooded in and time raced by, I revealed goodness within me that no man could ever take away. I discovered a rare form of self-sufficiency and strength that my bones were lacking. When I was hurt, the many times that I had been scorned, I thought that I was alone and the betrayal sat on my

154

head and mine alone. It was not until I started to meet woman with analogous and sometimes more heart wrenching stories than mine, that I determined that the world was full of confused and messed up people." Both of the ladies laughed, hesitantly.

"You are modest, Miss Evelyn," Leah managed to say with weakened energy. She slowly closes her eyes and sighs.

Evelyn looks at Leah, with no words escaping, and mind exploding with rambled sentences to share but nothing from her lips. "Where is your sister?" she softly said to break the silence.

"I don't know. She was here earlier."

"Earlier? She called me several times tonight."

"Tonight?" Leah asked in surprise.

"Yeah, she told me you wanted to see me," Evelyn said, wondering if she should have mentioned it or not.

"I told her earlier to call you and she promised me she would. She is such a flake. I told her that I was tired and she asked if I was dying tonight…what an idiot."

"I do not believe the insensitivity of some people."

"She just wants to know because they think I have some money hidden away. If I may speak frank…" she paused for a brief moment, and then continued, "I don't have a life insurance policy," she said with shame and regret.

"You know better than that," Evelyn said with mild fury.

"It was in my plan but I did not get around to it. You know me, researching everything, trying to find the right company at the right price, thinking I had forever. I did not think that forever would end this soon."

"Well, I should beat you, but it would only gratify you. I know you like it that way." They both laugh hysterically. A gruesome cough lingered in Leah's hand while she covered her mouth from the cough, but she kept on laughing.

"You are crazy. Don't you ever change," she said with repeated laughter.

Evelyn and Leah carried on like this for over an hour. Evelyn watched, seeing the diminishing body of her dear friend evaporate. She watched the lids of her eyes obstruct Leah's vision, closing periodically, relieving them to rest. She observed her lifeless breath, on occasion, take precedence over her energy. Her body, destabilized from the medication, weakened from the overtiredness of the illness, and weakened from the pain, had reached its limit. She watched in horror as the flesh pulled from her body. The cancer impacted her body like an express train with no instructor aboard. As she drifted under, in an effort to revive her, the nurses raised her body to pull the pillows from underneath her with her skin peeling off her back—catching onto the bed—it was no use. Her final wilted breath grasped onto the air, and silently relinquished all troubles of disparity from her body.

Leah vanished away from their lives in body but not in spirit. Evelyn would miss her friend, while holding on to the memories they shared. Those memories were good enough for Evelyn to keep moving. Still, she could not help but to think of the years prior to this day. The years before when Leah had to come to her rescue, from a mentally challenging ordeal.

Chapter

10

THIRTY-SIX POTENTIAL jurors entered the small Thirteenth District Courtroom at the Detroit Municipal Court House, simultaneously. All pouring in lined up behind one another. Some faces appeared to be angry about the entire ordeal, while others seemed excited, smiling as they entered with gleaming eyes focused at the prosecution table. They were summoned some time ago, perhaps nearly a month before. Most citizens dread opening the mail that read, *'Jury Services Main Office of Wayne County'* in the top left hand corner under the return address. They recreate the madness in their head from the times before—the long hours waiting; the grueling process of elimination questions being asked by the prosecution and the defense; the shuffling through hundreds of other summoned jurors fighting to not be selected; and of course the measly six dollars they were paid compared to their daily salaries. Just picturing the commotion was enough for any summoned juror to grunt in frustration because he or she had been selected to sit on a panel of potential jurors.

"If it pleases the court, Judge Larkin, Defense Attorney,

and our fellow potential jurors, good morning. My name is David
Hennessey and I am the Prosecuting Attorney in this case. How is
everyone doing this morning?" David Hennessey said, facing the
potential jurors.

Some grunts were heard toward the rear, some exhausted
sighs were exchanged, and some politely smiled and said, in low
voices, "Good."

"Wow. With the enthusiasm and carried conversation that
was heard as you were coming in, I thought this would be an
upbeat group and excited to be here," he said with energetic
excitement, waving his hands loosely to embellish on his words.
Mr. Hennessey was a typical lawyer character. His glasses
overpowered his face and the bright arrogant smile he wore could
be seen for miles. He wore a tan tweed suit jacket, navy blue pants,
with an oversized colorful stripe tie hugging his collar. His short
solid gray hair added years to his appearance but his facial features
suggest that he was in his early forties. The two Assistant
Prosecuting Attorneys that sat alongside of Mr. Hennessey were
glancing at the potential jurors, one by one, and scribbling on their
legal pads. One assistant prosecutor was a woman; possibly in her
late thirties, face fresh in the DA's office, legs crossed underneath
the table, and eagerly awaiting her turn. From what could be seen,
she wore a white blouse with a navy blue skirt. She looked more
tense and serious than her fellow colleagues, as she studied the
potential jurors' demeanor while they focused on Mr. Hennessey.
The other assistant prosecuting attorney was an elder woman, in
her sixties, who knew the law better than any attorney in the entire
DA's office. Her name, Willie Francis Howe, a prominent DA
Prosecutor who put notorious gangster Marty Jenke away for
ninety-nine years for drug trafficking and the gruesome murder of

a West Grand Boulevard prostitute, who died of asphyxiation. Howe was the lead prosecutor in the Jenke case, and she made a name for herself when the conviction rolled in, back in 1982. One could only assume that her assistance in this case would be more influential than not. But standing behind a table, next to his two assistant prosecuting attorneys, was Mr. Hennessey addressing the summoned jurors, as he started his questions.

"Well...how many of you want to be on a jury?" he said with an even brighter smile than before.

Silence!

"Wow...no one. Usually I get at least five or six people who would like to be selected. You guys are a tough bunch." He smiled and scooped up a clipboard, held it close to his chest with the clipped papers visible to the potential jurors. "Well, I'm sorry everyone feels this way, but without you we can not provide justice nor do our jobs. We need you to help us determine the guilt or innocence of this defendant. You will hear song and dance from The Prosecution's side and The Defense's side and in the end, you will need to decide if the Defendant, Evelyn McKenzie, is guilty or not. You will need to decide if we proved our case beyond a reasonable doubt." He went on for what seemed like hours to some of the summoned jurors, about wrong and right, and guilt or innocence, with some of the jurors hoping there would be a question forming any moment now. That moment lasted for over twenty-five minutes. "Mr. Wright...how do you feel about making the decision to convict a person for a crime and sentencing them to life in prison?"

"Well...I guess...it depends on what the crime was," the potential juror said hesitantly and surprised that he directed a question toward him first.

ALINA

"The crime is *murder*," he said, watching the expressions of the other potential jurors. Seats rattled, heads turned to face one another, and faint whispers floated amongst the potential jurors.

"Who did she kill?" Mr. Wright said.

"We will save the evidence for the trial, but right now we need to select a fair and impartial jury of thirteen to precede over this case and determine if the facts are enough to convict Ms. Evelyn McKenzie of *Murder in the First Degree*," he said with seriousness.

"I guess I could."

"Well, we really need firm answers from everyone. '*I guess*' will not give us a good determination."

"Yes," he said with little reassurance, looking over at Evelyn. Mr. Wright stared at Evelyn's attorney, then back at Evelyn. A respectful looking black woman, definitely wealthy, seated next to an obviously high priced attorney. He thought to himself, "She doesn't look like a killer. A little sad maybe, but no killer."

Mr. Hennessey flowed through his questions like rain. Over the next hour, the potential jurors were questioned by Mr. Hennessey and one of the other assistant prosecutors. The fresh face took her stand at the front of the room, facing the potential jurors and started her questions. It was quite impressive that she remembered all thirty-six of their names, their occupations, their spouses' occupations, and whether or not they had served on a jury trial in the past. Her graceful confidence roared through the room as she creatively asked her questions, which seemed more like general conversation.

After the prosecution presented its list of questions, the potential jurors had to focus their attention on the Defense

Attorney, Eric Shirer of *The Shirer & Frankly Law Firm, LLP*. Shirer was a cocky expensive flamboyant attorney, in his early forties, who first became recognized as the attorney who got Ricky *'Little Caesar II'* Grubbs off for the late 1980's murder massacre that stretched for three years over five states, leaving mutilated bodies along the way. Shirer got Grubbs off on a technicality—the first trial court appearance of his career. He got the case thrown out under the fourth amendment, which stated that it barred the use of evidence secured through an illegal search and seizure—along with other minor details but very applicable in the case and favorable to his client. The DEA, FBI, and other acronyms tried to pin a number of crimes of drug trafficking, prostitutions rings, and several other neighborhood murders on Grubbs after the case was thrown out, but none of their evidence was strong enough to stick. Shirer was a brilliant swift attorney who always remained a step ahead of the prosecutors. He stood here, in the case of the STATE OF MICHIGAN vs. EVELYN MCKENZIE *et al.,* for the gruesome calculated murder of Clarence Noltie, an ex-boyfriend of Evelyn's—with a warm smile and articulate speech. They called it a crime of passion. According to the autopsy, Clarence Noltie was stabbed seventeen times all over his body, with eight of the stab wounds delivered to his face, dismantling it beyond recognition. The coroner had to retrieve dental records to make a positive identification.

Evelyn, sitting only moments from the potential jurors, glanced across their faces with sadness. She mulled over how she could ever be in this situation. At forty-five years old and at the height of her career, sitting in a courtroom looking into the faces of the people who will ultimately decide her fate, was not how she imaged this stage of her life. She could not help but weep from the thought of going to prison for the rest of her life. She would live with the shame and guilt forever for this unspeakable crime, even if, she had no memory of what happened. She was not sure how her lawyer would set her case, given the fact that she claimed to have no memory, yet all the evidence pointed to her. She was found lying on the floor, partially propped against the wall in the living room next to Clarence Noltie's body, in a daze. When the police arrived, due to an anonymous call, they observed that she was in a trance, staring directly ahead with squinted eyes and little response to their questions. They found the knife, ironically placed several inches from her right hand that bowed over along side of her leg.

Just a year ago, Evelyn celebrated one of the happiest times in her life. She just made number six on the top ten list of Michigan's Top Real Estate Companies. It was a great honor and the publicity would send her business through the roof. Over the next several months, her real estate business revenue nearly tripled. She also owned a mortgage company called, *The Mortgage Bank* which specialized in creative financing. Her total year-end revenue for both businesses was reported at seven million dollars. Evelyn celebrated her news, at the Sheraton Hotel Embassy Ballroom with over two hundred attendees, including her dear friend Leah Sallad. Leah was always there for Evelyn and vice versa. Her presence was strongly known throughout the entire process of Evelyn's case, from the arrest to the trial.

Evelyn sat in her seat in the courtroom and reminisced on all the things she cherished in her life, and Leah was one of them. Leah had always been a strong brave woman, who believed that there was a plan for everything. She would say, "We need to put together a plan that will prove your innocence. There has got to be a way to prove this. Your past struggles do not automatically convict you of this heinous crime; it only proves that you could not have done this." Leah's comfort eased Evelyn's mind but nothing could be done for her guilty soul. Evelyn began to reflect on the many associates she had that hung by her side since the beginning, like her friend Lylie Frankly, the divorce attorney who happened to work with one of the most prominent defense attorneys in the country, Eric Shirer.

Upon her arrest, it was Lylie she called for advice. Evelyn met Lylie a year and a half earlier. Lylie came to Evelyn's real estate office looking to buy a much larger home than her current home because she wanted to start a family with her husband of five years. Lylie was told that Evelyn was the best. They exchanged a few laughs and two months later, Lylie was moving into her new thirty-eight hundred square foot home with promising hopes for the future. Evelyn and Lylie became very good friends before and after the sale of her current home. Then, six months later, Lylie phoned Evelyn and told her that she caught her husband with another man. Her devastation was beyond repair and she prepared her own divorce, with very little argument from her husband. It was Evelyn that taught her how to mend her heart and move on to forgiveness. But, sitting in this courtroom, on this rainy April day of the year 2000, she wondered if her actions could ever be forgiven. She could not fathom, for the life of her, how or why she could harm another human being. She could not come to terms with the blood that was spilled over her hands, nor find it in her heart that she even deserved forgiveness.

~

"Hear ye, hear ye, all rise. The Honorable Judge Henry Q.

Larkin presiding," the court bailiff said, as he stood near the chamber door where the judge entered from.

As the judge entered the room and took his seat in a huge black leather chair facing a room full of spectators, he said, "You may be seated." The onlookers, many of whom where reporters from the *Tribune* and *Today,* listened with open ears so they would not miss a beat. All awaiting the trial of one of the most sophisticated, humbly respected, well-known Real Estate Brokers in the state of Michigan. Most had voiced their opinions across the network, declaring that Ms. McKenzie could not have done such an unthinkable crime. Partners of affiliated businesses were shocked, while her company revenue augmented. Some thought her arrest would damage her company, but to much surprise, it flourished more. It flourished with people trying to show their support; people who wanted their fifteen minutes of fame—being interviewed, asking them 'why' they support Evelyn; and those that did not care what she was accused of, they simply wanted the best Real Estate Agent or Broker available. Although Evelyn was charged with Murder in the First Degree, her lawyer smoothly managed to have her released on bail throughout the trial period.

"Case number 32–6531, State of Michigan vs. Evelyn McKenzie, Your Honor," the court clerk stated, as she handed the case file to the judge.

"Good morning. The court will now hear opening arguments," the judge said.

Evelyn's body became numb and her eyelids seemed weighed down. She thought she would pass out right in the presence of everyone. Her body weakened from what she was about to hear. The Prosecutor, David Hennessey had set out to make her sound like a monster and wanted to make an example of her. He protested that she used her influential connections to try and get away with murder. Evelyn had not known how he intended to prove this, but she did not want to recant the events of that night which held little memory in her mind. The trial took place, only six months after her bizarre mental breakdown in late 1999. Evelyn wondered if her mental state had escaped her once again when she killed Clarence Noltie. Or did she kill Clarence Noltie? She didn't know. But, Leah tried to convince her that she could not have killed anyone and that she was over whatever mental slip her mind underwent.

In 1999, on a spellbinding comfortable night of seventy-two degrees in September, Evelyn found herself pointlessly wandering the streets of Birmingham for hours. A neighbor recognized her from the billboards, newspaper articles, and TV, and took her back to her home. The neighbor asked Evelyn what was wrong, but the neighbor was not given a response. Evelyn felt her throat move but no words would release. After several minutes of frustrating silence, Evelyn finally managed to whisper for the nice lady to call Leah.

Leah took Evelyn home and placed her in bed. She stayed for the night and knew that Evelyn would be okay in the morning, but that was far from the truth. Leah awoke the next day, at eight-thirty in the morning, only to find Evelyn had stripped herself of her clothing, genuflecting down staring strongly at a painting on the wall in the living room.

"Evelyn..." Leah approaching her in slow motion with little assurance, and she repeated, "Evelyn."

No response.

"Evelyn, are you okay?" Her answer was obvious, but what else could she ask.

No response, but she looked up at her with mad eyes. Though her brow was not raised, her eyes spoke of madness. They were glossy and red. Her stare was not direct, but was blurred in some way. Her movements were extremely slow and her demeanor was as if she was in an automaton state. She looked deeply at Leah, and then turned her head back toward the painting.

"The Devil's in there," she finally said. Eyes locked on the painting.

"What?" Leah said in disbelief with tears in her voice, but none fell from her face.

"He's in there and I will be right here when he comes out. I will not allow him to destroy me. I will not...I will not...let...him...destroy...*me*," she shouted as fury entered her voice with every passing word.

"Evelyn, I think you should come and have a seat on the sofa. Please, come on." Leah, moving closer to her, reluctant at first, but remembering that this was her friend and she needed her help.

Evelyn, still staring at the painting on the wall and kneeled down with both knees suspended in the air while she crouched down on the floor, and said, "You don't understand. You will never understand. I will not let him hurt me ever again."

Leah thought she was starting to put the pieces together. Recalling that several months before, Evelyn had just broken up with her boyfriend after a four and a half year long distance relationship. Mutually, they decided to end the relationship since neither of them wanted to make the move to a new state. Her ex, Sean, lived in Tampa, Florida. He was the Vice-President of Business Development of a well known company in Florida; Leah forgets which one. But, he made a lavish six figure salary, plus bonuses, while structuring business development plans for other independent clients in his spare time, bringing his net earnings to four hundred ninety-five thousand dollars a year. He knew Evelyn was well off, but did not know to what degree. But the beauty of their relationship was that money did not matter to them. They were in-love. Evelyn did not explain the details of the break-up to Leah but she suspected that he could not handle the long distance relationship, based on past debates that Evelyn shared with her. Leah would not surrender to the thought that this break-up would make her delusional.

All of a sudden, Evelyn jumped to her feet and ran, hugging the corner of the wall in the living room, several feet away from the painting. Her body shivered with fear and her eyes beamed a frighten stare at Leah.

"Evelyn...please tell me what's wrong," Leah pleaded.

"I can't let him get me. I can't. Please Leah, don't let him get *me*," she said as tears filled her eyes and gradually flowed down her cheeks.

Leah ran to the back to get a robe for Evelyn. When she returned to the living room, Evelyn was gone. She ran to the dining room, just off the living room, but she wasn't there. From a near distance, she heard a scream. Leah noticed it was coming from the guest bathroom. She ran down the hall to the guest bathroom, opened the door, and shock emerged across her face. She found Evelyn faintly hanging over the large garden tub, arms collapsed inside, with blood spilling from her mouth. Leah rushed to her aide in terror.

"Oh, Dear God. Evelyn...Evelyn...please tell me what is wrong. What happened?" she said in an erupted panic while kneeling down to rescue her head.

Evelyn was unable to speak. Leah could see that she was unconscious. She struggled to remove her from the tub and placed her onto the floor. After trying to reposition Evelyn's head, Leah's right hand grazed across the cold stone tile and she decided to move her to the closest room. With Evelyn being five feet eleven inches tall, weighing over two hundred and five pounds, it was difficult for Leah to drag her into the guest bedroom. She gave up on the idea to place her in the bed, so she opted to create a comfortable setting on the floor. She removed the pillows and blankets from the queen size guest bed, made a pallet, and positioned Evelyn on top for more support. She could tell that the blood was coming from her mouth, but did not know why.

Leah would sit and cry for the next two hours, debating if she should call the authorities or ride this one out. Her mind filled with horrific scenarios that left her at a loss for words. She could not determine what was happening to her dear friend—all she knew, was that she could not leave her this way. She called her boyfriend and told him she was going to stay at Evelyn's for the night and she would explain tomorrow. She had done this several times before, calling her boyfriend at the last minute, exclaiming that she would stay the night at Evelyn's; it was not out of the ordinary. Conversely, Evelyn's behavior was totally out of the ordinary. Leah did not know what to do. She lay by her side and waited until her friend woke up.

Leah had dosed off, one of many throughout the night until the morning, when Evelyn had finally awakened. Leah rested her arm on Evelyn's arm, so she would be able to feel her movements.

"Leah…is that you?" Evelyn said, appearing to be in a state of shock.

"Evelyn," Leah said, as her body jerked from surprise. "Are you okay?" She looked into Evelyn's eyes and her answer poured through. Leah knew she was not okay, but she did not seem as troubled as before.

"Leah, I don't know what is happening to me," she said with confusion.

"Hell, I don't either." She presented a subtle smile, hoping for the same from Evelyn, but her expression remained the same.

"Why am I on the floor? Why am I nude? Where am I?" she said, looking at her arms, glancing around the area.

These were questions that Leah could answer, so she did. She got up from the floor, and asked Evelyn if she wanted something to eat. Evelyn refused. She asked her if she needed to go to the hospital but Evelyn refused. Fear and frustration started to form in Leah at the same time. She was puzzled with yesterday's events and was not looking forward for today's. "Do you know what happened yesterday?" Leah asked with much concern.

"No, I don't. Do you know what will happen today?"

Leah looked in astonishment and said, "What will happen today?"

"He's coming," she softly whispered.

"Who is coming?" frightened from the words, Leah grudgingly asked.

"The Devil," she whispered and winked her eye.

"I hope not," Leah said.

"He's been trying to take my soul. But I won't let him." Suddenly, she jumped up from the floor and started running while looking back at Leah and saying, "I won't let him take me. I won't…" Then, she crashed into the wall. Her body bounced back to the floor and simultaneously, as if she knew it would happen, she quickly lifted her body from the floor and ran to the living room. She screamed obscenities at the sofa painting of eagles flying in the night, soaring through the moonlight and over a mountain view. Leah did not understand why that particular painting was the chosen one, but she knew it had to be removed.

After a few days, Leah decided to take Evelyn to the hospital. It became apparent that she was having some sort of mental breakdown and that she needed some psychiatric help. Then, feeling a powerful benevolent force sweep across the master bedroom where Leah and Evelyn had been resting for an hour now was unexplainable. Her face felt calm, her skin prickled from the cool draft that danced across her face, and her mind became lucid and unafraid. Suddenly, she realized that this, whatever *this* was, would not be a forcible nemesis to Evelyn. So, for the next couple of months, she took care of her friend.

During the course of the first month, she consulted an elderly woman who was a friend of her boyfriend's mother, and she advised her that Evelyn was somehow possessed. She stated that Leah needed to listen to Evelyn, and the words that she muttered would be the words needed to snap her out of it. Leah, not frighten anymore by what she had seen, set out to remove the pain that was inside of Evelyn, no matter how long it took.

Leah did just as the woman said and two months later, Evelyn was back to normal. Her body was severely weakened from the trauma it sustained everyday for the last two months, but her mind was moving in the right direction. Intentionally, but in a subconscious state of mind, Evelyn charged her body against the walls, fell over a dozen times inside the tub trying to wash the evil from her body, she said. Her nails had grown tremendously, and she used them as weapons to try and claw the eyes from Leah's face. Leah would awake with new scares on her body, until she got the opportunity to cut Evelyn's nails down to a safe length. Leah witnessed a understated calmness move into Evelyn's body on a late afternoon, fifty-seven days after the first incident, and released a long sigh of relief.

While listening to the radio, *Wild Flower* by *The New Birth* played and Evelyn stood up from the master bed and started moving to the music and said, "This is my song. Please, go get this for me. I have been trying to find this record for years." It was at that time that Leah new her friend was back. Leah, smiling at her friend while she feed her chicken soup, thought to herself, preoccupied by many unanswered questions, "Why did this happen to her? What does this all mean? Did this have anything to do with her ex-boyfriend? Will this incident ever happen again? I can *only* assume, we may never know."

~

With the trial being well underway, each lawyer giving their version of the events of that chilling day that Clarence Noltie died, Evelyn zoned out into her own persecution. She had already condemned herself. In her mind, she was as guilty as charged. She was not sure if her hand was at the other end of that blade that killed Clarence, but she wished him dead days before the incident. Whether she is exonerated of these charges or not, she will still hold guilt in her heart for the truth, and the truth is, she wished him dead. She could not conceivably accept that she killed a man, but she believed it was her desires that contributed to his death. Clarence was not a mean son-of-a-bitch that deserved to die, but rather a complicated man whose tactics would eventually lead to where he sits today, six feet under, she thought to herself. He was a gentle man when he and Evelyn first met. His magnetic light brown eyes undeniably melted her heart and interrupted her perception. His warm touch raised the faint hairs on her arms whenever he caressed her. She could still feel his lukewarm breath dusting across her ears from the romantic whispers, even now. Although his behavior shifted from a gentle breeze to a winding storm, Evelyn still remembered the nice thoughtful, on occasion gentleman, that masquerade in front of her wearing her oversized cream hat and three inch heels. She could not help but smile.

Rapidly fluttering her eyes trying to come back to reality, she glanced at the jurors. All of their attention was focused on the Prosecuting Attorney, Mr. Hennessey. Thank goodness. She would not want them to catch a glimpse of her smiling, giving the impression that this catastrophe was a joke. She regrouped herself and directed her attention to the trial. As difficult as it seemed, she listened to the horrible implications, the repeated words of how Clarence died and the final cut that ended his life. The prosecutors had massive evidence that showed how he died and fancy doctors that could break down his time of death to the very second. Evelyn wasn't a lawyer, but it did not take a rocket scientist to determine that the prosecution's case was merely circumstantial. They simply placed her at the crime scene, lying next to the body, but no hard evidence that would suggest that she committed the crime. But, a brief confession may be their strongest exhibit. Evelyn had no memory of the alleged confession, or of the crime, but she had to assume it was all true. However, her lawyer begs to differ. He denounced the real evidence...no fingerprints on the murder weapon, his client was delusional and was not coherent at the time to give a conclusive statement. He also proclaimed that they immediately were convinced that Evelyn murdered Clarence without the possibility of her being a victim too. "Their efforts were solely on making my client a murderer without considering the fact that she may be a victim," he said. Arguably, he was right, she thought.

Evelyn had not considered the possibility that she may have been a victim who lived through a frightening ordeal, but it still seemed a little too thin for her. Questions started to alleviate her mind as she wondered if her lawyer was on to something. Why weren't her fingerprints on the murder weapon? Why was she out for so long, what happened to her frame of reference before and after the murder? She felt heavily drugged, was she? All these questions and more raised a brow on Evelyn's face. The pain penetrated her head as she tried to embrace a hint of memory that would shed some light on these contemplative questions. Until now, she had condemned herself for this heinous crime without possible confliction of another. Her mind had been in a psychological state resulting from the often unconscious opposition between simultaneous, yet incompatible desires to manipulate her thoughts into believing she was guilty. Her mind became more alert and in-tone with reality. She listened intensely as her lawyer hammered away at *so-called* experts of this and that. No one seemed to have possessed pertinent information to the case that would suggest Evelyn was the killer. The perception in the mind of the jurors became inevitable as the evidence slowly shifted to favor Evelyn.

An unexpected sound, the courtroom door opened, and a messenger hurried with apologies to present a package to Eric Shirer. It was a thick yellow legal sized envelope with papers tightly bunched revealing sharp creases. Eric glanced at his assistant, an investigator on his team of professionals, who stated that he had exhausted all avenues of trying to retrieve any other favorable evidence on Evelyn's behalf. Proceeding with caution, he opened the envelope. To his liking, he quickly motioned to the judge for a recess.

"Please, Your Honor, if it pleases the court, we would like to have a five minute recess to examine some new evidence that has just come to our attention," Eric stated.

"What kind of new evidence, Mr. Shirer? This better not be one of your famous stunts because that type of behavior will not be tolerated in my courtroom. I have warned you of this," Judge Larkin firmly explained.

"No stunts, Your Honor." A serious staggered expression controlled the muscles in his face, as his eyes gracefully swept across the pages with intriguing wonder. "Please, just five minutes," he pleaded once more.

"Ok, Mr. Shirer. The court will take a five minute recess and not a minute longer." He motions his gavel and the clock started.

"What is it?" Evelyn nervously said, as she looked at the crowd gathered about, with necks fanning, trying to get a glimpse of what the mystery was about.

"Your life back!" Eric stated, smiling from ear to ear. "This is unbelievable. Where did this come from? Well, all I can say is somebody out there likes you." He turned to look at Evelyn, still smiling, mesmerized by his view.

"What is it? Who sent it? Does it have a name?" his investigator asked.

"No. No name, just evidence. Evidence that could set my client free," Eric said.

"There's no name?" Evelyn asked.

"Okay, we don't have much time. The judge has got to grant us a continuous on this, but we still need to move fast. This evidence suggests that the man in the house was not Clarence Noltie and that the real Clarence Noltie was found under a pile of wood in Southwest Detroit. It looks like the DNA was switched some how. Here, in my possession, I have DNA records along with dental records showing who the real Clarence Noltie was…"

Eric's assistant, Assistant Attorney, Lauren Blakeley interrupted, "But that only proves that she could have killed another person. It helps us, but it also confuses the situation. We need evidence that would place her somewhere else at the time of the murder."

"Be patience my dear," he said with a canny smile. "This evidence also shows the blood level in Evelyn's body at the time. There were traces of a Barbiturate and Gamma-hydroxybutyrate in her bloodstream that would suggest that she was not conscious during the attack. His time of death was argued by the prosecuting experts to be around one thirty in the A.M. but her blood results show that she was given a high dose of these medications which caused her to be unconscious for most of the day. She started to regain consciousness when the police arrived after two A.M., when they received an anonymous tip. According to the officer's own testimony, she appeared to be disorientated and her pupils were dilated and these are some of the side effects of the Barbiturates – possibly Quaaludes or Valium." He turns to face Evelyn, "And once I have time to analyze this paperwork, I am sure I will find more than enough evidence to get you acquitted of all charges," he said boastfully, then added, "I need you—" Directing his attention to the investigator, "—to go and check on a John Doe in the morgue that fit's the description of the victim, Clarence Noltie, who may have been killed around the same time as Clarence. It says here that you will be looking for a victim with a tattoo of *doves* on his chest. Just search for all John Doe's that died around the same timeframe and we will determine which one was Clarence Noltie through our own forensic analysis. We also need an expert to testify to the impact of these drugs and to the length of time she would have been unconscious. Hurry, I needed this yesterday," he pushed his words out forcefully.

"What does all this mean? I was drugged?" Evelyn said in disbelief.

"Yes, ma'am. And from the looks of this paperwork, you were framed. Someone wanted or needed you to take the fall and I intend to find out who and why. The judge may not want to grant a continuous, but he will have no choice," Eric stated, looking into the eyes of an innocent woman. He knew his fight had just begun. The hardest part of being a defense attorney was getting the innocent off. It was much easier to tear apart the prosecutor's case and creatively steer the minds of the jurors to a reasonable doubt, when the man accused was guilty, he thought. Here, before him, sat an innocent lady; he had known it all along but handled this case just as he had done many times before, with the presumption of guilt.

The judge, with uncanny favorable argument, granted a continuous and asked to speak to all counsel in his chambers. "What is this all about?" Judge Larkin asked Eric Shirer.

"I am not sure Judge Larkin, but I have reason to suspect that the body retrieved from Clarence Noltie's home was not his. Anonymously, this package was sent to me suggesting that my client could not have committed this crime and that other players may be involved. I believe my client was set up."

The judge collapsed in his oversized leather chair, with a puzzled look bewildering his face. He seldom expressed any emotions when it came to overseeing a case, but glancing through the mysterious paperwork, he could not hide its persuasion. Holding back his emotions, he said, "This is something…well, this is insane. You better be going somewhere with this," he warned.

"This is obviously one of his famous stunts, Your Honor. I think we should continue with the trial and grant this no more attention than it needs," Mr. Hennessey firmly suggested.

"No. My ruling stands. In light of this new information, it would be illicit of me not to give it the attention it deserves. After reviewing these papers, if any of this mess is true, it looks to me, you've got the wrong person on trial here. I suggest you start doing some homework of your own, Mr. Hennessey," Judge Larkin forewarned.

It was all true. A John Doe at the morgue was unmistakably identified as Clarence Noltie and the other body, the one found in the house next to Evelyn's comatose body, was Clarence's brother Clifton Nicholas Noltie. His complexion and build agreed with Clarence's. They were similar in weight and height, with the exception of the dental records; they could easily pass for twins. The dental records that mysteriously disappeared or replaced to convict an innocent woman, Eric thought. They had not uncovered who or why the dental records were switched, but Eric had his speculations. Clarence minor decayed body was found under a pile of plywood with old rusted nails hammered at the ends. His body lied in a pool of his own blood that spilled from his neck which indicated he had been strangled to death with some sort of sharp wire. His first two fingers on his right hand were nearly severed from his hand—sliced through the bone—which clearly stated that he put up a fight for his assailant. The left hand was chopped off, with many speculating that his death may have been the result of something he stole that was dear to someone he shouldn't have stole from. The new information also stated that Clifton was killed somewhere else. After careful re-examination of the evidence, the blood stains in the house and the positioning of the body indicated that he was not killed at that location. His throat had been sliced with the same sharp wiring that killed Clarence, but the knife wounds overpowered this unobvious fact. A forensics specialist, circumspectly analyzed the tissues and fragments removed from both bodies and found tiny silver particles lodged in the throats of both men, connecting the murders of Clifton and Clarence—proposing that they died by the hands of the same killer. Given the size of both men, Eric came to the conclusion that there had to be more than one assailant, and that his client could not have killed Clifton nor Clarence. "Someone else is working an angle here, Your Honor," Eric said firmly, as he requested for the charges to be dismissed for his client. He proclaimed that this case was bigger than Evelyn McKenzie.

"Prosecutor?" Judge Larkin looked to Mr. Hennessey for further insight.

"We have no more to add, Your Honor." Mr. Hennessey, standing to make his statement, felt a tap on his leg. He looked down and leaned in to converse with Prosecutor Willie Francis Howe. They whispered amongst themselves as the bystanders mingled intensely.

"Today, Mr. Hennessey! We are out of patience. Get on with your statement," Judge Larkin harshly stated.

"Yes...Your Honor. Yes. In light of the new evidence, the State of Michigan would like to dismiss all charges against Evelyn McKenzie for the murder of Clarence Noltie."

"Your Honor, I would like to add something." Eric quickly jumped to his feet, trying to be heard over the celebration from the crowd. "I would like to ask that the charges be dismissed with prejudice. I want my client to be free from this tangled labyrinth of deception and betrayal."

"Very well," the prosecution added.

The crowd roared with excitement. Most were strong supporters of Evelyn and knew in their hearts that justice would prevail. The judge pound his gavel several times to silence the crowd, but it was useless, they were overwhelmed by the outcome. Tears of happiness and laughter could be heard throughout the courtroom while supporters shouted, "We knew you were innocent Evelyn. We stand behind you *all* the way."

"Evelyn McKenzie, you are free to go," Judge Larkin added, firmly pounding his gavel to dismiss the court. He heaved a restless sigh and smiled. He had wondered how a lady of her stature be accused of murder in the first degree. The woman that stood before him seemed kind and gentle, not brutal and coldhearted. But in his thirty year career, he had seen them all, yet, it was something about Evelyn that pulled him in. He could feel the sufferings and strife that spilled through her body like liquid plumber down a clogged drain. His heart had not ached for anyone before, and his cases were never personal, but Evelyn's warmth was approvingly preferential and deeply felt from twenty feet away. Judge Larkin's mind was set at ease, as he watched a dazzling, respected and widely loved woman, gracefully walk through the courtroom doors, a free woman.

Newshounds swarmed Evelyn, requesting interviews and feelings. She smiled with little response—shock still wearing her face. Her attorney, Eric Shirer, did most of the talking and held a press conference on the steps of the courthouse shortly after the dismissal. He announced that justice was served for his client but that the real killers roamed free and that he would protect his client as best he could from any future attacks on her reputation—even if it meant that he would sue the city and the state for being wrongfully accused.

During the course of the years, Evelyn never found out who sent the envelope and why. Because of that act of courage, she was a free woman with nothing hanging over her head. Not a day goes by without bringing her to this time in her life. With all the trials and tribulations that she faced in her lifetime, the years 1999 and 2000 were the most difficult to swallow. Eliminating this episode from her memoirs would not be considered, in fact, it leaves her no choice but to remember the agony and fear of losing her freedom, which makes her a better person because of it.

Chapter

11

A STRANGER next to Renée in bed was all too familiar, but never a woman. She turned over, still naked, looking at The Stranger's innocence while she slept. Renée could see disturbance latent across The Stranger's face as she laid there, body partially covered in a satin sheet, hair stretched across two pillows lying on her stomach with her right hand neatly tucked away beneath her leg. Renée secretly climbed out of bed, put on her slippers, selected a silk robe off the hook of the closet door, and headed downstairs to the kitchen. She had planned to cook them a handsome breakfast, but realized that she promised her mother that she would pick the girls up by six P.M. It was three-thirty in the afternoon. Renée decided to call her mom's house and see if the girls were ready to come home. Her son had spent the night at his dad's house and was not expected until the following day.

"Hey, where's mom?" Renée said to Lolita.

"Hi, mom. Darianna's got a boyfriend, that's why she did not answer the phone. She likes him. She had a kiss with him. Gross, hah, ma'?" Lolita said with much energy.

"A boyfriend? Where is your grandmother?" she said with a hint of fury.

"She cookin'. Do you want to talk to her?"

Before Renée could answer, Lolita yelled through the mouth piece of the phone to the back of the house where the kitchen stood and her grandmother hovered over the steaming stove. Renée jerkily removed the phone from her ear and repositioned it again. "Girl, if you don't stop yelling." These words were never heard by Lolita, she was long gone, handing the phone to Renée's mother.

"Hello. That daughter of yours has got some lungs on her. And, the answer is *no*, I will not keep them for a little while longer which will turn into another night, *no*."

"Well, good day to you to mother. And how are you this morning? If you care to know, which I am sure you don't, I am doing fine too," Renée said with cynicism.

"You normally do not call in the middle of the afternoon, when you should be sitting in my driveway at this time, unless you want the kids to stay another night," she said with confidence in Renée's agenda.

"You are wrong this time, mother. Oh, wait, you are wrong often. I called to talk to you to see if you were ready for the girls to come home now. I wanted you to tell them to be ready when I arrived because I will not have time to come in this time," she said with sass.

"Yeah right," her mother said unsure.

"Just have the girls ready within an hour or two," Renée said with frustration.

Lolita yells from the background, "Mom can we stay another night. Please oh please. Grandma don't mine. Do you grandma?"

"Tell her that she will not stay another night and to be ready once I arrive," Renée demanded.

"Please grandma, Darianna wants to stay too. She doesn't want to leave her boyfriend," Lolita loudly whispers as if no one else should hear.

"Well, I guess they can stay one more night."

"Please mother, don't do me any favors. Tell them to be ready within a couple of hours. I don't want them to burden you," she still demanded.

"No, Renée, it's okay. I am not saying that you do not want them home, it's just, I don't want you to feel like you can call me at the last minute when you discover that you have something more pressing to do," she said apologetic.

"You can say *Hi* first before you start accusing me. It's not like I do this often. You must have something to do because normally you don't want the girls to leave so soon, that's why I called to check."

"I know. I am cooking right now. The girls are fine, I am fine, and we will see you tomorrow," she said hurryingly.

"Hey, Hey, Hey…before you go, what is this about a boyfriend?"

"Darianna has got herself a friend, that's all. It's harmless. She is an attractive girl, boys like her. She's also a smart girl, she'll be alright. I remember someone else at age fourteen, having frequent visitors wanting her to come out to play." You could feel the smile on her face.

"Yeah that's right mother and look where it got me. Pregnant with a good for nothing daddy, Darianna's daddy at that."

"Oh, stop it," she insisted. "You act as if your life has turned out so bad."

"I didn't say my life mother, I'm talking about men. I'm talking about the shit they put you through and all the while you believe the fickle stories they tell because they amuse you, while finding yourself staring at the ceiling resting on your back. I'm talking about the sweet nothings they whisper in your ear, telling you how beautiful you are and how you are the only one and how they will never leave you."

"Okay, I think you are going a little too far with this. For goodness sake, Renée, it's just a friend, that's all. That's all, Renée. I am sure she will not ride off into the sunset with him tomorrow, geese," she added with provocation.

"What I am saying mother, is that's how it begins. I was gullible, sometimes, I still am and I don't want her to think that it is okay to be that way. I need you to back me on this one for once," she added with tremendous compassion.

"Okay, okay. I get the point. I will watch them. I can't tell him to leave because he has been her for a while now."

"Then, it is time for him to go. If you do not want to be the villain, put her on the phone and I will tell her myself," Renée said with assertion.

"No, I am capable of handling this one myself. We'll see you tomorrow, dear."

Renée hung up the phone and studied for a moment. Her first thought was to reconsider allowing the girls to spend another night. Then, she decided against it. Remembering her childhood sparked the conversation between Renée and her mother. Her mother took life for granted when Renée and her sisters and brothers were growing up. Renée's mother was married to Renée's father for a short time. After their divorce, they still lived as a couple for as long as Renée could remember. Renée remembers her mother hosting parties, getting drunk, and fighting with her father. Before Renée heard that her father was the abuser many, many years ago, she felt pity for her father and resented her mother for being such a bitch. Learning more of the details, she felt her mother was justified for her actions.

Her mother was a stay at home mom, due to disabilities, but was not active in their lives as one would think. She gave them plenty of attention when she had a hangover from the night before and the noise pounded her head like a hammer. Her brother received his special attention, not in a good way, when he was arrested for the hundredth time on drug charges. After his imprisonment, she gave up on him entirely. Her vulgar language toward them was just the start. She was by no means a horrible mother, but she lost love for anyone else other than herself many years ago.

When she was a teenager married to Renée's father, she lost her self-confidence. She was always an attractive woman. Back then, she had long hair, just as Renée's; a figure to compliment any man's dream, and with a passive attitude. She never questioned their nightly behavior. She never questioned their overnight stays. She was a collective prize for any man, but her father corrupted her mind and body. He accused her of having affairs and vowing to destroy her beauty, inside and out, until he finally achieved his goal.

Rumor has it that on one cool night in the September month, that day was the *last* day she would endure the abuse. Renée's mother argued with her father for nearly the entire day. He started slapping her across the face, yelling all kind of obscenities, and charged her body with all his weight. Her father, five-ten, one hundred forty pounds, was strong with restless anger. His actions caused Renée's mother to lose her breath as her eyes watered from the impact. She slowly rose from the floor, being five-six, one hundred fifty-eight pounds she felt she could handle him. She had not decided to stand up for herself, but today was the last day. Today was the day that she could not take anymore. She stood with weakness and stumbled to the kitchen.

"Oh, you want to get a knife or something. Take your ass back in the living room before I kill you," her father said in a wrath of anger.

Her mother never said a word. Her father reached for her hair, aggressively pulled her to the floor and pounds her in the face like a stranger that just invaded their home. She could feel the force of his fist ripping through her skin. The sound pierced her ears like ripped stitching. Partially blinded by the blood soaked eye sockets, she reached for some support. She grabbed onto the handle of the stove, raised her knee to connect with his back as he sat on top of her stomach. His weight practically knocked the wind out of her body as he sat heavily on her stomach and chest.

Her powerful kick was enough to send him flying off her and he sat before her in amazement. His stunned facial expression plastered all over his face did not go unobserved. She quickly struggled to pull herself off the kitchen floor, using the stove for espousal. As he tried to charge her again, she grabbed the first thing in her reach, a little more than a half loaf of bread. She swung the bread sack with all her might. His face, overflowing with surprise, was at a standstill. She swung the loaf of bread until his vision blurred from the cut above his left eye that dripped with blood. Then, she charged his body. He landed on the dining room table a few feet away from the kitchen, back first. The candy dish, once used to hold candy and décor, was used as a weapon to destroy the man that was trying to destroy her, simply because it was feasible for him. He had no reasoning for beating her; he just wanted to be in control. Look how control works; it is sometimes a swinging door that can hit you harder than a ton of bricks. At least, that was the story that was told to Renée.

Her childhood memories revealed that her mother cared more about the men in her life than her children, except for the boys. Her mother favored the boys even all that she suffered by the hands of a man, her boys could do no wrong.

Renée could recall that her mother did not mind her children drinking before they were of legal age. She did not mind the boys that often stayed the night, even before Renée was fourteen. It did not bother her that her oldest became pregnant at sixteen, Renée's sister Sheila. Her mother's house was one big party for young and old attendees. She welcomed all the kids in the neighborhood into her home. Sheila attracted friends that always needed help and a place to stay, which led Renée's mother to take in runaways who were welcome to stay for a night or two. Even with the events that happened in Renée's childhood, she no longer held any ill-felt blame toward her mother. Life has taught her that her mother played her hand as best she could with the cards she were dealt. Still, Renée imagined a mother who had a greater appreciation for life and the things around her. She only hoped that she could embrace herself in the arms of a mother with an unforgettable persona of wisdom, intelligence and kindness—like her friend Evelyn.

When first meeting Evelyn, she was immediately attached. She was as warm, compassionate, wise, and sympathetic as Lylie stated she would be. Renée was in the middle of a tug-of-war with her ex-husband and examined whether or not to continue the estranged marriage, when Lylie suggested that she visit with a wonderful lady that could possibly provide a little insight on her situation. Lylie was Renée's divorce attorney. Her expertise was impeccable, and she managed to filter a sweet deal with Renée's ex-husband that would allow her and their children to live comfortably. From Renée's view, her ex-husband's finances seem dilapidated and he was not forthcoming with information that would not favor this perception —but, after shuffling through a mountain of tax returns, check stubs, bonus receipts, and independent income, Lylie was able to determine that the struggling view was deceptive. Her calculations concluded that Renée's ex-husband's income exceeded more than three hundred fifty thousand dollars a year, which entitled Renée to *half*. Not to mention the investment accounts that were tied up, earning interest for the next twelve years, currently valued at over a half of million dollars.

As this new information presented itself, Renée's ex-husband was more than glad to take the mediocre deal that Lylie offered. He had to pay her attorney fees, of course, just for starters. The agreement was that he would pay Renée a lump sum of sixty-seven thousand dollars, which amounted to half of an individual checking account balance he mysteriously acquired during the second year of their marriage. While their joint account had a total of eight hundred and something odd dollars by the time the divorce was in play, and on some occasions, carried a negative balance from overdrafts. He had been secretly swelling another account with positive cash flow as their joint account, the account that feed his kids, was riding on empty. Renée did not learn of this individual account until their second court appearance. The rest of the agreement would be for him to pay her alimony and child support in the amount of thirty-two hundred dollars a month, which only accounted for eleven percent of his income… "Peanuts," Lylie thought. But, it was what her client wanted. Renée only set after to be free from the marriage, have custody of her children and provide a comfortable lifestyle for them and at thirty-two hundred dollars a month she can do just that.

Renée was in pieces during the entire process of the divorce. She would say on numerous occasions that had it not been for her children and Evelyn, she would not have made it through the treacherous lies and deceit. Despite the ominous beginning of the divorce, her continuous meetings with Evelyn allowed her to feel more at ease as the case went on. There was something about Evelyn's demeanor and prudence of her tongue that suppressed the fears and rendered a glowing guidance that prospered with every step. It was because of Evelyn that she remained sane, not vengeful but appreciative, not bitter but content. Renée could easily be bitter and justifiably insane from the tormented relationship her husband put her through. Caught, sleeping with other women on a steady basis, several years after their marriage with little denial. Gone for days at a time, with Renée left to explain to impressible children, where was daddy? Trampling on Renée's feelings daily, as his careless voice carried throughout their small moderate house on Detroit's East Side; with their children crying and covering their ears from the high volume of cruel arguments bouncing from wall to wall. A mother who had always favored the man's side, insisting that Renée stay in her marriage and would say, "As long as he has not put his hands on you, you can deal with it. He's a good man. You need to figure out what you are doing wrong…" And the list goes on. Nonetheless, finding a way back to herself was all in credit of Evelyn McKenzie, a woman of great knowledge, experience and triumphs. A woman, Renée was glad to have met.

She awakened from the subdued trance and glanced at the phone again. She thought, once again, to call her mother back, instructing her to have the girls ready within the hour. Her right hand railed over the cordless phone, positioned on the base and paused. She thought to herself, "I will not let my mother spoil it for my babies. They love being over there, especially Lolita and presumably, Darianna now." She positioned herself comfortably on the sofa, leaned back and stretched her legs across the floor placing her feet on the genuine marble top coffee table. She smiled, thinking of her children, especially her girls. Relinquishing subtle breaths that slowly escaped her soft barely dry lips and evaporated into the air; and then she raised her arms, interlocked her fingers and rested them on the back of her neck. Briefly subjecting her thoughts to reflect on her new line of friends and Melissa came to mind.

Perhaps, if Evelyn had not helped Renée confront her fears of allowing her inner-self to be recognized, she may not have had the courage to speak to Melissa in the manner that she did. Renée struggled with being comfortable around people. When Renée's body collided with Melissa's as she walked down the hall of the Megan Building, she never thought that the timid frail woman would be one of her true friends. After extending great apologies for the collision and spilling hot coffee all over Melissa's ivory pressed suit, Renée offered to buy Melissa lunch.

But, she declined.

"Are you okay, Ma'am?" Renée stated with little concern.

"Yes, I'm fine. It's just coffee. I will have Marie take it to the dry cleaners when I return home. It is not a problem. No need to keep apologizing…it's fine," Melissa said with a warm smile.

"Well, I do apologize. It looks pretty expensive. Can I at least offer to pay for the dry cleaning?" Renée suggested.

"No, it is quit alright. Thank you for the offer," Melissa said, dusting her suit jacket with a white handkerchief from her handbag.

"I hope you have already been to your meeting. I would hate to be the cause of you missing something because of my clumsiness. Please, let's go to the restroom and try to wash some of this mess off your beautiful suit," Renée insisted.

Melissa, not really giving any regard to the suit, followed Renée into the restroom. She had hundreds of suits and all of similar style, so this was not a great concern to her. She thought, however, how intriguing Renée was. They formally introduced themselves and engaged in casual conversation. Renée told of her four precious children and Melissa told of her two children. And so, a friendship was formed. Several years after their candid introduction, Melissa explained her situation to Renée and Renée suggested that she meet with Evelyn. The one thing that Renée pondered over, but never asked—why was Melissa at that particular building. It was obvious that she was outside her city limits, close to downtown Detroit off West Grand Boulevard, where a woman of her statue was not commonly seen, if at all. She would not overwhelm her thoughts with curiosity, but focused on the shriveling confidence of a woman that with one final blow would send her soaring like pollen. With the undetectable depths of her pain, Renée only knew that she had to meet Evelyn. Renée knew, in her mind, that the delicate poison entrapped in her bosom would seep through her veins like blood flowing in a tube once she openly shared her troubles with Evelyn.

As Renée sat and reminisced, The Stranger was heard creeping down the stairs. "Good morning. Well, afternoon. What time is it anyway?" The Stranger said wiping her sleepy eyes.

"It's four thirty."

"What time did you wake up?"

"I've been woke for a while?"

Sensing tension in Renée's voice, The Stranger asked, "Are you okay?"

"Yes. I just have something on my mind. I just got off the phone with my mother."

"She needs you to come get the kids. I guess I can call me a cab so you can take care of your business," The Stranger suggested.

"No, it's fine. They will be staying another night. She is just so strange, it becomes ridiculous. It's okay. How did you sleep?"

"I had not slept like that in a long time. I would like to thank you for last night and your hospitality. I needed that last night…well…the talk, I mean…" She smiles at Renée. Renée welcomed the smile and smiled back.

Renée's eyes scanned The Stranger, then around the room. "You should really come to one of our networking events," Renée said, breaking the eerie silence. Then she added, "You know, I never got your name…"

Before Renée could finish her statement, The Stranger interrupted, "Who is this?"

"Who is who?"

"This lady in this picture?" The Stranger pulled a picture from the fireplace that she had not noticed before. Her eyes were glued to the picture as if she had seen a ghost. Her jaw faintly dropped and her breath was lost. Her mouth opened silently as if words were going to escape, but nothing did. Although Renée hadn't noticed the sudden change in The Stranger's demeanor, The Stranger thought she should pull her thoughts together and try to wait calmly for a response.

Renée bounced to her feet and walked over to the fireplace, and stood next to The Stranger. "That is my dear friend Evelyn. Evelyn McKenzie? That is the woman that I think you should meet."

The Stranger tried to appear calm, but she did not know if she pulled it off. Her legs felt as if they were going to buckle from underneath her. "Oh, this is the woman that you were talking about last night?" With nothing else to add, she assumed a question would be appropriate.

"Yes, that is Evelyn."

The Stranger did not have another response to add.

"So…"

"So…what?" For a transitory moment, The Stranger glanced at Renée.

"So, what's your name and are you going to the networking meeting?" Renée asked as if exhausted by the wait for a favorable response.

The Stranger thought she had noticed her intense stare into the photo, but feeling relieved that Renée remained unaware of her delayed reactions because of the picture of Evelyn.

"Veronica."

"Who's Veronica?" Renée asked foolishly.

"I am silly," The Stranger stated with a smile.

"Oh, my mind is somewhere else. Good. It is good to meet you Veronica!" Renée grabs her hand and gives it a gentle shake.

"You are silly." The Stranger laughed and placed the

picture back onto the fireplace and made her way to the sofa.

"I insist that you come to our networking meeting with me," Renée persisted.

"I don't know about that," The Stranger *(who we know as Veronica now)* said timidly.

"Why not? You should come. You have got to meet my mentor, Evelyn. She has helped me in many situations. Her wisdom is priceless. She is the most honest person I know. No matter what you want to hear, she'll tell you what you need to hear and some people can appreciate that whereas others shun at it. It took me a minute to embrace it because I was not ready to hear the truth; but when I stop fighting, stop being bitter, stop beating myself up, I became something else entirely. I still have a lot I need to work on, but I am a better person because she helped me to see that. I don't try to change the things that I can't change, like the situation with my ex-husband—instead, I make the effort to change the things that I can and Evelyn has given me the wisdom to know the difference. But, I am still learning and I have been a member for four years. Evelyn started the *MH Women's Club* about five years ago, when I first met her. It was right after she went through a nasty trial. But anyway, I think you would have a good time and benefit from the experience a great deal. As long as you are open, willing to grow, and understand that you are something more, then you will find the answers you seek. Come and go with me," she pleads one last time.

"Let me think about it."

Being persistent, Renée said, "I will not accept no for an answer and that is final." She smiles at Veronica and asked if she was hungry.

"You want to go and get something to eat?" Veronica said,

smiling from ear to ear.

"My cooking wasn't good?" she bluntly asked.

"No…no…not at all. I just thought we could get some air and go out to eat," she defensively said.

"Okay, we can go out to eat," Renée agreed.

Chapter

12

THE DOOR to the *MH Women's Club* seemed heavier than before. The grief and tears weighed down Evelyn's body like a magnet affixed to a refrigerator. Unknowingly, she had drifted in another place as she walked to the MH Meeting Room. Melissa strolled behind her, bewildered by the day's events. She had come to pour her problems on Evelyn's lap, but she did not intend to receive a lesson in *real* pain and suffering. Her problems were horrific, but her physical pain lasted for a moment and the wounds healed. Her emotional bruises lasted a lifetime but she did not suffer much physical pain like Evelyn's friend Leah, Melissa thought. She witnessed a courageous woman in unfathomable pain and yet she remained strong while maintaining her sense of humor.

Melissa watched Evelyn as she removed her purse from her left shoulder, tossed it on the sofa, crept to the refrigerator and removed a bottle of spring water. She watched her drag her zombie state body to the sofa and flop down with useless energy. Melissa did not know what to say, so she sat with Evelyn in silence for the next thirty minutes or so.

"I don't mean to be so restricted and self-consumed, please forgive me." Apologetic words blurted from Evelyn's mouth. "I am not dealing with this well. I had to deal with my great-grandmother's death last year and now I must deal with this too. They say the Lord never puts more on you than you can bear, but I think he forgot to stamp *'Paid In Full'* at my door so no other misery would find it's way in," she said while maneuvering a smile, which lightened the mood.

"I am at a loss for words. I do beg of you to allow me to do something for you. Do you need anything? Are you hungry? Can I get you some water?" Melissa's serious expression remained in place for a moment, and then she smiled when she asked if she needed some *water.* Both of the ladies smiled and Evelyn replied with no thank you to all of the above. Evelyn had not noticed that she was holding a bottle of water in her right hand. She also had not noticed that she had just taken a quick sip before the question was asked.

"I was at a loss for words when my friend needed me," she said with despondency in her eyes.

"I heard the words she spoke regarding your character and she adored you. I was totally blown away with the consideration she had for you. Your heroic nature is quite impressive."

"There is nothing heroic about me. I am a grateful *old* woman who has a lot of good friends that I respect and love. I am grateful to everyone whom I have had the privilege of learning from, even men. Had it not been for *man* disrupting my life with his doggedness and mindless games, I would not have founded this club and would not have met the extraordinary woman that I've met," she said modestly.

"Humbleness does come natural for you, your friend was

197

right."

"You are far too kind. I am just a simple honest woman that tries to live a simple honest life. Struggling with anguish and pain makes it harder to accomplish this life though," Evelyn said while arranging the pillows on the sofa to fit her comfort level.

"My anguish would have to agree. My family secrets greeted me all at once, one after another. I found out my dad's arterial motives behind giving my husband a job. My husband's motive for marrying me did not escape my long list of family secrets either." She looked over at Evelyn who had her cheek rested on a partially closed fist with her head tilted to the right side, elbows denting the top of the sofa. "Please accept my apology; I must not talk of my family problems now."

"No, please, go on. I have had many difficulties in my life and listening to others lets me know that I am human and everything happens to everybody. Please go on. I am totally interested." Melissa looked in vacillation. Evelyn continued on to say, "Please, I insist, this is the one thing that you can do for me." She smiled and welcomed her to continue.

~

Melissa went on to explain her story, with some unwillingness at first. She was not as nervous as she had been before, since seeing Leah. Leah inspired her to get to the root of her suffering so she could start a healing process, and she would finally be able to live *her* life.

"After our marriage, I discovered a few twisted events spiral in the misty air. By the time I delivered my first child Timothy, who's now thirty years old; my husband became verbally abusive toward me. Thirteen months into the marriage, his love turned to distrust, his frustrations turned to anger and Timothy was somewhere in the middle. Steven had not come from a family of prestige and wealth such as mine so he was unaware of protecting the family image at *all* cost. Letting Steven know that his colorful language and behavior would not be tolerated in front of my child resulted in a slap across the face. I will only explain to you that that was the first and last time he ever hit me. For a while, the verbal abuse eased and our house was on track again.

Several years later, we moved into a much bigger home, with the deed reading our names. I believe I was more excited than Steven. That same year, I was pregnant again and decided to attend college. Steven was furious."

"**H**ow can you go to school while you are pregnant?" he contested.

"I am only four weeks and I am already registered. I do not understand the difficulty in this decision," she said with resentment.

"Okay, fine. Don't complain to me about your feet hurting or your back hurting…or whatever," he said while walking out of the master bedroom, downstairs and to the basement. Steven spent the majority of his time in the *man's* basement. It was fully furnished with a black leather sectional and an oversized reclining chair with matching ottoman. A wet bar for entertaining with the boys, an eight foot pool table with net pockets and he especially enjoyed his twenty-five inch color floor model TV. His old habits of drinking and consuming large quantities of drugs did not die—he just had more money to make larger purchases. He, however, did not allow it to interfere with his work. He had a cushy job working for Melissa's father sorting paperwork. He was responsible for opening all mail pertaining to any Real Estate transactions for one of his commercial property complexes. All paperwork from taxes to tenant payments, hit Steven's desk first. Of course, Steven did not get his hands too dirty, with a handsome amount of the work shifting to his assistant, Erica. Unaware, Erica was there to watch over Steven at Melissa's father's request. He did not trust Steven. For that matter, he didn't trust anyone, especially when it came to his finances. Her father figured with the generous salary of $65,000 per year that he paid Steven in 1983, it would keep his hands out of the cookie jar. Not to mention the bonus money he paid to keep his daughter living comfortably. He did not suddenly develop a kind heart, but he knew Melissa was accustomed to a particular lifestyle and he had to protect his family's image. With that in mind, he demanded that Steven get his High School Equivalency and he did not frown upon the idea of Melissa going to college. In fact, he offered to pay for it. His daughter was a part of his image whether he liked it or not, so her attending a university was a notch on his belt. Furthermore, he was not particularly concerned with his son-in-law because he buried him so deep in a shabby back office, no one would recognize him except Melissa no how. But after a few years, Melissa's father began to shift more responsibility toward Steven. At the time, Melissa had no idea that the extra activities consisted of bribery drop-offs, extortion, bodily injury to another, and other criminal mischief that remained unclear to Melissa.

In the tense moments of the years that followed, Melissa stumbled upon a list of corruption that trailed from Steven to her father to many public officials. From the time she discovered her first piece of information, she was inquisitive about other facts that remained suspended in the air but too invisible to see. She wondered what other information had she missed about her husband and her father that she didn't know or ignored. At times her investigations led her frustratingly to a dead end with irrefutable conclusive evidence leading nowhere. Evidence suggesting the participation of unlawful cops, attorneys, and judges; all had their hands in the bank of the underworld—planting evidence, jury tampering, and throwing out cases. Melissa had not thoroughly understood the mentality of the underworld, or any corruption for that matter, but her search opened her eyes and she realized the inhuman characteristics of some men that existed in the world. Melissa had not known how far her husband had sunk until he admittedly revealed it to her.

Steven was adamant about Melissa not attending school. He got to her by ripping her homework to shreds. Another time or two, that she recalled, he ripped the chapters from her Accounting textbook and her English textbooks. She exhaustively fought with him about the textbooks, but simply knew that it was useless. She was determined not to let Steven hinder her. While she was in school, it became her time of peace. She did not have to think of the lack of love and attention at home or the situation with her parents. School became her sanctuary.

After working diligently on a class paper, they got into another argument about Melissa cheating. She had no idea where the argument initiated from but she assumed he had to justify the rage inside him instead of admitting that he was high and foolish. She finished typing the paper, closed her books and sat her hard work on the desk in her office in a neat pile, all prepared for the next morning. Steven entered the room, blood shot eyes and rapid breathing as if he'd jogged a mile while smoking a cigarette.

"You love school too much. You must be seeing someone

there. Who is it?" he hissed slowly, as his chest rose with every breath.

"You're crazy and high. Just go back down to the basement. I really don't have time for this today. Now move out my way, I must check on the children," she said while pushing him to the side like dough.

"You think you are extra smart...now that you're a *university* student," he said with sarcasm, moving his face closer to hers as saliva sprayed across Melissa's face.

Melissa wiped her mouth in disgust and slowly responded, "You are high and you need to remove yourself from my space." He moved to the side so she could walk past him. Melissa had made it to the hallway when she heard a ripping noise. Standing a few inches from the doorway of the office, she looked back. He was slowly ripping all the pages of her fifteen page term paper she had typed for her English Composition class. She was furious. She lodged at him swinging. She hit him so hard he fell to the floor. She grabbed him off the floor by his shirt collar and pressed his back into the custom built bookshelves leaning against the wall. "You son-of-a-bitch, I can't believe you." She released his shirt. He tried to get up but stumbled back to the floor, hitting his head against the bookshelf. As he lay on the floor with blood moderately running from the back of his head, he laughed. Lips swollen from the mighty blow, and still he smiled with much delight.

"Teach you. I advised you that school was a bad idea, one day you will listen to me," he said still soaking in his smile of irony.

She picked up her work and tried to piece it together but it was no use. He had destroyed the paper. It was due the very next day. She took the pieces and placed them in a sandwich bag and took them to school with her; timidly presented the paper to her teacher and insisted on an extended timeframe so she could rewrite the paper. The professor, never feeling sorry or pity for any of his students before, saw the desperation in her eyes and agreed.

Eventually, after three long hard years, she attended the ceremony for the Associates of Applied Science Degree achievers. She wanted a piece of paper to reflect every step of her hard work and sacrifice. Then, she headed for the next step, a four year degree in Accounting.

During the course of her studies, after four years, her husband gave up on trying to make her quit. His efforts were pointless, plus, she started doing most of her homework in school and brought mostly reading and note taking material home with her.

Some time in the fall of 1988, just when another monotonous semester started, her husband had yet another secret to unfold. The green leaves had just begun to turn an orange, reddish-brown color, with an intimation of yellow splashed across the uniquely shaped foliage that sheltered the grass. With a maddening summer ending, Melissa was inundated by the fallen leaves that crowded the concrete stumps that created a path to the garage. Melissa had started to mind the little things and her emotions displayed aggravation. Monotonous, would be an understatement because she had grown tired of the same drama with her husband—if it weren't school it was the men at school. He also accused her of having relations with her professors, male or female. This fall, Melissa and Steven had an argument that explained a mountain of bottled inside emotions. Steven had been in the basement that morning, smoking grass and who knows what else. His good friend Bull came to visit. Melissa thought that over the years Steven would have grown less fond of Bull and his tactics. She suspected that Bull was the reasoning behind the verbal abuse, the accusations, and the frequent stays in the basement.

After escorting Bull to his car, Steven entered the house in a stagger. His eyes exploded like fire and his pupils were dilated. Sweat perspired from his forehead like he was fresh into his work-out and he reeked of alcohol. His bottom lip was slightly slanted like a homeless drunk. Melissa determined that he was higher than she had ever seen him. She thought she would need to call 9-1-1, but her father would be frantic. Publicizing their family affairs was *not* tolerated. If at any point she considered calling for help, she would only be permitted to call her father first. She sensed a debate would start and she was in no mood for it tonight, still, she mentally prepared herself for what was anticipated. She recalled that Timothy was spending the night at a friend's, and Kathleen, the youngest child, was staying the night at Steven's sister house in Eastpointe, not too far from where they currently lived. Being thankful to herself that the children were not at home was a tremendous stress relief.

"You whore," he said with slurred words.

"Every time he comes over, you behave in an intolerable manner," she said, shunning him out her face.

"I know this is about him…that's why…that's why you're a whore," he persisted.

"What are you talking about? Lying down will do you some good at this moment," she stated, trying to keep the situation under control.

He looks at her, still standing in the narrow hallway a few feet from the door leading to the garage, where he directed Bull to go through to get to his vehicle, and said, "You know what I am talking about." He walks toward her and head butts her in the forehead. Standing in the kitchen leaning against the granite countertop, she stumbled. She was caught off guard with the head butt.

"Are you sick? You have been warned about putting your hands on me. Please do not take this madness to another level," she said firmly.

"You have been warned…yeah, yeah," he repeated mockingly. Laughing as he embraced the back of the kitchen chair, and finally took a seat, "You disgust me."

"Okay," she said, taking a seat adjacent to his. "Let's get to the bottom of this. I am not familiar with the facts surrounding this hostility toward me and Timothy as well. Is it because you are not his father? You took hold of that responsibility when you agreed to marry me. And what have I done to you that is so bad that I deserve this cruel treatment? My ears are waiting on answers because my mind is fresh out of them."

"Why must you talk like that? That is one of the things that drive me up the wall. Your language! What's up with that?" he said with more apathy.

"What do you mean? This is the way I speak. Please do not try to change the subject. Do not play me for stupid," she said with aggravation.

"You know why I can't stand you? 'Cause you are a whore. I don't dislike Timothy, he's my boy."

"I'm a whore. And that is based on what? Explain my convictions. Please, enlighten me."

"You are such a smart ass bitch. Enlighten me…yeah," he said in a pretense tone repeating her words and tossing them back.

"Just get to the point. Why do you hate me so much? In the beginning of our relationship, your proposal was more than acceptable, now your behavior is irrational." Melissa was tired of the charade and wanted answers, she demanded answers.

"Don't you raise your voice at me," he said emphatically. "I should be the one complaining here. I'm not the one that slept with my friend. You whore."

"Your friend? What friend and what are you talking about you freaking lush?" she asked with intense anger. Melissa felt her blood boiling and the longer it took for Steven to spill his guts, the more she wanted to punch him in it.

"You know you slept with my friend."

"Whom are you claiming?

"BULL!"

"You must be insane. That piece-of-shit means nothing to me. I thought after nine years you would part from him, but I am convinced now, more than ever, that you are just as sick as he is. I will not listen to this nonsense." She removes herself from the kitchen chair and proceeded to exit.

"Don't walk away now…it's just getting started," he slightly laughed and raised his voice louder. "I know you had sex with him because I was there, Melissa. You probably slept with them all. You ran to your daddy saying you were raped but you loved it, every damn minute of it!"

She became enraged and vaguely looked over her shoulder with her back facing him, "What did you say. You saw what?"

He looked at her with a smile written in his fired red eyes. Words not pulled together, disoriented, and said, "I was there, I saw you."

She turned completely around then added, "You son-of-a-bitch, you saw what was happening to me and you did nothing. I can't believe you let that happen to me. Now, after nine years, you feel the need to release this information. So, Timothy is Bull's son, is that what you are trying to say? *Is it, you sick son-of-a...!*" She gagged and ran for the kitchen sick. Her stomach boiled with nausea but nothing exited. "I don't believe you," she quickly added—breathless. "I don't believe a word that escapes your lips. You are a sick bastard."

"And...you...you're a whore," he said while trying to swallow, gasping for a breath of air. He had been holding this secret in too long and he could not hold it any longer, he thought.

"Look at you. You are high! If this is true, why tell me now?" she angrily asked, releasing her words in infuriated curiosity. "I marvel the fact that you can say that with a smile upon your sick face. Let me explore...if this is true and you are so eaten up about it, why marry me? Why accept Timothy as your own? *You sick bastard.* Why put me through this holly hell of a life? You uttered your everlasting love to me and in the same breath you despised me. What is the deal?" Her high pitched voice screamed in a rage. Frustrated by his performance, her rage took over the conversation. "If you feel this way, then let me out of your life forever. If you feel that you can't look at me without recreating the memories through your mind. How do you think I feel? It happened to me dammit. *You sorry piece-of-shit!* It happened to *me!* How do you think it affected me?" Anger built inside her and the tears fell frantically. "Can you answer that question, Mr. Know-it-all?" she deplored with sarcasm.

"Yeah...yeah...I can. You loved it, that's how you felt. I put up with your shit because I love my kids and..." he paused, and then Melissa interrupted.

She straightened her face and said with a firm voice, "...and what? What were you going to say? Spit it out you little shit. You can't stop now, you're on a roll," she said with strong demand.

He paused and did not say a word. His silence infuriated her. She began slapping him across the face and punching him in the chest, nearly knocking him out of his seat. "Hey, hey…you better…" He tried to fight off her attack, but his body was too flaccid from intoxication. He was unable to complete his sentence due to the punch in the lips that sent a hint of blood soaring across the room and onto the kitchen wall.

"You sick bastard. And what? Tell it!" she demanded as the adrenaline went rushing through her veins.

He said in an antagonistic voice, "I made a deal with the devil. In exchange for your hand in marriage…I would be set," he finally managed to say as he laughed, cleaning the blood from his lips with his rough, burned fingertips. "I made a deal with the *Devil*," he repeated louder.

A look of shock took over her facial expression. She paused in the middle of her enraged hits, and shook her head in disbelief. This could not be true, she thought to herself. Her body stumbled back a step and halfheartedly, she asked, "Who's the devil?" Feeling in her heart she knew the answer, but she needed to know for sure.

With a big bright smile, showing almost all his blood stained teeth, he said with keenness, "*Your Father!*"

Her muscles paralyzed. Her body dropped to lean against the edge of the granite kitchen countertop—motionless. Her expression released the convoluted emotions traveling inside her. Her thoughts escaped her and a suitable remark of ridicule could not find her lips. She repeated the ferocious words to herself in Steven's voice, just as he had said them, and they went through her stomach like a dagger. The ambivalence that Melissa felt toward her father was confirmed by the cruelty of her husband who proclaimed his love for her. Unsurprising, she was not as perturbed with her father as Steven, because her father had announced his lack of love for her many, many years ago without hesitation or misunderstanding. But Steven had once told her he loved her and the words leaked from his romantic lips gracefully. At least, that's how it sounded in her head. Maybe, it was the sound of desperation that transformed the words into delightful words she needed to hear to render the decision to marry him. Suddenly, with thoughts in every direction, she gasps for a breath. Holding her chest tightly with her hands angled across, while balling over in frantic tears, she starts to breathe heavier and heavier. The power of her emotions soon got the best of her, as she reached out her arm to catch her balance.

Steven got a glimpse of her distress, and the fire was fueled. "Not so bad now…that's right. You thought you were too good for me with your fancy talk and your university education. You tried to cover up the fact that you are nothing more than a cheap whore that spends daddy's money." He laughed in great enjoyment. Even with that comment, she was still unable to speak. She knew her dad was rotten, but she did not believe, could not believe, that he paid Steven to marry her. Several minutes had passed and she pulled herself together. Trying to clear the tears and interrupt the emotional trauma that took her mind by storm so she could seek the truth, was emphatically difficult. "Yeah, your good old daddy paid me handsomely to marry you. It would ruin the family name for his daughter to be unmarried with a child, he said. Oh, he ran the whole story down for me. That's right…he paid me thirty thousand up front and a very generous salary for shuffling papers in one of his back offices, along with other odd jobs that I did for the family. Yes, he goes through great lengths to protect his family's name and his reputation. I was paid nicely. A small price to pay, don't you think?" He smiled with a smug facial expression and wiped some more blood from his mouth. He was wiping more spit than blood, leaning with an arrogant slump to his left side in the chair away from the table, waiting on a response from Melissa. "Of course, it was not easy dealing with you, but the grass kept me going." He laughed uncontrollably.

"I bet you and my father had a loving time entertaining yourselves using my misfortunes?" she said in a low psychotic voice while unbendingly magnifying her words with careful selection to discard the tasteless unscrupulous trickery. She continued with unpredictable strength and said, "Yes, you are right...daddy's money has been well spent, including the booze and drugs you buy with it. Let me ask you something, how much do you think daddy will pay to know about your nightly habits?" Not a flinch in sight, she looked him directly in the eyes and continued, "You and my father got a good laugh at my expense. Now, it will be my turn to laugh." She moves in closer to Steven. Her face so close to his that she was inches away from a kiss. "I have a few tricks of my own, but you're too drunk, too drugged up, and too stupid to apprehend the perplexity of what I have been aiming for. Don't play games with me Mister. I woke up long before you, so don't fuck with me. You and my father think you can out smart someone, well, we'll see about that. You may have contributed to my desolation and your self-indulging behavior has caught me by surprise, but your coldness will not obstruct my goals. You piece-of-shit! You tormented me the last eight years because you think I slept with your sorry ass pathetic, good for nothing friend. Oh, you bet your sweet ass that things will start looking up from this point." With a calm, sharp firmness in her voice, she added, "And please remember; I am my father's daughter, so don't underestimate that the apple doesn't fall far from the tree. I will eat you alive." She pressed her index finger in his chest and spit in his face.

"You bitch. Yeah, you may have an upper hand over your daddy's money but it will not change the fact that you are guilty…just admit it."

"Guilty of what? Well, as if I really care." She shunned him away with the wave of her hand as she walked over to the chair across the table to have a seat. Her insufferable emotions had withered out and exhausted her strength. She could no longer indulge Steven, not even with the news to come.

"I was there remember!" he repeated for the last time.

"You've consistently proclaimed this notion, which begs the question as to why you did nothing. Because you are a coward, that's why. You let Bull run all over you. Your movements are useless without his input. Your mind does not function; it simply wanders when you are not in his presence. You have never been your own man, and you never will be. The mere fact that you are still friends with a repulse asshole like Bull, especially after he raped your wife says a lot for your character. Your inaction is comical to him and he explodes with laughter every time he sees you. You are amusement to him, I'm sure." Her hateful words exasperated him.

"Yeah, I'm sure you know. I laugh at him because I had you first," he said in anger.

"Sure. The drugs and the alcohol have scalded your brain," she said with mild humor.

"I was first," he repeated in a hostile voice. "No one

211

touched you until after I went first. Those were the rules," he confirmed with a conceited look upon his face.

She looked in skepticism. She goaded his senses to the point of confession. It was apparent that her nonchalant attitude was testing his patience. He confessed to the pills that were slipped inside her drink to paralyze her body. He confessed that he hated her for allowing him to do that to her. His confession, however, did not admit to being wrong—he confessed in spite and to justify his guilt that he felt he did not have. She was mortified by the words that bounced through her ears like a piercing gunshot blast. Glancing at his thin decade body, disgust was all she could muster. The shock of her father paying the repulse animal to marry her was all the shock she could handle in one day so the gruesome words that followed left her practically expressionless. Her demeanor reflected stunned, but she quickly pulled herself together and that angered him more. She was not going to fuel the fire again. "And to think, you were paid handsomely to wed me. Now, you are going to pay me handsomely. I don't suppose my father is aware of this crucial information. To make him out to be a foul for paying the man that raped his daughter to marry her, especially a young uneducated idiot like you. Can you understand how imperative it would be to get rid of you, forever? It would be detrimental for someone if this vital information just slipped out during supper. I am sure I don't have to make you aware of my father's friends in high places, well, and in low places too." She swiftly walks over to him as a smug look entrapped her face and said, "You are going to pay for everything you put my mind and body through. I am going to get every nickel I can from my father and you are going to help me do it," she demanded.

Before long, Melissa had received over two million dollars from her father within a five year time span, not including the money he willing paid for her college tuition and books. A deal he would have never made if Melissa had suggested it herself. Melissa's plan to extort money from her father was easier than she originally thought. The biggest bulk presented itself when Melissa advised Steven to inform her father that they wanted to buy another house—that they never purchased of course—but Melissa's dad never came to visit so this was a perfect scheme. Of course, she did not look at it as a scheme. She was rightfully getting what she had coming to her, especially after the misery they put her through. With the eight hundred and ninety thousand dollars they received from Melissa's father, it put her capital just over two million. Steven did not reap the benefits of the money because the understanding of their agreement was that he would not. Melissa built an empire with her daddy's proceeds, opening a loan consulting firm which specialized in assisting business owners in obtaining financing for new business ventures or financing for existing franchises. Combined with her father's business power, his money, and her intelligence; her business grew to one of the largest loan consulting companies in Michigan with revenues averaging over seven point five million within the first two years of business. Melissa's income went over the top, just under a hundred million dollars in profit and assets. In just under eleven years, when she decided to branch into another area of expertise—becoming the lender of some selective business loans, her revenue soared.

Now, Melissa faces another dilemma in her lifecycle, trying to divorce her husband after thirty years of marriage without giving him a dime.

~

"That's the easy part!" Evelyn said excitingly.

"What is?" Melissa was unsure of the statement.

"How you will divorce your husband without giving him a dime?" she said with more enthusiasm.

"*How?*" Melissa's eyes widen with curiosity.

"Simple. Naturally, he is your husband and what's yours is his, but you can get around that in one of two ways. First, offer to buy him out. Don't let him know that's what you are doing. Just give him a few choices, like you will leave him the house and the car in exchange for a divorce. Of course he will want spending money for his nightly expenses, so you have him get it from your father or you make a deal to give him one lump sum once the divorce is finalized. Your second option is to sell your business or businesses to a trusted trustee or friend, if possible, and divorce his ass and he'll get a portion of your profits from the sale of...let's say...fifty thousand dollars. The second option is tricky but it can be done, legally. You can set conditions that you remain an active member of the board and a few years later, buy the business back or a portion of the business." A big smile formatted across her face as if she had solved the case of the century.

"Well, that was quick thinking," Melissa said as she briefly considered the options and continued, "Option one sounds more like one he would certainly go for. I don't want to go through the trouble of extra documentation, contracts and the like regarding my business. Something tells me that Steven will not be too much of a problem given the information I have on him and that my father is not in the best of health, so he may think extorting more money out of dad may be a good way to go." A puzzled look captured her face. She looked at Evelyn, slowly blinked her eyes and nodded in appreciation and said, "You may be right. I did not think of that. I guess the answer is truly in front of you, you just need to look a little harder to see it."

Evelyn smiled and agreed. "Now, we both need some relaxation. What do you say to us relaxing in the sauna for an hour discussing anything but problems and turn in for the night or the morning?" Both women laughed and headed for the SQ Room to get changed.

"You have a really nice facility here."

"Thank you. We try to make it a relaxing stress relief facility that we call *home*."

"You have done a marvelous job. I must feel relaxed, revealing my mind and body in your presence." She smiled while slipping on a thick fluffy cotton robe, still holding the hefty price tag of two hundred seventy-nine dollars, from Evelyn's member closet. Melissa was convinced that Evelyn's since of style did not come overnight. If you were on the outside looking in, you would believe that Evelyn was born with a silver spoon in her mouth, Melissa thought. It is amazing how two different worlds share the same stories, she continued her thought.

"We are having our fifth annual meeting in September, you should come. Or better yet, you should attend the networking meeting on the nineteenth of this month first."

"A bunch of women getting together to discuss problems...I am not sure if my heart can take any more stories of anguish."

Evelyn smiled then added, "Not really discussing problems but discussing our encounters with men."

"Oh, like male bashing!" she said with more interest.

"Not quite male bashing, although some of our members have been known to get a little heated during these discussions and some of their friends or associates they bring are more angry than most."

"It sounds interesting. Let me think about it."

"It will be great. We cater different cultural food at each event and at this meeting we will be presenting the face of Italy, my favorite place, besides the United States of America." Both of the women laugh and lean back to enjoy the hot vanilla aroma therapy mist from the sauna. Their faces flush with moisture and sweat oozing all over their body from their gently disturbed pours. Twenty minutes of silence passed and Evelyn continued, "Our networking meetings create a calm soothing atmosphere for our members to eat, entertain, converse, and share insight of our stories with our guest. Each member typically brings a friend, relative or colleague to the meeting for food, fun and conversation. It's really a great event. You should come."

"I think I will. Thank you. It will allow me to let my hair down and have some fun for once, since...since...damn, I don't know when." She looks over at Evelyn with tear filled eyes and starts to laugh. "You never think about living life until you have seriously thought about it. All the time we spend living for or through someone else, we never take the time to reflect on living for ourselves. Isn't that funny? We think that living for our children, our husbands, or our parents is what life is all about."

"But, if we don't learn to live for ourselves, we can't provide the means necessary to help someone else. We can't live their life for them, so why sacrifice your own just to make them happy. When you live for yourself, joy, will always come in the morning—at least that's what they say. Living your life doesn't mean that you must live selfishly, it just means that you need to take care of yourself first to create the stable foundation needed to help or support others. The successful business woman that you have grown to be still leaves you with an unhappy heart because you lived your life through the eyes of your family."

"You can say that again." Melissa smiles and relaxes her neck to firmly place her head against the wall.

Evelyn faintly laughs, relaxed her head in the same gesture and said, "The networking meeting is next week, don't forget. If you need any help with your divorce, let me know. One of our members, Lylie Frankly, is a great divorce attorney. She works in the Megan Building, near downtown Detroit. Although you may not have to go to court, but just in case, she is one of the best and she will have him begging for mercy." Both ladies smile with confidence and enjoyed the sauna for another forty-five minutes before heading to bed.

Chapter

13

"THE FACE OF Italy," Melissa thought. Holding on to the words Evelyn said regarding the theme for the networking affair. Remembering her savior, Charlie, initiated a wide smile. She mysteriously ran into her hero while conversing with a classmate outside of the University of Michigan. Their minds were fried from the long hours of complex discussions and vigilant research for their dissertation for the Masters Degree Program. It had taken Melissa over eight years to make it this far, concentrating on the operations of her business and tolerating the tactics of her husband. Although, his behavior was not as bothersome as before, he still managed a hint of destruction every now and then.

Old deaden brown, partially crumbled leaves danced across the ground like little children in motion. The debris was subtle and was left behind before winter had settled. The snow had melted a month before, but rainstorms tunneled the air with no end in sight. It was almost dry on this day. It had been much cooler this April than the previous year; in the twenties with a high of thirty on occasions. The buds from the flowers had not yet started to form and the leafless trees were still bare from the grueling winter. It was spring. Karen, Melissa's classmate, searched vigorously for a lighter to light a cigarette, adding to the polluted air. Exhausted by Karen's efforts, Melissa asked, "Are you sure it's in there?"

"Yeah, I put the damn thing in here this morning. This really pisses me off when I can't find something," Karen said with much irritation.

"Maybe you left it in the library, you know, where we were seated," Melissa suggested.

"Na...it's in...damnit, here it is," she said, as her face calmed. Melissa watched; as she instantly lit the cigarette, not mindful of the handbag loosely dangling from her broaden shoulder. She inhaled as if it were her last. The gray dampness of the climate, which mentally infringes on your mind with sadness, had not entered her moment of beautified fulfillment. She had abandoned the atmosphere around her and for a brief space in time she was content, until she opened her eyes to exhale. The smoke spiraled through the air, dissolving in the wind. There was a delicate wind blowing to the North that tickled their faces, forcing their eyes to blink rapidly. The suede jackets they wore were no match for the cool breeze.

"It's getting a little chilly out here; I think I will go back inside. I'll meet you back in the library."

"Okay," Karen agreed. Before Melissa could make it back inside the building, Karen quickly announced with enthusiasm, "Hey...Melissa wait, I see my brother coming. I want you to finally meet him."

"Oh good! I finally get to meet your brother. You've told me so much about him," Melissa stated with much excitement as she headed back to stand next to Karen to get a better view.

219

Karen's brother pulls up to the curb, quickly gets out of the car, and embraces his sister with a huge hug—spinning her around in circles. He glances over at Melissa and slowly brings his boyish hug to a still motion. "Who's your friend? She looks familiar," he asked in a calm tone.

"This is Melissa, the lady that I've been talking about. You know, I said how smart she is and…"

He interrupts Karen and extends his hand to Melissa, "I'm Charlie. Charlie LaGuiarro."

Accepting his proposal, she shakes his hand and said, "Nice to finally meet you. My name is Melissa Contour."

His eyes widen with surprise, but his reaction went unnoticed by his sister. There was a warmness about him that Melissa immediately felt. She felt as if she had already known Charlie. "So, what are you ladies getting into today?"

"Researching our asses off for this darn dissertation. Why does school have to be so damn complicated?" Karen said, releasing a lengthily sigh.

"That's what you get for having all the brains, sis—a Master Degree. I am really proud of you…have I ever told you that?" he said, winking his eye.

"Na…I don't think you have," Karen replied with a big playful smile. Charlie expressed how proud he was of her everyday but it was always music to her ears.

"Well, it was good to finally meet you. I have heard so much about you. Karen talks about you all the time."

"Don't believe everything you hear."

"It was all good things."

"In that case, it's all true." He smiles and looks at his sister.

"I will let you two catch up. Karen, I'll meet you in the

library, okay!" Melissa said as she started to walk away.

"Wait. Don't go. Let me take you hard working ladies to lunch or dinner tonight," he suggested.

"No thank you. I really need to finish this research and I have a family to get home to," Melissa stated with a regretful voice.

"I am sure you can tear yourself away from your studies for one dinner," he pleaded.

"Come on Melissa, it will be fun," Karen begged.

After several minutes of study, Melissa agreed to go to dinner with Karen and Charlie. Melissa felt compelled to go and something was drawing her closer to Charlie. She found herself straggling in his shadow like a school age teenager following a football jock. Melissa felt pathetic, but safe. She secretly cuddled under his wing and embraced his sensitivity with open arms. Instantly, she felt attraction for Charlie but it was not because of his masculine, muscular body. His dark memorizing eyes, placed on his handsome face swallowed by his charming smile. It was not his dark short hair style that made him look like a fierce gangster. It was his warm inviting personality that captivated her curiosity and forced her to accept the engagement. It was just something about him that would not be known until later.

~

It was not until that summer when Charlie confessed to Melissa that he was the gentleman that rescued her and sat on a mountain of steel to insure her safety for the remainder of the night.

"Why did you stay until the morning?" she curiously asked.

"I didn't want those guys to come back and do more harm to you. I wanted to kill them, but it was not my fight. Well, I had not killed a man before, at least not in those days."

Melissa was afraid to pursue that response, so she let it go. "Why didn't you take me to the hospital? Not that I was not very, very grateful for what you did for me; I just wondered why you didn't take me to the hospital?"

"I would have had a lot of questions to answer. At the time, I was about nineteen and high. There would have been a boat load of questions that I would not have wanted to answer. Not to mention, they would have wanted me to describe the fellows that hurt you and I could not have done that," he said with reassurance.

"Why?" she said baffled.

"My family is not your ordinary family. It's in our blood, Italian blood. You don't rat on anyone, no matter what. You take care of the problem yourself. Although, I did not hurt those guys for hurting you, I knew I had to stay for the night to be sure you were okay. Once, many years ago, for the first time, I saw a man die. It was not a pretty site. My uncles beat this guy until there was nothing left to beat. I never knew why or what he did, all I needed to know, according to my uncle, was that he double crossed them and there was a hefty price to pay. This was after those guys did that to you and I felt the rage build inside me again. I wanted to do to them what my uncles did to that guy, but I couldn't. Then, I thought I would never see you again, so I let it go. I never told a sole about what happened that night, but it always stayed with me. Primarily because I felt weak. I should have done more, but I didn't."

"When I fell on the ground and looked up, it was you that I saw, wasn't it?" she said with a blunt smile.

"Yes it was." He smiled back.

"When I first laid eyes on you, I knew it was something

222

magnificent about you. You saved me and I could never thank you enough," she said with tear filled eyes.

"You already have. I am so glad to see you and especially glad to see that you are safe," he said, reaching down to stroke her smooth delicate face.

She slowly closed her eyes and allowed the touch. She motioned her cheek in the palm of his manly hand, giving in to his sensation. Melissa had never thought that she could feel so passionate about a man. She wondered, "Is this how it was suppose to feel?" As he massaged her shoulder length hair, his hand gently places it alongside her ear. She feels the warmth of a gentle breeze sweeping across the rim of her ear as he whispers softly. "I have thought about you for years. I never stopped thinking about you. Can I please, just hold you closer to me? I want you to feel safe. I want you to feel respected. I want…" His words were loose and shaky. It was as if his soul ached for Melissa. She had never felt so empowered before. It was gratifying.

They had met at his home in Eastpointe. Finally, after several months of pleading with Melissa to have dinner with him again, she agreed to meet him and they continued to meet every week after that enormously hot day in July. Melissa had not cheated on her husband before, although, long after they were married, she suspected he cheated on her. By the time this occurred, she didn't care. He became a business agreement. She needed him to get what she wanted from her father and his carelessness assisted her in her investigation on collecting evidence against him and her father. Evidence that would be used in her favor to get what she wanted and possibly get her husband out of her life for good. With Charlie, she strongly considered wrapping herself in his arms and making mad passionate love to him, to get a glimpse of what love *really* felt like.

"I have not been forthcoming with you," he said suddenly.

Melissa looked up at him with surprise. Her body thrusting forward from a calm position snuggled under his arm as they relaxed on the sofa. "What do you mean?" she asked, reluctant to hear the response.

"I have not told you the whole story?"

"What whole story? Story about what?" she said with more concern.

"I saw your husband. When I was leaving your office, after bringing you those roses, I saw him. Is he on drugs or just tired from being an asshole?" he said with aggravation.

Melissa was uncertain where this was going, but he had her husband down to a T. She was unsure as to the response he was looking for her to give, so she said, "Yes," with much hesitation.

"I should have told you this months ago, but I wasn't sure how to say it. I am not one who drags around the world, so I will just say it. You're husband was there with those guys that raped you." Melissa felt his firm body congeal even more. His heart raced rapidly, visibly seen through his silk shirt. The lost expression on his face suggested uncertainty on what should be said next.

Melissa eased his mind, relieving the distress encumbered upon his face and said, "Yes, I know."

His eyes filled with shock. "You know. But…how?"

"He told me," she said, dropping her head with shame.

"He told you. *What kind of…what kind of piece-of-shit is he? What? What was he trying to do, rub it in your face?*" he said angrily.

"Yes, as a matter of fact, he was. He was really high that night and everything spilled out of him like a leaking faucet. And that is not the worst of it." She looked up at Charlie with restless tears and continued, "My father paid him to marry me." At this point, the tears were uncontrollable. They rolled down her cheeks one after the other. After Steven broke her heart with this despicable news, she had vowed to throw it out of her mind and move on; and telling the news to the Charlie freed her of the anguish that was trapped inside her.

"*What?*" He jumped off the sofa in a rage, clenching his teeth and said, "That is ridiculous! What the hell was your father thinking? That has got to be the most absurd thing I have ever heard. What kind of family do you have?"

Melissa almost burst into laughter, but he was so passionate, she would not dare to humiliate him with foolish insensitive laughter. She stood up and calmly assisted in positioning him back on the sofa so she could explain the entire story. "You must know that my father has never been a father to me. He had confessed his true feelings for me many years back. You must understand that my father will do anything to salvage the reputation of his family name and when I became pregnant and unwed, it was a slap in the face. I was not aware of this betrayal until years later. My father, on the other hand, does not know that it was my own husband who raped me and fathered my first born. My husband blamed me, naturally. He not only ripped the innocence from my body but he distorted my mind. He had challenged my sanity for many, many years and sometimes I felt my troubles proved to be an asset to my state of mind. It has taught me to be tougher, be more assertive, and go after what I want. I will admit that his tormenting acts forced a breakdown of my confidence for several years, until he confessed his undying love for me by bragging that he raped me and took pleasure in doing so. I don't know what happened, but something came over me and suddenly I could see more clearly. I knew what I had to do."

"I still cannot believe that any man would do something like that. And then, to be married to you all this time and feel no sense of guilt for what he had done, it's preposterous," he said calmly.

"Believe me, he felt guilty. That's why I had to suffer through the mental and physical abuse. Well, he hit me once and tugged on me another, but, he got the message that physical abuse would never be tolerated," she said firmly.

"Can I ask you a question?"

"Sure."

"Why are you still with him? You said you found out years ago, why are you still being bothered with his bullshit?"

"It's a business agreement. I look at our relationship as a business. You get the customer's business but you don't have to sleep with them," she said with a bright smile.

Charlie was puzzled and it showed, but he smiled back. Melissa was deciding if she would tell Charlie the rest of her story but she thought that one confession would suffice for tonight. It was getting late, so they said their goodbyes, embraced their first kiss, and Melissa headed for home.

~

Sex disguised as love making became plainly known to Melissa as brutal sex. Her sexual encounters were limited to two men in her lifetime, Steven and Bull. Her stomach turned with weakness at the very thought of Bull invading her sacred body, leaving his musty intoxicated smell embedded within her. At the age of thirty-four, she had not made love to a man before, a *real man.* In her mind, she never lost her virginity. She felt that her sacred garden would not flourish until she had opened her buds to allow the sunshine and rain to seep through. Charlie would be the sunshine that lit up her life with promising love and redemption.

Standing by the enormous bay window, Melissa was in all of the panoramic view of the Lakefront. Breathing in the tranquil, fascinating pond in the courtyard of the building neighboring to Charlie's house, captured her senses. It was an extravagant showcase that featured four dolphins symmetrically proportioned across one another, sprouting water several feet in the air and perfectly meeting together, descending to the center of the pond. Palace Creek was marvelously crafted with masterfully planned homes, newly developed, and offered a variety of beauty. This community's atmosphere seemed peaceful and breathtaking. She was extended an invitation to rendezvous with Charlie a few days prior, and she accepted. A spectacular moment of billowy forms racing aimlessly across the overcast sky, resting a romantic array of glowing light captured from the set of the sun, was interrupted, but welcomed, by the soft touch of a warm embrace. Charlie entered the spacious living room, with windows uniquely angled to the back of the home, and found Melissa standing in silence. He approached her motionless body and wrapped his strong arms around her. Her heart melted with satisfaction, placing her arm on top of his, forming a tighter hold.

"It looks so beautiful out here," she said titling her head to the right as Charlie neatly positioned his chin along side of her neck.

"Yes, it is. It looks like rain, though," he agreed then added.

"Yes. I think you may be right."

They stand in silence for several lingering minutes. "Let's have a seat on the sofa. Or, we can go outside on the patio, if that would be better," he suggested.

"Yes. It is still warm outdoors. But I think we better stay in tonight. Instead of the sofa, can we go to the master suite? I would like to lie down for a while," she said, as the words softly escaped her lips but with a wearisome tone.

"That's fine. Whatever you want to do is fine with me. Would you like for me to run you some bath water first or you could take a steaming shower. It usually helps me when my body aches from the day's dilemmas," he said as he smiled, still holding her tight, viewing her reflection in the window. Melissa intrigued him. He could not understand why the memory of Melissa left an everlasting impression in his heart for so many years. A woman he barely knew at the time. To hold her tight and never let go, is how he imagined this night. His thoughts were challenged by the guilt of leaving her in pain sitting inside that tiny car until morning. He had thought that he could have done more, but what?

"You look deep in thought," she said, glancing at his reflection.

"Yes. Thinking about you," he replied with an enchanting smile.

"You have the most beautiful smile," she said sharing one of her own.

"And so do you, along with everything else. I don't understand how any man could do nothing but love you. You are so beautiful, sophisticated, pleasant, and modest, if I may add."

Her heart became overwhelmed by his words. She turned to face him, staring directly into his magnetic eyes. For the next intense moment, they shared gazes, then a kiss. With every

228

interminable second that past, it felt like minutes, then hours. Her heart raced rapidly through her chest muscles, and her breath shortened with every moment. Slowly, she glanced at him in a peak, his eyes remained closed. Even with his eyes closed, she could see the intense undisputable love he felt for her. Her eyes smiled with envy. She pulled his body closer, as if they could possibly get any closer, melting their body heat inside one another. Their passionate kiss ended with a soft connection that delayed for a second, as their lips partially pulled apart with the bottom maintaining faint contact—their eyes connected and smiles were exchanged. Melissa had never kissed a man like that before. She had not felt the adrenaline she was feeling now. Her pulsated heartbeat became irregular and her lungs practically collapsed from the excitement. She took a immerse breath and said, "I think I will lie down now."

"Okay. I will run you some bath water. Trust me, you'll feel much better after havin' taken a hot bath," he cleverly demanded.

"That will be fine. I will lie down until the water is ready," she insisted.

"Okay, follow me." He motions for her hand and guides her into the master bedroom.

Charlie was right. Melissa felt like a million bucks after she removed her body from the large garden tub of *hot* water. Her body seemed scald when she first entered the tub. She questioned in her mind whether or not she would be able to stand the pressure, but she convinced her mind to relax. Relaxing, trying to clear all the thoughts from her mind was a tough challenge, still, for a few minutes, she managed just that.

"Wasn't that great!" he said enthusiastically.

"Yes, as a matter of fact it was."

"Come, lie down now, and rest."

"My mind is so tired..." she said exhaustingly with Charlie interrupting her sentence.

"As it should be. You have been through a lot, mentally. I think you are a strong woman."

"Thank you, but, sometimes I don't know."

"No, you should not feel that way. With everything that has happened to you, you can count yourself blessed for being able to pull through. You are a strong woman and don't you let anyone tell you different," he demanded with a smile.

"You have been so good to me these past few months. Well, I guess our relationship started over sixteen years ago."

"As anyone should. You are a beautiful flower with delicate leaves amplified through a sensational garden which should be admired and appreciated with delicacies. I have loved you since a month after I met you. I have been fighting with a feeling of guilt or pain, or both. I cannot comprehend if my love for you is because of the guilt or the pain that I felt in my heart for your troubled heart. Maybe, over years, I have felt your pain and I suffered too. All I know is that I have loved you from the beginning. I haven't been able to keep a woman because I was constantly thinking of you. It became apparent to me that my prosperity and meaning would not reconcile until I was with you. I do not know that my infatuation for you lies in the bosom of your delicacy, but my heart contemplated your worries and my first duty was to keep you safe. I am not sure if my words are making any sense to you, but I want you to understand how I feel. At least, try to understand, so we may know together— 'cause sometimes, I'm confused." He smiles, anxiously awaiting a response.

"I do understand what you are trying to say. You are a

good man, Charlie. And I thought of you every waking hour that I could, because had it not been for you I may not have lived through that nightmare. I don't have the answer to the question you seek. I can tell you what I feel now...and I feel your love for me. I can see it in your eyes. I can hear it in your voice. I had not felt that before. The only person that I ever cherished in my life was my uncle, and he died when I was twelve." She reached across the bed where they were sitting up facing the master bath, and gently touched his face. "We will always have a connection, you and I. We will always share the same emotions—confused, tormented by a treacherous past, disoriented by guilt, and the love we feel today. We cannot help the way we feel, but we will work through it," she said, in a soft spoken reassuring voice.

He smiled, pleased by her response, leaned over and kissed her sweet lips. "You are a peach," he whispered.

"You *are* amazing," she responded.

He smiled and boyishly tapped the tip of her nose with his index finger. "I know I asked this question before, if you don't mind...why are you still with that piece of shit?"

She smiled and said, "It's a business contract, pure and simple."

"What exactly does that mean?" he said inquisitively.

"After he abruptly delivered his confession, I made a plan. It hit me, right in the middle of the agony and pain; it hit me like a freight train. I demanded that he help secure my future. Since my father was the culprit that insisted that I be married, at all cost, I thought he should have to pay for it. So, with my husband's efforts, I was able to get the capital I needed to start my company and a new life. Now that I have what I need, divorcing him seemed favorable; however, I still had to think of my children. My son,

Timothy, will be off to college soon and my daughter is a few steps behind him. I know that that may not be a good enough reason to stay with him, but it is for me. If I had not learned anything from my father, I learned that we must secure our family. Of course, he only cared about his family's name, and perhaps so did I, but in time, I will make the decisions necessary to end this tragedy."

"You are a very clever girl," he said with deep appreciation.

"It happens from time to time." They exchanged laughs and she continued, "My husband is killing himself. In the beginning, I felt a sorrow for him and a part of me wanted him to get help. Now, I concentrate on self-preservation. Even my children don't want me around, it's that funny?" she said with sadden eyes.

"No, it's not. Why do they feel like that?"

"I don't know. Timothy thinks I contribute to the self inflecting abuse his father does on a daily basis and my daughter, Kathleen, blames me for my own sufferings. She is hotheaded like I was—can't wait to leave the nest."

"So what will you do after your children are away at college?" he asked with curiosity.

"Not sure." She breathes in deeply, then releases. "I have contemplated on that very same question."

"Do you want me to get rid of him for you? Because I will."

"No, it would only complicate things even more," she said seriously, smiling finely.

"I will do whatever you want, you just say the word."

"Thank you. But I need to handle this on my own. I'll come to a peaceful conclusion, I know I will. It will be a matter of time before he kills himself, anyhow. I would not want you to be put in that position, and risk your conscious on a man that is not worthy of living anymore."

"He shouldn't have been graced with your presence all this time," he harshly stated.

"You are so sweet. You have a good heart and that is what I like about you." She reached her arm out to touch his face. He rested the left side of his face deep in the palm of her hand, shifting it slowly searching for comfort.

"I want to hold you tight and don't let go." He reached across the bed, as they carried for what seem like a monumental distance between them as they sat on the edge of the bed, and he hugged her tightly. "I know you are tired, so, let's lie down for a moment. Do you want anything to drink or eat?"

"Water would be great," she suggested.

"That's it? No food? I've got some homemade *Chicken Fettuccine* with savoring herbs and broccoli and creamy *Al dente* sauce. It's delicious, I made it myself. I must warn you…you will not be able to stop eating it," he insisted, sanctimoniously.

"Since you put it that way, I will try a little. Not too much though. I am not really hungry," she said.

"Eating is not to be indulged when you are hungry. You must eat for nourishment. You should never wait until you are hungry to eat. By that time, it is too late. You no longer get the same appreciation for food, plus, it's not good for your system," he explained.

"I didn't look at it that way. But still, just a little. I really need to rest," she insisted.

"Fine. Just a little and I will leave you alone so you can get some rest. I apologize for all the nagging, I feel like a woman sometimes," he said gesturing a smile.

ALINA

"Yes, we have our moments when nagging is a form of art—we can be very creative." They share a laugh and he heads for the kitchen to warm up the food. Their connections were miraculous. Melissa knew that this would not last forever, so she relinquished her mind of all uncertainties and exhaled. She would savor the flavor of this rendezvous, just as she demolished the delicious taste of Charlie's authentic homemade recipe. Despite the ill-fated beginning, their relationship had blossomed into a promising new love that only lasted for a moment in time.

~

Franticly awakening from a nightmare, Melissa's body jerked with intensity. She found her body embraced in Charlie's arms, safely positioned, and locked into purity. She released a long sigh and her sudden movements triggered Charlie to awake.

"Are you okay?" he asked with sleepy eyes, barely lifting from a deep sleep.

"Yes. I am fine now." She grabs hold of his arm tightly wrapped around her thin waistline and felt secure, just as he wanted her to feel. She was lost inside him, aimlessly, weakened by his delightful tantalizing touch. Surrendering to his instant affection and attention, she was mystified by his princely aroma of lavender body wash, while illuminating her mind with romantic thoughts. Before another word could be spoken, Melissa rolled over to face Charlie, and in an instance, their lips interlocked in a mad kiss. Her breath collapsed inside his mouth. She kissed him with full compassion and she did not want to leave that moment. She wrapped her right arm around his masculine body, caressing his muscles with her hands while moving toward his handsome face. With lips intertwined, she softly motioned her hand across his smooth skin, glancing through a tiny window of her long lashes to sneak a peek at his intense gestures; she was glorified. She slowly escaped the kiss, stared into his smiling eyes, and kissed him again. The rhythm of her breathing switched from an irregular deepened flow to a calm sensational relaxation. Her soul gradually melted in his arms. Her thoughts slipped into an unimaginable heaven of delight. The desire to capture of glimpse of his gestures had subsided and her emotions roamed freely. She closed her eyes and took in all of him, mentally and physically. She would only allow herself to feel. To feel his strong embrace, his muscles flexing with every stroke, his warm winded breath dancing across her skin, and his gentle touch that shocked her body.

Together, they shared a love that either of them had not known but so desperately tried to find. A love that they had longed for in the early years, but were unlucky to find. As Melissa pressed his body closer to her bosom, submissively, she answers *yes* to the question inadvertently displayed across his face. Without a word, their actions were understood. His eyes lit up with glee. With several passing minutes of foreplay, his face asked another question, "Are you sure?" Silently, with no words escaping her lips, she answered *yes*. She nodded her head in an upward motion, with shimmering eyes captured by the late moonlight, and pulled him closer. His glowing face and breathtaking smile leaned in forward to kiss her again. Before long, Charlie had successfully captured her approval, slipped inside her precious sacred zone, and began his gentle thrusts. His body moved up and down with the flow of his breath. The deeper inside her he got, the heavier his breath carried across the room. Melissa tightly closed her eyes, anticipating the pain, but it never came. She opened her eyes for a brief moment to see if he was real, he was. Her face smiled with enjoyment and enormous satisfaction. After several deep breaths, the rhythm of her body started to change. The more relaxed she felt, the more she moved. Soon, her body thrust forward, *as he lay on top of her*, to connect with his motions—surprise engulfed his face. He handsomely smiled and continued his slow steady countless cadence, exceedingly pleased by her efforts. His energy spilled over into her and unconsciously she wanted more. She softly uttered the words, "don't stop…please don't stop." Releasing a soft cry, she pleaded for the motion to never end.

Chapter

14

AT NINE fifty-five in the evening, most of the members were just starting to show up at the networking meeting. Even for a Saturday, the majority of the women worked long hours and had families to tuck in before exiting their homes for the night. The networking event normally lasted until three A.M. with some members choosing to stay for the night in the SQ Rooms, which could hold a capacity of twenty-five to thirty people comfortably.

The meeting room was eventually swallowed by rich women, middle-class women, high government officials, lawyers, doctors, nurses, million and billion dollar businesswomen who clawed their way to the top of a male dominant society. They roamed around the room mingling and filling the room with laughter and confidence. Self-pity never seized the room, not from these ladies. If lack of self-confidence was an attribute that any of these women possessed, tonight was not the night that it would be unveiled. Their hearts may have gleamed with grief from the trials they endured, but tonight no weakness would be implied seeping a hint of a dysfunctional disposition. Unconsciously, secrets would be exposed, but none that would hinder their impeccable perception of themselves and how everyone else saw them. Conversations of politics and sports channeled the room for the first few hours of the night and the subject on relationships followed to take center stage. Even so, the meeting was always a night to remember with some who have yet to miss a single meeting.

Appearing with a smile of appreciation, covered in a stylish navy blue *Cartier* skirt suit holding a favorite drink of choice—imported V.O. and coke—Evelyn examined the room. Establishing eye contact with most of the women in the room, she started her routine promenade to indemnify everyone was enjoying the ambiance and food. Occasionally, joining casual conversations, leaving an everlasting opinion and moving on to the next set of sophisticatedly splendid women discussing topics of what seem to be of similar interest.

"Are we going to have a speaker to give us pointers on how to deal with these sorry ass men or what?" one guest stated to the member who accompanied her.

"No, it doesn't work like that. See the lady standing on the other side of the room with the gorgeous blue suit…" Pointing toward Evelyn.

"Where?" The guest asked.

"Over there, next to the woman in the red suit. She is the president of this club and she is hosting this event. First, we mingle, and then we eat. She will speak later and some of the members will get up to briefly tell their stories. The entire night is more insightful than anything else. Of course, we do some male bashing." Both of the women start to laugh.

"I can't wait until that part."

238

"Well, no need to wait. See the lady across the room with the generously long beautiful hair, wearing a black top and the long fitted skirt..."

"Yes!"

"I guarantee she is talking about a man right now, just go join the conversation." The member smiled as she directed her hand toward Renée.

Obviously, Renée was the attraction for this meeting. Her loud mouth and opinion of men always attracted the attention of most of the guest at every event. Her aura attracted men and women to crowd her like smog. Many were cautious to approach her because her personality was unreadable, but speaking the language all too familiar to women, no-good men, was enough to work up the courage to any participate who wanted to join in on the discussion.

"I appreciate your perspective on searching within ourselves to see what we are doing wrong that would allow a man to do what he does, but, I got to say, some men are just assholes. We can't account for all their actions," one member, Wilett, a doctor from Ohio, who moved there two years ago but still attends the networking and anniversary meetings.

"I am not proposing that we blame ourselves for the actions of men. I agree they must take some responsibilities too. However, I believe that we create our own problems as well. We allow them to treat us like they do," Renée said with reassurance.

"See, that is the problem now. We are letting them off the hock again. A woman gets raped, immediately she's blamed for allowing herself to be in that position and scrutinized as a tramp. A man gets us pregnant, immediately we take the blame for that as well and assume all responsibilities during the pregnancy and after having the child. I agree that some liability lies on us, but do we have a choice. Our choices are not the same as men. They can go along for the ride or leave us high and dry. Why is all the sin placed in our laps and we are not left with a choice whether or not to stick and stay," another member jumped in, Alicia, an accountant from Berkley, Michigan.

"That's part of our responsibility, holding them accountable. You are right! We don't seem to have as many options as they do. Or do we? Does it have to be that way? One of our first steps should be to hold them accountable. Since more and more women are coming forward after being raped or molested, the law decided to take us more seriously. In the past, domestic violence was a joke, now there are tasks force put together to end the violence. These are small baby steps, but they are steps in the right direction," another member added, Katy, an Oakland County Police Officer.

"The programs are a good start, but you hear about more women dying at the hands of their lover more than ever before," Wilett noted.

With most of the ladies nodding their head in agreement, Renée added, "That is true. That's why we must do some soul searching. Our behavior attracts the same behavior. They say ignorance is doing the same thing over and over again expecting different results—well, if you attract womanizers and you don't search within yourself and discover a way to change, you will continue to attract them."

"So, because my ex-boyfriend took a cast iron skillet and hit me over the head so hard that it put me in a coma for three days, then that's my fault?" Alicia asked, seeking a lucid response.

"No, I am not saying that's your fault. My question to you

is…did you learn from that experience or have you put yourself in that position again?" Renée confidently responded.

"No I have not. I didn't think that my behavior was a result of his ignorance. He was simply a jealous man and my profession frightened him. He thought I was having an affair with my clients. It was absurd," Alicia added.

"But, what have you done differently since then? And, what did you do then that you thought you should have changed?" Renée asked.

"Now, I am not as trusting, which has left me alone. At times I feel very alone and want to seek the comfort of a man but I am too afraid to put my trust in any man again, at least for a while. This happened only a year ago," she added with much despair.

"Can you remember any behavior that you noticed before it got that far and what do you believe you should have changed?"

"Now that I look back, he was jealous from the start. I was working over sixty hours a week—really did not need or have time for a relationship—but I was lonely. What started out as a few dates here and there and something to fulfill my lonely nights, ended up in a two year mess that almost got me killed. I should have listened to my first thought, to have a one night stand and move on, but I didn't. What was supposed to be a seasonal relationship, I tried to make it a lifelong relationship," Alicia said with repeated sadness in her voice.

"Why are you turning it on her? She can't possibly blame herself for that idiot's action," Wilett said with anger.

"We are not stating that she is to blame. The signs are always there in the beginning but we choose to ignore them to satisfy our own wants and desires. We need to start listening to what the man is saying and not what we want to hear. We need to stop interpreting his horrific actions as something else or to fit our own purposes and observe his behavior around other women and his friends. These are all the things that will divulge him to us within the first few days, and with very clever slick men, within thirty days," Renée said firmly, and then added, "we stay in a relationship too long because we think the poor bastard will change or even worse, that we can change him."

"But some men are just assholes. You've got to admit that," Wilett added.

"I will be the first to agree. However, if we don't see the asshole coming a mile away we will end up being the one screwed, literally," Renée added with a vague smile.

"Whether they are assholes or not, we still need to be cautious and more fearful of our lives. Some women don't value their lives as much as they do his. I have a friend who married a man and years later discovered he was on the DL, sleeping with other men. She did not make this discovery until it was too late. She contracted genital herpes from him. I also see it every day were a man is beating the daylights out of a woman and she goes right back to him. I don't understand what the hold is, but whatever it is, it's strong," Katy shared.

"Some of us are not taught to love ourselves. Love is in all of us, but somewhere in the mist of things we forget the true meaning. If love does not live in our environment on a daily basis and we are not showed love in early childhood, it trickles down to create a self-destructive pattern, unintentionally. We accept all kinds of abuse from men for many different reasons. The first reason is that we were not taught to love ourselves first and foremost. We ponder whether or not to stay in certain relationships, providing all the necessity reasons, but not the lucid reasons. We want to stay for the children or he doesn't have anyone else and the list goes on," Evelyn stated, joining the ladies in the debate.

Silence crammed the back corner where the ladies stood conversing over the subject of men as Evelyn stated her opinion. Eyes glued to her lips and they motioned their head and body with every word that escaped from her mouth.

"How does a woman like that rescue herself from a relationship so tormenting?" Katy asked.

"She releases her emotions and walk away," Evelyn said with assurance.

"It's not just that simple?" Alicia said grudgingly in disbelief.

"I'm afraid it is that simple. The catch is that she has to be willing to do it. She has to say enough is enough. Just like the movie, *Enough* with Jennifer Lopez. When you begin to fight back, people listen, especially your opponent. Most abusers feel it in their soul that their wife or girlfriend is afraid of them. They treat you like a victim and helpless because that's what you show them. Most of them are not quick to stand up to anyone else except you, because you are predictable and they know how you will react and what you will say before you say it. They know they can count on you to defend them—defend their actions because you have shown what a faithful spouse you can be. They know they can depend on you to take them back after everyone has tried to intervene to separate the two of you," Evelyn answered.

"So, she will stay until she determines that she doesn't want that life anymore?" Katy confirmed.

"What about the woman that tries to leave and he still locate her and kills her?" Wilett asked.

ALINA

"Some men are persistent and insane. They cannot take *no* for an answer. I don't have the answers to all situations but some of the answers lay in the woman continuing to trust him. She has left the building but still continues to pay the rent, if you understand my meaning. She believes he will harm her or maybe kill her but she trust in his words one last time which overpowers her judgment, letting down her guard and ultimately resulting in her death," Evelyn responded while tapping Wilett on the shoulder to console her as she gradually sneaks away from the crowd.

"I believe men that cheat on you are putting your body at more risk than a man that abuses you. His need to fill a void can cost you your life with various diseases crawling around out there. In an abusive relationship, you will always have an option to change your mind, but when you contract a disease like AIDS; your options no longer exist," a woman from the crowd proclaimed.

"That is undeniably true. We stick around too long hoping and wishing that he would change. We condone his behavior and reward him with our continued support. We have this crazy notion that getting married or having a child by him would make him change, when in fact, it creates a heavier issue. If he cheats on you once, he will most likely do it again. And when he is done cheating and he is ready to move on, you will not have to hide behind the bushes to uncover the story, he'll tell you. When his empathy for you turns into a fight, a blasé attitude enters his personality, and he no longer denies his activity; he is ready to let *you go*. Our problem is that we hold on too long and for women so inquisitive and intelligent, we pretend to not have read the signs," Renée said.

"Pretend! We don't pretend, we know but we are willing to accept it. Some of us are afraid that we will be alone so we put up

244

with anything just to keep him around. We insist that we put so much time and effort into the relationship and refuse to give up without a fight, but the only person we are fighting is ourselves. His love has already moved on and our hearts need to learn to do the same. Why are we so confused and flabbergasted when he explains that he no longer wants to be with us?" Wilett asked, not particularly seeking a response.

The women motion their head in an agreeable fashion, each taking a hefty sip of their drinks watching Wilett make her statement, shake her head in disarray and takes a drag from a half light cigarette.

"Men in general seem to take center stage in today's society. Getting off the subject of abuse and moving to the business world, where they still dominate. Take for instance the Martha Stewart situation. Men have been conducting insider trading since the test of time and when a woman comes along and benefits from their so-called secrets, it becomes a problem," Lylie said, an attorney and active member of the MH Women's Club along with several other women organizations across the country.

"That's true. The problem arose when this ordinary woman develops a multi-billion dollar company off everyday household domestic items. Big shot businessmen are scratching their heads wondering how this one got past them. She didn't need their big business money and influence to make hers, her products and services sold without it. She became a threat to them, *plain and simple*. An ordinary woman masquerading as a business*man* was too much for them," a member's guest added.

"She was a threat. They thought they could rip her business from under her, that's why they put her in jail. They wanted to make an example out of her to show the businesswomen of the world what could happen to them if they dare to tread on their ground. I am not taking up for her or condoning what they *say* she did, but I am on the side of any woman that stands up to the masculine male dominating society heads," Lylie stated.

All the women laugh and toast their drinks to big businesswomen standing up to big businessmen with tiny business minds. If it were not for the millions of secretaries and the women that kept the books in line, most of the big businessmen would be small businessmen on the down slope to failure, thought Lylie, with everyone agreeing. With the conversation just getting warmed-up, Evelyn makes her way back to the front of the room.

"Miss. Evelyn! Evelyn, I want you to meet another friend of mine. She had some tough questions and I advised her that you may have the answers," Renée stated, flagging Evelyn from across the room.

"Where is she?" Evelyn asked, eyes searching over the crowd.

"She went to the restroom. I will introduce you to her when she returns. She is a little shy, well not shy but a little quiet."

"One doesn't have a choice when they are around you," she said with sarcasm.

"I see we have jokes. I am equally impressed with your sense of humor these days as you are with my wit." She gave Evelyn a bright smile and flagged down another member, racing off to include herself in another intriguing conversation.

Renée approached a small group of haves and have not's—a public official and a small town floral shop owner who seemed to be in a conversation way over her head. The look on the owner's face told the story. She watched them exchange words of a similar nature, but the florist lost without a fight. Registering their tones and a fleet touch of a partially cut off sentence created an opening for Renée. The florist tried to follow, even when the subject matter spilled into death, but she remained under antagonistic interrogation from the public official. Renée approaching at a perfect time of interruption, as the public official sited a quote from Moby Dick— "some dying men are the most tyrannical and certainly, since they will trouble us so little for evermore, the poor fellows ought to be indulged."

"Indulge, how?" Renée intervened.

"Well, he merely stated that we should allow them to rule since they are dying anyway," the public official said trying to justify the quote with little success in Renée's view.

"But why? Chances are he was a pain in the ass during his time of good health, why should we grant him or indulge him any farther?" Renée added, seeking an explanation.

"Well, it is a fact that men still continue to rule the world. Being a senator, I should know. It will not change. We should get what we can out of it and move on. Let them have their power. As long as we get a little out of it, then I don't understand why there should be a problem," she hesitantly responded.

"See, you are not really making any sense. Being a 'Senator,' you should understand the importance of women in power. Your influence could mean the difference between women getting dealt a fair hand or not. You can use your reputation and influence to make a difference and change the stereotype that men are the rulers of this earth. Yes, men have ruled since forever and the world is round and so what. Scientist, which some are women, are seeking ways to develop new substances, medicine, and discovering new worlds but we can't get our government, in one country, to develop a plan that will create better positions for women or at least gain more respect from men. I think that is a problem and women like you make it worse, with your male chauvinistic mindset believing that men are inferior to women. You quote from Moby Dick, a man of course, that we should indulge a dying man's need to stay in power, are you serious? Why should we care about his dying need?" Renée's hostile voice carried a few feet away, sparking the curiosity of another group of women. Soon, she had another crowd forming on the opposite side of the room from where her first discussion began earlier.

"That is why I take no prisoners. If he doesn't want to get with the program, then he is history. I rule my own kingdom," Ashley said, one of a member's guest.

"Dear...you are young and you have that luxury. Men will always rule, no matter what we do or say or put them through. They will get what they want in the end—they always have," the Senator said.

"Maybe in your world, but not in mine. I have always gotten my way with a man, because that is how I present myself. See, they can see your weak ass coming a mile away. Your presence is on the edge of invisibility which keeps you absent from his mind when another woman leaves an unconquerable impression on him that forces you to vanish from his mind completely. They will run over you before you can speak your first words...because you are predictable," Ashley said with aggression.

"I just don't believe you have to dog a man to get his attention. I absolutely do not consider myself weak, simply because I do not question the things that we know men to do. Men will be men and some things we cannot change. Men do not care about sex or money it is the power that drives them. Men have an itch that needs to be scratched and once that fulfillment has been fulfilled, they move on. If they can gain power by having sex with you, then that will be done, but do not misunderstand that it is the sex they are after it's whatever desire they are trying to fulfill at that time. And some would contend that sleeping with a man for money or things would be a form of prostitution," the Senator said.

"Why can't we change...?" Renée said.

Before Renée could finish, Ashley interrupted. "I do not dog men and I definitely do not sleep with them for money. I presume the world would be a big prostitution scandal because that is what prostitution is—everyone's trying to negotiate a deal in exchange for something. I don't try to change them. I let them know that I am not in the business of raising a man that should have been raised long ago; I have children of my own. Letting them go is not the same as dogging them. I don't waste my time with foolishness and I address that in the beginning. I don't walk over them and I damn sure do not let them walk over me. I don't try to change them I just let them know that they can't change me. And for the record, I take pride in myself and respect my body, that's one of my biggest assets," Ashley added with conviction.

"Someone once told me a joke...with today's society I'd rather be a prostitute, at least then I would know I was getting screwed from the start." Words drifted from a voice in the background. Laughter echoed the walls and was heard over the low volume sounds of Teddy Pendergrass, *Come Go With Me*.

"Are you married?" the Senator asked, directing the question to Ashley.

"No."

"Everything changes when you get married," the Senator proclaimed.

"Why does it have to?" Renée asked, and then she continued, "When I was married, I felt trapped. When I got divorced, I came alive. I realized that I was worth more than what he offered me. I did not prosper until after my divorce."

"Nothing changes when you get married; the issues were there before you got married. You knew he was cheating on you when you walked down that aisle and because you showed that you would accept this behavior, he would not change. Why should he? You knew he was a mad man before you said 'I Do', and yet you still turned a blind eye persuading yourself that he would change. If your husband got comfortable, it was because he knew you would allow that. And I don't have to be married to understand your story; you wear it on your sleeves. I can see right through you, just as he did," Ashley said with very little consideration.

"How can you talk about something that you have never experienced? What do you have to show for all your talk besides that rock and your fancy suit?" the Senator said.

"First of all, I normally don't respond to women who try to question my life because they hate their own, but since you put it out there, I will indulge you. I am very selective for starters. I don't jump into any relationship because I know what I want and what my needs are and I am not afraid to be alone. I have boundaries that I do not allow greedily sensations to adhere to nor overpower my standards. I have respect for myself and my body, along with my dignity and I will not let any man take that away, that's another one of my assets. My physical accomplishments and successes would be the love of my life, my two beautiful children. I have never worked a day in my life, except for volunteer work, yet, I own three properties including an apartment complex; I own two vehicles, a Benz truck and a Lincoln Navigator; and the home I reside in *(not included in the three properties)* is approximately fifty-eight hundred square feet storing over seventy thousand dollars worth of furniture inside. But all that is of no importance to you. I guess that makes me a High Priced Hoe," Ashley said calmly.

"You go girl," Renée said.

"That's what I am talking about. Everyone is out for something, why not get what you want in the process, hell, the government pimp us every day. I believe we are all priced hoes…not sure on *High* priced, but we are unquestionably for hire. I want to be just like you when I grow-up!" a voice in the background said. Everyone starts to laugh to relax the mood.

"Well, I guess you told me," the Senator said casually, bowing her head to Ashley, as they toast their drinks. "That is a stunning ring you have there. I meant to tell you that earlier."

"Thank you," Ashley politely conceded.

"Yeah, girl. That looks at least three carats," Renée added.

"It's about eight," Ashley confirmed.

"Wow. You must tell me how you do it. I am afraid I may be a little jealous," a member, Mrs. François said approaching the women to intervene in the conversation. She was dressed in a cream sleeveless *Azzaro* evening gown that gracefully swept the floor as she walked with a matching Shaw and a wallet size *Jimmy Choo* handbag with genuine diamonds across the closing snap. Her broad cheekbones and prominent jaw was noticed as everyone moved with her full pouty lips that faintly exposed the wrinkles on either corner of her mouth as she smiled. Her discreet elegance did not go unnoticed and her strong arrogance remained fearless. There was no exaggeration of her prominent lifestyle with very little implication of remorseful thinking. "My husband's a tight ass, but I am deeply spoiled so I demand particular items that will keep me at ease—for a while." All the women laughed as they concentrated on the large ring that accompanied Mrs. François's right hand that motioned while she spoke.

"From the looks of it, you have no reason to be jealous," Ashley said with a bright smile.

"On the contrary, you've made your argument of getting a man to do what you want, when you want it, but it has taken me a number of years to reach this status. My husband is a billionaire and still I live like you. My age doubles yours, and still we live the same. My dear, I must congratulate you on finding out at a very young age how powerful women really are. We have always held the power in the palm of our hands, but we did not have the knowledge or the courage to use it. I take my hat off to you." She raises her glass, revealing another splendid diamond of eleven carats worth over two point five million dollars. Her royal demeanor silenced the rest of the ladies as their energy spilled over into her. Her graceful appearance captivated their minds and refreshed their souls. They could not help but sigh as Mrs. François walked away.

"What I would kill to have a lifestyle and a figure like hers when I am her age," a background voice blurted.

"She really knows how to dress," another voice added.

As the conversations progressed, Evelyn took the stage and welcomed everyone to The MH Women's Club Networking Meeting of 2006. Everyone roared to a collective stop, eyes beset on Evelyn while searching their areas with blind hands for a seat. Her passionate voice was known to trigger motionless stares. Her calm swagger suggested that she had not been affected by the abrupt silence. She presented her stories, her encouraging words, and insisted everyone enjoy the food and be merry for the rest of the night.

~

Renée spotted Evelyn amongst the crowd and gradually fought through to introduce Evelyn to Veronica. Almost thirty minutes after Evelyn's speech—stories surfaced, the warmth of the room heated up in several small group debates with the subject of *men* still remaining the topic of choice. Renée reached Evelyn engaged in an intense conversation, gathered around a group of wealthy businesswomen—mature, all whom had been around the mountain a time or two. Their ages ranged from forty-nine to sixty-six, appearing as youthful as someone in there early thirties. The sophisticated Armani and Chanel suits presented the serious lifestyle of the women, but the relaxed facial expressions revealed the calm contentment they carried in their hearts. These women had lived challenging lives, but found a way back to themselves from a lost world of cruel and unusual punishment, through prayer and wisdom. Among the liberating women that stood before Evelyn was her newly found pupil, Melissa. Each of the women were discussing different issues with the woman beside them, while Evelyn's attention geared toward a muted *tête-à-tête* with Melissa at the time Renée tapped her on the shoulder to interrupt.

"Miss. Evelyn, excuse me for interrupting, I would like for you to meet my friend," Renée said with a big unsuspecting smile.

Evelyn holding a subtle smile during an enchanting conversation with Melissa soon dropped and incredulity filled her eyes when she faced Renée and Veronica. She slowly raised her hand and gently placed it across her chest nurturing a stunned reaction that the surrounding crowd of sophisticates seemed to notice. After ignoring the voice of Renée, asking "are you okay?"–Evelyn managed to respond in a whisper, "I am fine dear." Evelyn unknowingly reached out to shake Veronica's hand with piercing eyes glued to her face. She had prayed for this day to come but was not prepared for it on this night.

"Miss. Evelyn, are you okay?" Renée asked again with deep concern.

"Yes. Yes. Can we go to one of the SQ Rooms and talk for a moment?" Evelyn struggled with her words that appeared extremely difficult to muster.

"Do you need to speak with me or the both of us?" Renée asked pointing to herself and Veronica.

"Both of you," Evelyn calmly demanded, and then she added, "Excuse me for a moment ladies. I will return in a moment Melissa, I must speak to these ladies at once."

"That's fine. Please, do not rush on my account. I will be fine," Melissa said in an understanding voice.

Evelyn led the way to one of the SQ Rooms, advised Renée to shut the door behind her and directed the ladies to have a seat in the seating area.

"What is the matter, Evelyn? Is everything okay? Are you sure you need to speak to both of us?" Renée said with even more concern.

"I'm afraid I already know your friend," Evelyn said while cautiously running the palms of her hands slowly across her face. With perspiration forming on her forehead, her nervousness became obvious.

"What? I don't understand? What is going on here, Renée?" Veronica said with a subtle smile across her face, trying to hide her fear.

"Your name is Veronica Zellman," Evelyn wrestled to say.

254

"How did you know my name? Who are you, lady?" Veronica said looking at Renée in wonder.

"Yes. That's a good damn question. What's going on her Miss. Evelyn?" Renée insisted, trying to assure Veronica that she was just as confused.

"I have never been the one to beat around the bush...so...I will just come out with it and try to explain along the way. I am your sister. We share the same mother. I recognized you from the pictures I received from mother over the years. The last time I physically saw you, you were just a toddler running around with a saggy diaper." She managed an awkward smile but her tears poured like rain.

Veronica sat in silence for a moment. She thought the picture on Renée's fireplace was familiar but she would not believe in her heart that it could possibly be her sister Evelyn. She turned to glance at Renée and back at Evelyn. With her mouth slightly opened in disbelief, her sad water filled puppy dog eyes bounced from Evelyn to Renée and back again several times before she finally spoke. "Are you serious? What are you trying to do to me? Is this some sort of set-up or some sort of sick joke?" she said with widen eyes and grave concern, facing Renée.

"I had nothing to do with this, I promise. I don't understand myself. Please, Miss. Evelyn, tell her I could not have known about this, please." Renée pleads with Evelyn to confirm her words.

"Veronica, I did not know Renée knew you, let alone intended to bring you to this event. My heart dropped when I turned to see you standing in front of me. I prayed for this moment just some time ago but did not know it would come so soon. I could not have imagined it would take twenty-three years

255

for us to meet again. You don't know how many times I wanted to let my presence be known to you but mother thought it would be best if I stayed away," Evelyn contested.

"I don't understand. Why would you not want to see me? Why would mother say that?"

"It goes deeper than you can possibly imagine. Mother and I have a very, very long history together and that was one of the reasons for my departure," Evelyn responded, looking out the window with her arms neatly folded across one another. Her mind spun sequentially slower than before, short gulps of labored breath catching the nightly air from the partly opened window that faced a colossal yard flooded with mature trees and gorgeous blossomed assorted flowers.

"Enlighten me," Veronica demanded with anger.

"I understand that you may be upset, but..."

"Upset...upset...you can't begin to know how I feel. You could have helped us. You were too busy living in your fancy house with your fancy club and your fancy friends. How could you sit there and let a man pound on your mother and do nothing. He *killed* her. Can you get that around your swollen head and your fat rocks...he killed her!" The tears flowed uncontrollably down her flush cheek trembled face. She shoved her generously long hair to the back trying to gain control of her shaking hands. Within seconds of fighting with her emotions, she could control them no longer. Her speech moved more rapid and her voice rose to the high ceilings. She stood from the chair to move closer to Evelyn and continued, "How could you do that?" Pasting the floor back and forth as she continued, "Why didn't you come to help us?" she asked, wiping her tear filled cheeks, searching for an honest response.

"You are right. I could not possibly know how you feel. And back then, I did not want to know how you felt. I did not care how mother felt, I just wanted to get as far away from her as I possibly could. My understanding of your feelings was not a part of my immediate reality—just as you may not understand how I felt when mother killed my father." Evelyn malformed her body in the loveseat nearest to the window and rested her arms over her thighs with her head facing the floor. In the position she sat, her tears uncontrollably rolled off her face, soaking the plush light beige carpet.

"She did *what?* I can't believe that," Veronica muttered.

"It's true. One of the McKenzie secrets. When I was younger, I witness my mother stab my father to death. Sure, I knew he was beating on her, hell everyone did. I was a daddy's girl so I thought she provoked him. After the incident, I lost respect for her. As if she did not feel bad enough, I wanted her to feel worse so I rubbed it in her face each time the opportunity presented itself. It was not until I reached my late twenties—after I was already in self-destructive mode—that the story was explained to me by my grandmother on my father's side. My father's mother told me what I should have been told many years prior. My mother killed him in self defense. It was really an accident. She did not intend to use the knife. She was cutting some tomatoes when he started hitting her, so she raised her arm for protection, not realizing that the knife was still in her hand and it went through his throat. I entered the kitchen just as the knife went in and she pulled it out. I had never seen so much blood. Blood spilled out onto the walls and when he dropped to the floor it poured like spilt grease. I walked over to my father, kneeled down to cover the wound, feeling his convulsions travel through my body. Shock settled in my head for a year. The real trouble began when reality stopped me cold—realizing that I would not be able to see him again."

"So she had it in her all along. Why didn't she use that strength to stop *my* father from beating her? I am not like you. I hated him for everything that he did to my mom and when my stepfather killed her I blamed my father," Veronica infuriately added.

"It was not strength that she exhibited, it was merely an accident. She lived with that for the rest of her life. She did not believe she deserved to live after taking someone else's life. Nothing your father could have done, she felt, would be enough to avenge the life that she took. Furthermore, my torment did not allow an easy road to recovery for mother. I will have to live with that for the rest of *my* life. She tried to kill herself once, but the Lord was not ready for her. The only positive motivation that kept her going was you. She did not want me to interfere with the relationship that you had with her. She needed you to stay strong. Secretly, she was using your stepfather, or any man for that matter, to do what she failed to finish, killing herself. Until you have taken someone's life, you could not possibly understand what she was going through, not to mention, she loved him with everything she had. She loved my father more than she loved herself and when he died, he took her soul with him. Everything else was totally irrelevant, until you were born."

Chapter

15

EVELYN LONGED for her father's affection. His death was not true in her mind, even though, he had been gone for over a year. Months after his death, she would often go to the closet in search of an old T-shirt that he would often allow her to wear, to find it bare. He knew they were too small for him, but he would declare, "I want my shirt back when you are done, don't be tryin' to keep it." He would inaudibly laugh, and continue reading the Sports section of the *Detroit Newspaper*. It was one of their little games that Evelyn found herself thinking about on the ride home from her grandmother's house. She was twelve. During the past year, the shock of seeing so much blood had not worn off. The gaping hole from the knife lodged in his throat significantly blocking his airway, had not subsided from her memory. The shock that spilled across his face, blankly, had overwhelmed her heart. His body shivered from the sudden impact that stripped away his life. She could still hear his choked breath struggling for a word, watching his eyes roll in the back of his head. She stared intensely at her blood covered hands as she clutched hard, adding pressure on the wound to make it stop, but it never did. She looked up at her mother with despair, still holding the knife as the blood dripped from the tip of the knife to the floor. Her mother's mouth was widening, with the knife strangely positioned in her right hand and an absent gaze dominated her facial expression. What she had done had not been confirmed in her mind. The final jerk had moved stealthily through his body, neutralizing his sighs, and Evelyn refocused her attention on her father, as he painfully slips away. The nightmares came and went for more than a month, but the reality of her father's death was still not conceivable.

By the spring of 1967, Evelyn's world seemed as if it would crumble to the floor. Through her sad filled eyes, her heartache emerged. The forceful trauma was felt in the pit of her stomach, knots tied like a bow, as her legs weaken from the pain. Suddenly, she was hit with the realization that her daddy was no more. She would never see him again. No more wild nights of pillow fights. No more screaming and running around the house like a mad girl from the imitated monster. No more fighting lessons, showing her how to defend herself against attackers. She mentally visualized all the wonderful things her father had taught her and the activities they would do together. The playful secretive innuendos that would only be shared amongst them would be no more. Her drunken stumble into the *real* world, made her feel intoxicated. She seemed small, trapped inside an enormous world of promising hope, now irrelevant with the vacancy of her father. Her mind use to be filled with useful wonder, youthful anticipation, and thriving on connecting with the strangers she would come to meet, but now she sits only in sorrow. Evelyn extricated herself from the world, locking herself in her room for hours at a time, vowing to never converse with another again. Her childish curiosity had diminished while her mind beckoned for a purposeful meaning, trying to make some sense of it all. Imagining life without him was impossible. She was a daddy's girl and felt she would always be that way. But, sometimes, life is more complex than fiction.

~

"**My** mother became meaningless to me." Evelyn wrote in her journal. A journal she started writing a year and a half after her father's death, to occupy the time consumed in her bedroom with the door tightly fasted and a chair propped against it. The distinct pain she felt for her father was in little comparison to the hatred she felt for her mother. She launched her vengeful tactics on paper as they played in her head. She thought in many ways how to punish her mother for the pain that she caused her and for taking her father away from her. She did not know, at the time, that her mother's pain was more unbearable than hers. Evelyn, moving pointlessly for a year with no reality of her father's death, was not aware that her mother was undergoing psychiatric treatment for killing her father. Evelyn had not wondered where her mother was for over six months after her father's death—she didn't care. She did not understand the magnitude of her mother's pain in being responsible for taking the life of another, especially the life of a man she loved more than she loved herself. Her mother was never the same after that day.

Their arguments flared in the coming years. Five years had past, and Evelyn decided to leave the nest. She practically ran out the door, shoes in hand, and an ex-boyfriend waiting in a new Cadillac Deville.

"Goodness, I could not wait to get away from her. Where are you going? Who's that boy? You think you're grown! So many damn questions…she's pathetic," she said, firmly placing her body inside the car and beckoning for him to speed away.

"Yeah, parents are something," he said.

"I am so not coming back to this dump. I mean, look at this block…it's a dump." She erratically waved her hands, pointing at the passed houses.

"So, where do you want to go?" he said.

She looked at him with wondered eyes and said, "Anywhere, I just wanted to get out of there. I can't breathe around her." She had not given much thought to where she would go. She was seventeen, with little money, and no place that she would care to go. She thought about her aunt's house in Southwest Detroit, in a rough part of the city that no one should be permitted to live in, but decided against it.

"We can go to my house for a while. My brother is there taking care of some business, but I am sure we can chill in the basement," he said, glancing over at Evelyn. His eyes periodically drifted to the revealing cleavage that bulged from her blouse. Sweeping his eyes across her gorgeous legs and admiring her healthy figure. At seventeen, she was physically fit—subtle muscular arms, big shapely calves, voluptuous breasts, and a plumped butt. Men loved her bedroom eyes and her unforgettable stride.

"What kind of business?" hesitantly, she asked.

"Just a little business that doesn't concern me or you," he said.

"I hear that. I just said how my mom was asking too many questions and here I go. I guess it is in the jeans." She manages a smile and he smiled back.

"It's cool. As long as we are out of his way, he won't care," he added.

"Whatever. It doesn't matter to me," she said tenaciously. She had pondered on the lavish clothing that Myron wore and the fancy vehicle that he drove, which he indicated it belonged to his brother. She suspected that they sold drugs or something, but none of this concerned her at the time. His wistfulness was one of the major things that annoyed her about him, so, he moved from the boyfriend list to the acquaintance list. His controlling behavior was another reason. She had her suspicions about the strange manner in which he conducted himself, but past it off as a unique guy. Her suspicions were confirmed when she caught him outside the grocery store peaking through the windows. She had broken a date with him earlier that day because her mother insisted she pick up a few items at the store. He did not believe her, so he followed her. But, on occasions, she dealt with his unsavory behavior, strictly to get what she wanted. He was nineteen and one of the only *friend boys* that was not in school at that time of day—so she called him to pick her up, right away. Being on time was one of his great qualities. He did whatever Evelyn said, when she said it.

Evelyn bounced from house to house, from boyfriends to *friend boys*, for a couple of weeks. She had simply disappeared from her mother's radar. For a week, her mother called all her sisters and brothers, aunts and uncles, cousins and nieces; no one had seen or heard from Evelyn. By the end of the week, her strength weakened from the search. Her energy had not fully been restored from her sufferings and in a strange sort of way she was at ease with Evelyn being gone. She no longer had the death of her lover staring her in the face. Evelyn carried his mesmerizing eyes and his shiny smooth jet black hair that always stayed neatly in place. His aggressions were also forced upon Evelyn, and her mother was not particularly fond of it.

Eventually, Evelyn phoned home to relieve the pressure from her mother's heart. She told her she would stay at a friend's house and that she was okay.

"When are you coming home?" she asked Evelyn.

"I have made arrangements with my friend and I will stay here and split the bills with her," she said firmly.

"Oh. I see. So, you don't want to talk about this?" she said emotionally.

"Talk about what mother? There is nothing to talk about," Evelyn said, raising her voice. Then, she remembered her manners, and continued, "Look mom, I will be okay. Okay! It is time for me to stand on my own two feet. I got a job at the supermarket and I will make enough to pay my portion of the bills," she stated calmly.

"The supermarket? Honey that will not be enough to make the bills. You will need something more than a cashiering job," she said with much concern.

"I won't be a cashier. I am working in the office adjacent to the market. I will be handling Mr. Ashton's real estate paperwork," she said.

"Oh…and how did you get that job?" she said with sarcasm.

"There you go. As a matter of fact, his son asked me if I wanted a job. He said that he noticed how I am always adding up the groceries before the register does…he thinks I am smart. So, he asked if I would consider working for his father handling his property tax papers and I agreed, with a nice suggested salary of course."

"Well, I am proud of you."

"Yes. You know I am my daddy's child, and I have to see

the money first." They laughed and ended the conversation. *Click.*

It was perhaps a big break for Evelyn, being offered this position. Working with Mr. Ashton, she learned everything there was to know about Real Estate transactions and more. Mr. Ashton was a wealthy Real Estate Developer. She had not known it at the time, but he was the developer who designed the Nichols Plaza off West Six Mile Road, where she worked. With little significance to her at the time, she was made aware that he owned nine strip malls and over five hundred residential properties throughout the city of Detroit. Several apartment complexes and a dozen vacant lots would be added to his net worth a couple of years later. Evelyn's primary position consisted of handling all property tax papers received from the city of Detroit and generating a payment schedule to pay the bills. The diminutive things were the most important to Evelyn. Simply learning how to write a check was astonishing to her. The aberration of it all became heavily entrenched in her mind as the years past and she had come to the conclusion that she was where she needed to be. She had not felt comfortable around Mr. Ashton, being of Arab ethnicity. The locals knew him as a kind generous man, but Evelyn, in the beginning, did not know him at all. With increasing responsibilities, she soon came to know Mr. Ashton very well. Despite the profitability of his establishment, her compensation was not as lucrative as the duties she upheld. However, Evelyn counterbalanced her pay with the skills she learned from Mr. Ashton. It was because of his patience, guidance, knowledge, and reputation that made Evelyn the top Realtor in the state of Michigan ten years later, owning her own business, with consistent revenue of seven million plus, per year.

Evelyn's acuity on life had been altered by a wonderful,

simple man. She felt purposeful in life again and knew where she wanted to go and what she would do to get there, all because of Mr. Ashton. In the essence of finding her own salvation, she lost sight of something more important, humanity. She became self-absorbed. Her tender heart had leaked its purity, draining it from her body. She distinctly traveled down the forbidden road, with little acceptance of the consequences of her actions, snarling at those who tried to forewarn her. Assuming, vigorously as she did, that she had all the answers and her thorough understanding of life had taken its form several years before. It was not until the death of Mr. Ashton, that reality, once again, had hit home. Working with Mr. Ashton for seven years, they developed a close-net bond. Close enough to name her in his *Will*.

At his funeral, an enormous crowd mingled about to pay their respects, from the locals to the Governor. Mr. Ashton was a well-established man, kind and loving. His son, Shimed, who suffered from a drug condition, burst through the doors of the funeral home thirty minutes late. His old dirty torn clothing, red beady pierce eyes, and scummy hands with motor oil shoved in the creases of his nails; brought an uncharacteristic display to the attention of the attendees. Their hearts filled with grief for the son and for Mr. Ashton. Evelyn, on the other hand, was unsure as to how she should feel. She tried so diligently to focus her attention on herself that she had not thought of anyone else. She justified her feelings by rationalizing her unacceptable behavior toward others, encouraging her mind to believe that it was because of what she had lost. She tried to close out the world, which ironically led her to another world of dark and lonely nights. She had not realized that she used Mr. Ashton to monopolize her time so her nights would not be spent alone, with only her mind to keep her company. It was not until the next day after the funeral, that she realized she was alone again. She had shut her mother out of her immediate life, with a call every once in a while, just to let her know she was okay. She had not indulged herself with a boyfriend because having a man was not a part of her plan. She thought of Mr. Ashton, wondering at this moment, how he truly felt about her. Much too late to ask now, but as the thoughts scrambled through her head, she mulled over many questions that she should have asked. A momentary reflection of her life flashed before her eyes, as she struggled to regain her thoughts, finding it difficult to capture a relative moment of peace while her heart filled with disappointment. Evelyn found herself running again, but this time, it was from her own transgressions.

~

Evelyn inherited a gold mine, a rich source of wealth from her respected employer, Mr. Ashton. His wife had passed several years before and his only child was a heroin addict, who eventually went to prison for assault and battery. Mr. Ashton left his businesses, his investments, and all his money to Evelyn, which came as a shock to her. She would not have guessed in a million years that she would retrieve such wealth from a hundred and fifty dollar a week job. She was shockingly grateful. Nevertheless, all of the riches in the world could not instill the warmth and acceptance back into her heart. Deep within, she was grasping onto a world that had became a figment of her imagination. Her heart longed for the love a man, but her mind would overcome the fight. She would struggle with this abnormality for sixteen more years.

Each waking hour was eventful for Evelyn, with challenging scenarios that kept her on her feet. Being the owner of an establishment she knew so very little about and she discovered that it was much more difficult than it looked. Mr. Ashton had taught her everything there was to know about real estate, but so little about the grocery business. Now, she was the owner of a supermarket and things were falling thru the cracks. Her struggles were enhanced by the couple of men who came into her life for a season.

"Look, I can't run this damn place by myself. I need everyone to participant. Look, if we do not do our jobs properly, this business will go under and every last one of you will be out of a job. I don't need this mess. I can pack and leave any time I want to. I choose to stay because I believe in this store. Mr. Ashton would want us to put our best foot forward, and he would not have it any other way," Evelyn said, one morning in an employee's meeting.

Joe, the Meat Manager, raised his hand and added, "I'm willing to do what it takes, 'cause, I need my job. I can't afford to be out of a job. I have a wife and two children to support."

"Good! How about the rest of you? Do you care about this store? Moreover, do you care about your jobs?" she said with firmness.

"Yeah," a sheltered voice from the crowd of employees said.

"Yes, we do," another said.

"Then, let's make this happen. We need to work together to bring customers back into the store. How do you suppose we do this, Rahem?" Evelyn asked.

"We can have a big sale and put a sign out front that would say that we were under new management. Customers like to go to places that are under new management so they can see how different things are," Rahem suggested.

"Great idea let's do that!" Evelyn excitingly said.

Bill, the security guard who patrolled the strip mall interrupted, "Excuse me Ms. McKenzie, but there is a gentleman downstairs who wishes to speak with you at once."

"Did he say who he was?"

"Myron. He said."

"Myron?" She begged the question, with an astonished facial expression. "What the hell! How did he know?" she said to herself. "Whatever. Tell him that I am in a meeting and I will call him later."

"I suggested that he come back when the store opened and that you were in a meeting but he insisted that it was urgent."

"It is seven A.M. for goodness sake. What the hell is he doing here this damn early in the morning, anyway?" She had an alienated look upon her face, and continued, "very well, tell him I will be down in twenty minutes. If he cannot wait...too damn bad. Now, as we were saying before I was so rudely interrupted."

After the meeting, thirty minutes later, Evelyn strolled downstairs passively to confront Myron. "Why are you here so early and how did you know I was here?" she said angrily.

"Everyone knows you're here," he said calmly with a sarcastic smile.

"What do you mean by everyone?" she said more infuriated than before.

"Don't get your panties in a bunch. It made news, that's all. Look, Mister...whatever his name is, was a famous man, and everyone speculated that you and he had a thing together, I guess they were right." His smile carried the weight of his words of sarcasm.

"Oh, that's ridiculous. He was three times my age and what business was it to everyone anyway. He was like a father to me. You know...the one I never had or only had for a few years. You know the story. What's your problem anyway? I mean, why are you here this morning?" she questioned.

"I wanted to see you," he calmly stated.

"After seven years?" Surprised whisked across her face.

"Yeah."

"Where have you been? You look like death warmed over." She smiled, watching his movements. Myron did not appear as handsome as before. His subtle beauty was still seen in his eyes but they were more distant now. Unlike seven or eight years ago, his eyes were inviting and warm. His rugged appearance was something new to Evelyn. He had always been remarkably dressed and impressively tasteful with his choice of clothing. It was just before eight A.M., daylight, and he was dressed for a midnight run with an unsavory outcome. His muscles were more built than Evelyn remembered. His physical appearance was obvious to the naked eye, but his emotional dilemmas were yet to be seen.

"I've been in prison," he replied with ease, as the words smoothly slid from his tongue.

"Prison! Why?"

"For assault and battery...well, attempted murder was the charges," he said matter-of-factly.

"That still does not answer my question, why are you here," she said, exhausting her patience.

"Damn...I just came to see you."

"Well, you should have cleaned up first. Did you just get out this morning?" she said with little remorse and a hint of derision.

"What! Am I an embarrassment? Does my appearance not meet your standards for your high and mighty new friends?" he yelled, glancing over at the security guard, Bill, who did not leave Evelyn's presence.

"What are you talking about? It is strange that you show up here, looking the way you do, and expect for me to wrap my arms around you and embrace you with love when I haven't seen you in seven or so years. I mean, who does that. Normally, when someone visits someone this early in the day, it is of an important nature. I am simply baffled by this interruption."

"Interruption. So I am interrupting your establishment. I see," he glanced at Bill again, and continued, "Can we go somewhere private to talk?"

"To talk about what?"

"Us," he profoundly said.

"There is no *us*. We were a long time ago and *we* are no more. This was understood a long time ago, before you went to prison," she said firmly.

"So it's like that?" he said with a dynamistic smile.

"Yes," she said with no empathy. An insinuation of concern withered her mind, but she did not want Myron to notice. She had a feeling this was not going to be the last time she saw him. He was not giving up that easy.

Evelyn headed back into the store, business as usual. Days had past before she saw Myron again. He hung around the store, secretly searching for Evelyn to get a glimpse of her beauty. It was months after their morning meeting, before he said another word to her. He came to the store to purchase items of no interest to him, but nothing over ten dollars. He was moderately dressed, with a young vibe that attracted the youthful ladies at the register. They were surprised, of course, to here he was once involved with Evelyn.

"Damn, who wasn't she sleeping around with," one of the cashiers stated, watching Myron stroll out of the store.

"I know. That's how she got this store. And she wants us to work with her ass. She don't give a damn 'bout us, only about that mighty dollar." They high-fived each other and childishly laughed.

"I hear she's freaking rich, and we get paid this pathetic four dollars an hour. What a bitch. She's too stuck up to appreciate a good thing when she had it, hell, I need to get him," another cashier said.

"You should do that, girl." All the girls agreed. They laughed and continued ringing up the customers. Since the new *simple* remodeling, the store's business had doubled within two months and everything seemed to run more smoothly than before.

One morning, in late August, nine months after Evelyn and Myron's early morning meeting, he showed up again at the store just before it opened. The security guard, reluctant at first, beckoned for Evelyn to come to the door. A strong suspicion came over Bill, especially concerned with his attire on this warm muggy and ominous morning. It was seven fifteen in the morning, but the temperature had reached seventy-eight degrees, with a high of ninety-two. Myron was dressed in a dark thick sweat suit, covered in a long thin trench coat which seemed to be shelter from the rain that wasn't there. His sneakers were muddy from the long walk across the Red River Park off Lasher and Five Mile Road, four miles from the store where Evelyn worked. Each time he came to the store, his journey was the same. He traveled along Lasher Road until he reached a relatively small river stream, Red

River, picking up rocks and sticks tossing them into the river as he walked through the contiguous park. On this morning, in August, it had rained the night before and Myron was still dressed accordingly.

"Myron, why are you here this morning?" sighing tiredly.

"I wanted to see you," he calmly stated.

"Look, I thought we were clear on this several months ago, hell several years ago," she angrily noted.

"No. I want you and I don't understand why you don't feel the same way. Why do you insist on making this a difficult decision? It wasn't so difficult when we made love the other night."

"The other night! The other night! Are you nuts? I haven't seen you in months. I occasionally see you when you come into the store, pretending to be interested in the many selections of bread. But, we haven't been together since I was eighteen. Are you mad, or something? Look, you really need to get some help," she said with anger as she turned to walk back into the store, waving her hands to his following remarks.

Suddenly, he pulls a shotgun from his hip, pointing it at Evelyn. Bill, the security guard, yelled for Evelyn to take cover. Before she could grasp what Bill was saying a shot went off. A near miss of Evelyn's head as her body leaped to the floor. She was wedged between the outside world and the doorway of the store, with the automatic doors repeatedly crushing her side. Bill, standing outside next to the patrol car, rushed over to Myron and struggled to take the gun from his hand. Bill would not have normally persisted with such action but he had a fondness for Evelyn. Most men did. It was her charm and charisma that captivated the hearts of the men around her. Other women were in disbelief that a woman of her size could have men balling at her feet. She was not your average size four, but a size sixteen. Before her nineteenth birthday, she wore a size ten, and before she turned twenty-one, she had reached a voluptuous size sixteen with everything in the right places. Evelyn was a full figured woman, and liked every inch of her body, and so did every man she came to meet. It was like she was a movie star; men were mesmerized by her beauty and followed behind her as if she were queen.

As Bill and Myron struggled with the gun, Evelyn crawled into the store. Her body pressed tightly against the cold ceramic tile on the floor, and her breath was running short. She tried to hold her head up to see the commotion that trampled behind her, but she was too frightened and stunned by the forcefulness of the first shot. Then, she heard another shot. Her eyes flustered in her head and her fear weakened her motions. The commotion ended, but she was not aware of how it ended. She laid there, motionless and startled, hoping for the madness to end in peace. Soon, she was able to raise her head, looking back to see Myron standing on the outside of the door, trying to force his way in. There was a special way you had to open the door from the outside, but he didn't know it. Myron had not paid any attention to how Evelyn opened the door. His patience was running cold, so he grabbed the shotgun from the ground and reloaded. He pointed toward the doors and forced a shot. The glass was bullet proof but the shot gun was too much of a blast. The force from the blast pushed the glass in but it did not shatter. With the edge of the gun, he pound on the door until a hole emerged. Before he could successfully force his way in, the police arrived.

From the loud speaker, Myron heard, "Put the gun down. Put the gun down." He had not realized he was holding the gun until he heard those words. He looked in the store to see Evelyn's shaken body leaning against the display of Pepsi's hovered around the front entrance of the store. He slowly jerked his head while blinking his eyes rapidly, twitching from incredulity. A delicate calmness drifted in his body and he smiled. His lips moved, motioning the words, "I loved you. I loved you more than you'll know." He looked at the police that surrounded him, with silence piercing his ears. No sounds were heard. No police sirens penetrated through his mind. Through the smog, he saw a clarity not to be described, and a restrained smile flashed across his face. With the blink of an eye, he raised the gun and blew his brains out.

Evelyn watched in horror as Myron's brains splattered forcefully onto the immovable sliding doors. She quickly covered her eyes and turned her head as her stomach turned sickeningly from the explosion. She lay on the floor, motionless. Not a thought in her head.

The workers watched from the corner of the entrance in shock. The cashiers, who once found him irresistible, looked at Evelyn's lifeless body and glanced at one another in sadness. They could not understand why she had let this one go, but the events today were too clear to be ignored.

Evelyn's head bled from the fall to the ground, but her heart bled for Bill, who lost his life trying to save hers. She wept for many years after that event and had her share of true stalkers. A police officer, who would not go away for over a year; a millionaire who tried to buy his way to her heart, not knowing that she was wealthy herself; and a construction foreman with a wife and two daughters. None, who wanted to let go after the relationship had severed.

Evelyn felt like she was going out the world ass backwards.

She realized that she was missing something in her life—her family. She missed her mother and her sister's on her father's side. But, after visiting her sister's, she understood why her mother did not want her to make frequent trips to see them. Their lives were shattered by broken promises from their men and the confidence that was stripped from their minds. They lived a life of crime and mischief. Their primary activities included selling illegal narcotics—not successfully, but enough to keep food on the table and alcohol in their bloodstream. Their police records were several inches thick from numerous minor busts over the years. Evelyn came to know them but kept them at a distance.

After discovering that her mother was married again with another child, she felt compelled to get to know her younger sister, but her mother was against that.

~

"Why couldn't I have at least met you or knew you existed?" Veronica asked.

"I don't know. She made me promise not to interfere. I told her that I would not, on one condition, that she would keep me informed of your whereabouts and send me updated pictures regularly. I knew someday we would meet and I wanted to be prepared."

"After mom died, why didn't you come to find me? She's been dead for ten years now." Veronica glanced at Evelyn and quickly moved her eyes back to the floor, speaking in a sad slow tone.

"My first thought would be to fill your ears with irrational excuses, but my heart will only allow me to speak the truth—I don't know. I struggled with so much in my life that I forgot about

276

yours. When I put my life in the hands of God, I was able to find my way or I should say that He helped me find my way. I prayed that some day we would meet again and I released it from my mind. I could no longer dwell over past events, I had to find myself, get over it and live. It took me forty-four years to figure out how to live life and now I live with little worries. I still live with pain, but little regrets." She turned to Renée and said, "I have been meaning to inform you that Leah passed away. I was going to announce it during our departure prayer."

"My goodness, you must be devastated. I am sorry to hear that. How are you holding up?" Renée said with compassion.

"I am making it, what else can I do! But I will dearly miss her." Tears clouded her eyes but only a single tear gently dropped from her left eye and rolled down her flushed cheek.

"Who is Leah?" Veronica asked with scanty concern.

"Leah is Evelyn's best friend. She was fighting breast cancer and she was only thirty-six years old," Renée confirmed.

"She was a brave lady, much braver than I. Many things still frighten me and I have learned to accept the things that I cannot change, but what frightens me the most is that I may miss something that I could have changed. I felt it was more that I could have done for Leah but she insisted that I had done enough. Sometimes you wonder what enough is. When have we really exhausted all options or avenues? Just as with you and mother. I don't know. Unanswered questions that may not need an answer, I suppose. Women, we are often our own enemy. We will analyze something until we make it true when it was meant to be false." Evelyn takes a deep breath and leans back resting her right arm on the plush arm of the loveseat.

"So, where do we go from here?" Veronica asked Evelyn.

ALINA

"Where do you want to go from here?"

"I don't know. I will need to think about this. Give me some time to swallow this and clear my head."

"Fair enough. Maybe we can take it one step at a time. I would like it very much if we could have dinner soon," Evelyn suggested with caution.

"I'll see. I need some time to think. Some things I understand while others I struggle to comprehend, but still, I can not ach for your troubles—at least not know."

"Sure. I mean, we don't have to have dinner tomorrow, but I want to be sure the offer is on the table," Evelyn confirmed, trying to dismiss Veronica's last statement.

"That's fine." Veronica looks over at Renée and said, "Can you take me home now? I need some time alone."

"Yeah. Are you okay?" Renée asked disquietly.

"Yes, I will be fine. I think my body needs to rest." Both ladies smile and head for the door.

"Can I ask where are you staying now?" Evelyn hesitantly asked.

"Downtown Detroit."

"Downtown…at the Lofts?" Evelyn said with surprise.

"Yeah, the Lofts. Why, are you surprised?" Veronica said with sarcasm.

"Quite honestly…yeah," Brief laughter filled the room as Renée and Veronica exit the SQ Room and headed for home.

Chapter

16

THE EVENT slowed down at one thirty AM, much earlier than past networking meeting events. Melissa's eyes swept across the crowd to make connect with her friend Evelyn, but she was nowhere to be seen. Evelyn's moment turned into hours, so Melissa decided to locate her. She moved smoothly down the long hallways, trying to appear familiar with the building, until she came across an ajar door with a faint whisper of what sound like crying. She placed her fingertips on the door knob and slowly pushed the door in a few inches to capture a momentary look. She witnessed Evelyn sitting on the loveseat with head in hand and sniffles echoed into the air. Evelyn had not heard the door open, nor saw Melissa standing in full form as she entered the room and began swiftly walking before her.

"Are you okay?" Melissa said with grave concern.

Body jumped from surprise, Evelyn held her head up, wiped her face and smiled. "Yes, I am fine. I did not hear you enter. I am a little shaken up right now," she softly said, barely a whisper.

"I apologize; I did not mean to frighten you," she said with a quick smile.

"It is perfectly alright. Please have a seat for a while." Evelyn motioned for Melissa to sit down in the sofa adjacent to her.

"What happen to Renée and her friend? Are you sure you are okay?" Melissa asked again seeking reassurance.

Evelyn, still fighting back the tears said, "Yes. They are gone now. Do we still have guest in the Banquet Hall?"

"Yes, but only a few. I overheard some mentioning the SQ Rooms and how they had had too much to drink."

Evelyn smiled and said, "That was probably Marilynn and some of her associates and Katy will probably stay the night too. That's fine—we usually have several guest that stay until the morning." Evelyn stood up, slowly slid her hands across her clothing, held her head high and continued, "That's what the rooms are for, now I must get back to my guest and see them out the door."

"Can we talk about why I found you crying?"

"Yes we will, but first, I must tend to the guest. Although they may have had several drinks too many, trust me, they have definitely noticed that the host has been missing for a couple of hours." She smiled, exited the room and Melissa followed.

The guests were narrowed down to a handful. Evelyn insisted that the waiters take the remaining food with them. She sat at the bar, overseeing the cleaning process. As everyone departed, the warm inviting room had turned drafty and lonely. Silence clutched the air as Melissa sat on the barstool beside Evelyn sipping a lemon-lime Margarita. A waiter broke the silence and said, "Will that be all Ms. McKenzie?"

"Yes. Thank you Albert. We will worry about the rest in the morning."

"Shall I stay the night and hold you accountable for the explanation you promised?" Melissa said with a feeble smile.

"Yes, of course. Come, I will need to soak in a warm bath first. You may do the same if you so desire. I am sure it may only be seven to ten ladies that actually decided to stay the night so we should have plenty of room in the SQ Room on the north end, closest to the MH Meeting Room," she said hopping off the barstool as she removed her suit jacket.

~

"**N**ow that your body is relaxed and calm, would you like to explain to me why I found you crying?" Melissa asked.

"This has been an exhausting month for me but it will only get better, I am sure of it." Evelyn persisted and said, "I had the distinct pleasure of meeting my little sister for the first time in a long time."

"That young lady was your sister? How?" Melissa eagerly said.

"My mother's daughter. I had not seen her physically since she was three or four years old."

"But why?" She said in an unsure tone.

"My explanation to her was not enough I believe, so I hope that I may find comfort in explaining the story to you," Evelyn said as sadness packed the room, leaving her almost breathless.

Melissa, standing near the bathroom door, walked over to the bed where Evelyn lay and sat down on the edge. "Try me," she said benevolently.

"With the passing of time I must say that I had long

forgotten about my sister's existence. It was not until I visited Leah in the hospital that she came back in the light. Although I dismissed her from my mind, my heart would not allow the thought to go free. Many decisions I've been faced with in my lifetime, but nothing as great as the decision to plead for her to come back into my life. For a moment, I thought it was impossible for me to demand such a request—but, I knew that if I had asked of the Lord, he said it would be so. I realized that I had not had an exigent dilemma such as this since my body was smothered in the arms of two brothers.

My oldest daughter was conceived by one brother and the other brother, Mitch, relationship came several years later. After a few years, we mutually decided to end the relationship. In spite of everything, today I wonder if I made the right decision.

The decisions we make are not always the easiest and sometimes we can only hope that they are correct. But we'll never know because we chose a path of distinction on the contrary of being complacent, hoping to avoid the accumulated adversities of life. With the infinitesimal knowledge we know and understand about life—seldom—seemed too often to get it right. I struggled with the decision to end the relationship for a long while before Mitch ever knew. Nonetheless, my pathetic family remarkably influenced my decision yet again, but I hold no blame to them because it was my own voice that I eventually listened to.

Leah's existence helped me realize some of the things that I had been missing. Her love impacted my decisions but it also left a sense of emptiness inside. After leaving Leah at the hospital, I silently prayed that my presence be known to my sister. Forgetting her was not a cruel gesticulation, but a relief. Pretending that she was a dream allowed the rest of my past life's cruelty to be a dream too. Still, a growing void drifted into my heart and the memories would linger in mind forever.

It's amazing what we try to escape from, only to find ourselves deeper inside the frustration, lying in the depths of it with no room to breathe. Gasping for a joyful fulfillment that only comes in the evening when all the lights have simmered and no one can see the darkness that lay inside you. She was one sister that I held dear to my heart for many years, but after a while, the memories started to collide with each other making it impossible to distinguish one memory from the other. I had forgiven my mother for killing my father but so how I regretted it ever happened. For a while, I resented my sister for being born. I had other sisters on my father's side, but Veronica was something all together different.

After my foolish emotions subsided, I began to feel or I should say miss the sisterly connection that sisters have. I realized that my ignorance bound my ability to reach out to her and my mother too. It was not until my early thirties that I stopped running and decided to face the music. I contacted my mother again and asked to see her and my sister. She refused to let me see Veronica, fearful that the past would corrupt her, but I was able to see pictures of her. I know now that she had not shared our family secrets with Veronica and that was her reason for me to stay away. We debated for a long while with why's and why not's, but we soon came to an agreement.

After my mother's death, I was unsure how I should feel. I loved her deeply but my pain still lay in the way of my emotions. Mother died ten years ago and I still find it hard to speak of her. Over the years, guilt had sat inside me and stayed. My heart was full with guilt because I was part of her suffering. I encouraged her stupidity. I do not blame myself anymore for letting that man take her life. It took years to come to terms with the fact that I was not the blame for my mother's behavior. But it did not settle in my stomach until I was almost forty. I do not understand and may never, why I did not try to find my sister after mother died. I guess, finding her would mean that I would have to come to grips with the past."

A silence entered for a while and Melissa reached over to give Evelyn a tight hug. Evelyn, being utterly surprised by the hug, hugged her back. During an emotional steady hug shared by Evelyn and Melissa, they heard a muffled tone playing from a distance, seeming to have come from the seating area of the SQ Room.

"What was that noise?" Evelyn asked.

"I am not for certain," Melissa said with wandering eyes.

They listened more intimately and there it was again, stretching from a distance. Evelyn mastered the sound and determined it may be someone's cell phone. "Could that be one of our cell phones?" Evelyn asked, assured she knew the answer.

"It very well may be. We should go check."

"I believe the sound may be coming from your purse or jacket. Besides, my phone is on vibrate mode—this time," Evelyn said.

Melissa ran to the seating area. Given the late hour, she franticly thought it could only be disturbing news. By the time she reached the phone, the ring came to a stop. As she tried to view her missed calls, the ringing started again. At half past four A.M., she answered the phone to hear the melancholy voice of her mother on the other end, slowly chanting the words, *your father has passed.* Melissa's body remained steady and her eyes charged straight ahead, looking at nothing in particular. Then instantly her emotions lingered toward sadness but with repressed anger. Sadness was the only emotion she could muster for the man that controlled her life and everything in it; while anger bottled inside for the woman she called 'mother' who expressed that her breath was controlled by his. Though his deceitful tactics of dishonesty and betrayal led to her unforgettably miserable life for thirty plus years, she still loved him because he was her father. Visibly, her expressions were still, but her mind was racing rapidly with the images of a life so tormenting. She could only feel sadness for the death of a man, not of a father. Pretending to be more than sad, as you would for a colleague or friend, not as one dearest to you, would be an act of duplicity and that would make her as disgraceful as her father, she thought. Because of Evelyn, the blame is no longer shifted on her father's head and taking responsibility for her involvement has led her to the road of forgiveness.

Her mother had not partaken in the special arrangements made by her father, but forgiveness for her somehow seemed unusually hard for Melissa. Evelyn tried to explain to Melissa that her mother did the best she could, given the circumstances and participating in a life beyond her control was not a choice for her but a demand. In her heart she tried to forgive her mother for allowing her father to dominate her life, but it became harder for Melissa to excuse the insignificant role her mother played throughout her life. Disappointment was harder for her to forgive, but what she did not know was that it did not have to be. Trying to thrust forward, presumably hoping that time would allow her to gradually work on forgiving her mother, but time was running out.

"I am sorry dear. I am sorry," her mother repeatedly muttered words that were unexplainable.

"Why are you sorry mother?" Melissa asked with

ALINA

stupefaction.

"I am so…sorry." Her words were slightly slurred and trampled.

"Mother, are you alright? What's wrong?"

"I am sorry about your uncle."

"Uncle? What does he have to do with this?"

"I did not want to be the one that told you that your uncle was killed. The smoking gun usually has the fingerprints of the one closet to you," she said, essentially besieged to find her words.

Melissa's hands trembled, trying to organize in her head the words her mother devastatingly put together. "What are you trying to say, mother? What about uncle and what does he have to do with father?"

"Your father killed him, alright. Is that what you wanted to hear? He killed my brother." She broke down in tears. Melissa could hear her uncontrolled breath fading from her ear. She pressed the phone harder against her ear, struggling to capture the rest of the story. Her mother's words seemed to disappear in the night. She couldn't understand why this was of importance to tell her now. Melissa had her assumptions that her father was the root to all evil and that he possibly had something to do with her uncle's mysterious death, but she had moved passed that. But, just hearing the words from her mother's lips made it difficult to swallow. Assuming the truth and actually knowing the truth were two different feelings and Melissa wasn't sure how she was supposed to feel now.

"What are you saying, mother? I don't understand. Why would father want to kill my uncle? Why would he do that?" She wept for an explanation, but one was not forthcoming.

"I can't live without him. The difficulty of his painful exit is

286

too much for me to bear. I am sorry, dear. I am sorry." Her voice slowly drifts away from the phone again.

Melissa stepped on it. Spinning her wheels eighty miles an hour; trying to make it to the house to talk to her mother. Before she made it to the Contour Estate, she received another phone call, this time it was from Ramon.

"Ms. Melissa, you must be on you way," he said urgently. His thick accent made it difficult for Melissa to understand him, because her mind was flustered by mixed emotions.

"Yes, I am. Mother called me a moment ago, is everything alright?" she asked, dismissing a trivial moan, trying to calm her nerves.

"It's your mother...she has taken a lot of pills and I can't wake her, what shall I do?" he said franticly.

Melissa, rambling around in the car as if she needed to pick up something; with cell phone in one hand, her thigh guiding the steering wheel, and her right hand shuffling around her purse. She tried to prepare an answer, "Oh...she did what...oh my God. Please, Ramon, don't wait, call the police. I mean an ambulance," she said with confused fear.

"I am so sorry Ms. Melissa, but your father state that we must request permission to call any type of authorities," he thoroughly tried to explain.

"That's fine Ramon. It's okay. Hang up *now* and call an ambulance."

"Right away Ms. Melissa."

Melissa finally arrived at the Estate, thankfully in one piece. She drove erratically, racing to make it to her childhood home where she had not set foot in over ten years. The yard had not been maintained for several months, with her father being ill and all. Small fallen branches from the neighboring trees had taken their position along the front walkway brushed against the walls of the house. The double glass doors leading into the house were fogged with dust and debris and appeared to not have been cared for in over a year.

As Melissa approached the double doors, Ramon opened them to greet her with tears of crushing despondency. It had only taken Melissa five minutes or so to arrive at the Estate after her phone conversation with Ramon, but by then, it was too late. It had been a little over an hour and a half since Melissa spoke with her mother, and she felt that should not have been enough time for a devoured bottle of Vicodine and sleeping pills to take effect.

The autopsy—which was standard procedure when someone died in the home—disclosed that Melissa's mother had taken the pills at least an hour or so before she phoned Melissa. Large doses flowing through her bloodstream, suggesting that she had been taking the pills for a couple of days. An autopsy on her father made the determination that he had been dead for two days, still lying in the bed in an upright position, with two pillows propped underneath him. His cause of death was classified as *Natural Causes*. Melissa's mother was found in the dining hall, in a Queen Anne wingback chair, sitting by a roaring fire with a half empty bottle of Scotch by her side. On the floor next to the chair laid the empty bottle of sleeping pills that ultimately took her life. Her cause of death would be an overdose of prescription medication, chased down with a bottle of alcohol—a deadly combination, the coroner stated.

Regrettably, Melissa never got the chance to mend the relationship with her mother. Nor did her mind penetrate forgiveness, leaving emptiness inside pondering on arbitrary thoughts of a relationship that could have been. Arguably, silencing her forgiving heart was the most disappointment she would ever face alone and vowed to never feel this disillusionment again. Disjointed, boundless ignorance helped her discover that the love for her mother was stronger than she originally felt and her passing became intolerable to bear. Only emaciated fragments of memories circulates Melissa's mind with hopes of finding a peaceful memory of forgiveness to help ease her pretentious thoughts so that life may find her again.

~

The death of Melissa's parents made headlines, but with powerful influences, the reporters were only able to capture what Melissa wanted them to which was that both parents died of *Natural Causes*. Through learned behavior, Melissa knew to conceal the family's private affairs and leave speculation afloat. The reporters had made no scientific discovery, but stated the obvious; to include that Melissa was now one of the riches women in the world, inheriting the Contour Estate with all its amenities—totaling over fifty billion in assets.

Guilt had not set in, since Melissa forged the documents that changed her father's *Will*. She accidentally discovered that he *Willed* his entire estate to an underworld charity. They used the charity as a front for laundering money and to finance political campaigns—thriving on the support of the people with misleading promises. Melissa was not going to allow fifty billion dollars, plus a private retirement fund worth over two billion, go that easily. Everyone suspected that she would inherit the kingdom, but Melissa knew her father all too well. After careful planning, she manipulated the family's attorney into drawing up another *Will*, at her father's request of course. Melissa intercepted the papers that were on their way to the Contour Estate for her father's signature. She had the papers re-routed to her establishment and forged her father's signature, and with practice, it was a perfect match. She gained control over the Contour Estate and spread the wealth, accordingly. Melissa felt that after the love and devotion that Ramon and the other servants had shown her father throughout the years, it was only right for them to inherit part of the Estate as well.

With little contemplation, Melissa signed over the deed to her family's estate to Ramon and advised him to do as he pleased. Naturally, she suspected he would sell immediately which would increase his net worth to approximately eight and a half million dollars or so. Given the publicity, scrutiny, immaculate condition of the property, cosmetic work needed of course, and *the somehow attractiveness of death adding value to a home*—it very well my increase the homes value to over fifteen million. Melissa had not grown fawn of the place and her wealth had surpassed tangible paper, moving to collective feelings captured inside her soul. She enjoyed the day-to-day operations of her own business. Keeping her father's businesses would not be as rewarding and possibly too much for her to handle, so she sold it and donated most of the proceeds to all *Hemophilia Foundation* charities. The rest was set aside for a rainy day.

Chapter

17

"YOU HAVE been so open and honest with me, I must make a confession to you," Melissa said, looking Evelyn directly in her eyes.

Evelyn baffled by these words, could not contemplate what she would need to confess to. She faced Melissa with a grave look upon her face, and no response.

"I have not been totally honest with you. I've learned directness from you, so, I will be direct and come out and say what I need to say." She paused, and then continued, "I have been divorced from my husband for more than two years…"

Before she could continue, Evelyn interrupted, "Why would you lie about that?" Evelyn's mind began spinning in different uncontrolled directions. She blinked twice, shaking her head in disorientation. "But, I don't understand," she added in a crumbled voice.

"I needed a reason to meet with you. When I bumped into Renée at the Megan Building, I was on my way to see Lylie Frankly. I did not confess that to Renée at the time because it was not known to me, until much later, that the three of you knew each other. It was of urgency that I met with Attorney Frankly, concerning your case. As I walked to the restroom with Renée to clean the hot coffee from my suit and she mentioned your name, I thought it was an act of faith." A surprised look engulfed Evelyn's face. Melissa glanced at her, feeling like she betrayed her in some way, and continued. "Please, allow me to explain," she pleaded.

Melissa went on to explain, delicately, about a man she came to know six years ago. A man she looked up to, but in little agreeable terms she still considered him to be her father. Explanation could not explain the rare appeal that Mr. Contour had for his daughter, and perhaps, there weren't any. He was a pigheaded Irishman that catered to his own needs. He would go to great lengths to protect his reputation, including murder. The information she uncovered about her father was more than troubling, it was psychotic. His criminally insane psychological behavior undoubtedly was too in-depth for Melissa. Her mind could not come to grips that her father was a notorious man who bludgeoned a man to death with the butt of a pistol because he threatened to expose his deception to the world. Her father's underworld activities had remained far below the police's radar, which made him powerful. His influential decisions were as powerful as the Irish American Gangsters of the late twenties. Complicated stories of mayhem splattered across the newspapers about the brutal massacres that compellingly resembled the St. Valentine's Day hit in 1929. But, it was his hatred he proclaimed for the whites, blacks, and any other man that was not Irish that infuriated Melissa. However, his business forced him to consult with the very people he claim to hate.

Her father's underworld secrets surfaced, when she found

bloody clothing in a trashcan in the basement next to her husband's collapsed body. He had stumbled in from one of his drunken spells, buckled on the floor next to the trashcan. Melissa thought that was a sight for sore eyes—trash, taking out the trash. She slowly removed the clothing from the trashcan. She inspected it with mixed emotions, not knowing what she would find or what she needed to see. In the pocket of the left pants leg was an address off Joy Road, on Detroit's West Side. Strong curiosity got the best of Melissa, so she drove to the address to find out who lived there. She had not prepared herself for what she would see. She didn't know how.

As she approached the residence, around two-thirty in the morning, her eyes were blinded by the rapid motion of the police lights. Their sirens had silenced, as if they had been there for a while. She pulled her Bentley over to the side of the road, blocking the driveway of a neighboring house. Spectators surrounded the scene, gawking, searching for any information that would make for an interesting morning discussion. Some noticed Melissa, pointing, as if she should not have been there. Profoundly drawn to the situation, Melissa had not noticed their stares of curiosity. A number of minutes had past as the intensity grew amongst the crowd and Melissa, as they waited edgily for the unknown. Ripples of fear tore through her body like a sharp blade. Anticipating the unimaginable could not be foreseen in her eyes. So, she sat in the warmth of her vehicle, on this chilly night, and waited for something to happen. She became one of those spectators, gawking, searching for any clarifying information. Why did her husband have those bloody clothes? What were Steven and her father up to? Erratically, the questions flooded her mind with full force. In the final moment of her cycle of endless questions, a body was carried from the small house. She looked in dismay, and a minute later, a figure, what appeared to be a woman, was escorted to a police vehicle and placed in the back seat. She picked up the bloody piece of paper to verify the address again. She could not see the address from where she sat, but the surrounding homes were in-line with the address scribbled on the tiny piece of paper. A troubling expression flashed across her face. Her snooping had only led her to more questions, and she needed answers. She worked up the courage to get out of the car and flagged down an individual who would be willing to talk to her. She had to think quickly, so, she stated that she was looking for a friend and the friend's sister told her that she would find her here. Eyes reluctantly looked at her with curiosity, then, one woman said, "What is your friend's name?"

"Her name is Cassie," Melissa softly whispered.

"I don't believe we know no Cassie around here. Lady, are you sho' you in the right neighborhood?" one of the men stated, glancing over at her Bentley.

"Yes. Well, she told me she would be on this street. 4 - 2 - 9, was the address," she stated, cautiously looking around, hoping someone believed her.

"Well, I guess you picked the wrong night to go looking for your friend. 'Cause the woman in there is Evelyn McKenzie, the famous real estate queen," one of the lady's replied.

"Evelyn McKenzie?" Melissa asked.

"Yeah...you don't know Evelyn McKenzie. I thought all you white folks knew her," another lady barked.

"I have heard of her, I am just shocked that she could be in there," Melissa struggled to say, when in fact, she had not heard of Evelyn before this day.

"Yeah. I don't think all the money in the world could get her out of this mess. Then again, you rich folks have a way of surprising us po' folks all the time." The others laugh and Melissa smiles to keep with the moment.

"Well, thank you. I guess I need to call my friend's sister to be sure I have the correct address," Melissa said, walking back to her car, holding her breath.

"What a strange lady," one of the bystanders suggested.

Melissa quickly flopped down in the soft plush leather seats of her vehicle and sighed in relief. She slowly pulled off and headed for home.

The more complex the story got, the more nervous Melissa became. She tussled briskly to find the words to say to Evelyn. How could she explain that her father was a man of many evils and he was the cause of her temporary incarceration? How do you explain to a genuinely splendid woman that has skirmished to find redemption within her, that she was framed by a man more powerful than she could fathom? Melissa culminated her struggles and embraced the words that spoke from her heart.

"I needed a reason to see you, so I could apologize for the wrongdoing my father caused you. I know that my sympathetic nature could not compare to the hardship that you endured, but I was not going to rest until I successfully completed this mission. My father was a cruel man, and my interpretation of him was obstructed by promising hope that filled my heart daily. I knew he was an evil man, but I turned the other cheek when I got a whiff of his tormenting scent. It was not until I saw your loving face splashed across the *Channel Eight News* that my heart mourned for your redemption as I vowed to remove your mind from that dilapidated state. I sent the package to the courthouse, revealing the findings of an independent investigation. I hired one of the best private Criminal Investigators in the country to uncover this evidence for me. I knew my disgraceful husband had something to do with the murder of Clarence Noltie, but I could not prove it. My father may not have been the man that withered the life out of Clarence, but he was certainly the man that ordered it to be done. This treacherous story falls deeper than I care to recollect, but my father, whose punishment should have been swifter, was the man behind it all. It was discovered that Clarence tried to pull off the biggest heist of his career. He distinguishably slivered his way into my father's domain, and secretly tried to manipulate my father into paying him nearly two million dollars. The exact details of the blackmail or deception remained unclear, but whatever it was, it cost him his life.

The investigator also uncovered the fraudulent manner in which the reports were disbursed to your attorney and the prosecutors. It seemed that someone switched the cause of death and swopped the records that identified the bodies. With a handsome suggestive figure of two hundred thousand dollars, I persuaded a nurse to confess what she knew. Although she was unyielding about testifying, she was able to direct me to the places I needed to look in order to find the evidence we needed that would ultimately set you free. She had been forced to keep quiet by the attending physician who worked for my father, performing this same operation on numerous occasions. The nurse was at her wits end, seeing this corruption up close and personal, so she quietly left town. We caught up with her in a small town in Arizona. It took some time to convince her that we were not thugs coming to end her life, but friends that were trying to save another life. She stated how she watched the trial on *CNN* in horror, wishing she could do more for you. But her fears stopped her at the door. Months later, after your release, I got an anonymous letter in the mail at my office, postmarked from Oklahoma. It stated…

"I want to thank you for what you've done. I wish I demonstrated courage such as yours, but I don't. For many years, I watched crooked politicians and criminals get away with bloody murder, and I did nothing. Evelyn is glad to have friends like you and from what I saw on the news, she was worth the effort. I hope her life is blessed with more happiness than mine and for years to come. Although you brought me no harm, I still watch over my shoulder in fear. I am not working now, but fearing for my life seems to be a full time job."

Sincerely,

The Nurse

A few months later, I had the private investigator locate her again, where she had moved to California. I had him give her one point five million dollars for her bravery and told her to stop living in fear because I knew who killed Clarence and she need not worry about that man ever again. I am not sure if it relieved a small portion of her troubles, but I suspect it lifted her spirits just a little higher." Melissa managed a quaint smile and turned to Evelyn whose face was sheltered by the palm of her left hand.

"Just when you think you have heard and seen it all, another lightning bolt strikes you down," she whispered.

"I am truly sorry for lying to you about my husband. Everything I told you about him was the truth, unfortunately. But, my divorce to him was finalized in 2003 with the help of a dear friend, Charlie.

"Charlie? Who is Charlie?" Evelyn inquisitively asked.

"He was my hero. The man that saved me from the

despicable rapists', including my husband, and hauled me to safety. I met him personally when I was researching material for my dissertation. It turned out, he was the brother of one of my classmates," she said with a widened smile.

"Really! Your smile is much too bright; did you have an affair with this man?" Evelyn softly asked. Her saddened muscles had disengaged releasing a much needed smile.

"Yes I did. I had been a virgin all my life until I met Charlie. He showed me what it was like to be a woman. He respected my body and my mind," Melissa said.

Suddenly, Evelyn's shocked expression turned into curiosity. Talking about Charlie was her way of not facing the horror Melissa sprung on her without warning. But what type of warning would she give? This was a story that Evelyn could not swallow, so she forced herself to ask questions about Charlie until she could discover some answers.

"So…what happened? Are you two together or what?"

"No. We thought it would be best if we went our separate ways," she said softly.

"Whose idea was that? His or yours?" Evelyn reluctantly stated. Assuming it was his idea, her lips curled in disappointment.

"It was my idea. I could feel that his love for me was strong and undeniable, but my mind would not allow me to forget the first time we met. After I divorced my sorry-ass husband, I vowed to find salvation within myself, not in the arms of another man. My older appearance has discreetly sneaked into my reflection, and although, my beauty doesn't fall far from splendid, I still see the unhappiness I share to the world through my eyes. His comforting pleasure lasted for that moment and I awakened to find myself wanting something more. Traces of my past stood before me, and for the first time in my life, I did not feel compelled to stay. It was that moment that I felt rejuvenated. Then, I met you and everything became atrociously clear." Melissa looked over at Evelyn, who was leaning against the headboard of the queen size bed, and added, "Had I not met you, I would not have found me."

"You went through all this trouble just to find me?" Evelyn said with skepticism.

"Yes, I did. I knew I had to set the record straight. I had secretly harbored a criminal, two criminals, in my life and I could not let them get away with it. Charlie offered to kill Steven, but I advised him that that would not be necessary. I had other plans for Steven. I worked out a sweet deal with him that he could not refuse. I gave him the house in exchange for my freedom. Of course, he waved his hand dismissing my offer until I placed a pad of conspiracy evidence on the table forcing his acceptance. Charlie insisted on coming with me to make sure everything went according to plan. I did not suspect that I would have any problems out of Steven though. He was a drug addict and a low life so any mention of him going to jail or being killed was enough to terrify him. It did not take long for him to agree to the terms.

I knew that he would sell the house as quickly as possible, even if it meant for pennies on the dollar. Our home was worth over a million dollars, but with the tight market, two weeks was much too long for him to wait, so he accepted a worthless offer of four hundred seventy-five thousand dollars. That was his second deal he made with the devil. A blind corporation bought the property for nine hundred eighty-five thousand dollars from a Realtor in Grosse Pointe Woods. The Realtor convinced Steven to give him a kickback for repairs, points, insurance, and closing cost in the amount of five hundred ten thousand dollars. He did not want the transaction to diminish the value of the home by stating a selling price of four hundred seventy-five thousand dollars. That blind corporation was one of my partners. My heart had not grown fond of the home, so I told them were they could get a steal from a desperate, pathetic, drug addict who would sell his mother if the price was right.

Several months later, I found out that he quickly went through his money, as I suspected he would. Although I must say, he lasted longer than I calculated. He was arrested a few weeks after, during a liquor store holdup. Isn't it ironic how the door swings both ways?" A subtle smile formulated across her face.

"Yes. Indeed it is," Evelyn said, releasing a delicate exhale, noisily. "I still cannot get over the fact that you went to all that trouble for me," she added.

"I could not let you go to prison for a crime that you did not commit. My heart would have been flooded with guilt and I would not have been able to live with myself if you had been convicted," she said convincingly.

"I see the Lord was looking out for me, yet again. He brought you to me in my time of need and now, he has brought me to you in your hour of need. He definitely works in mysterious ways." Both the ladies hail with laughter, practically falling from the bed as they embraced one another to prevent the fall.

"Yes he does. Regrettably, he took his time with my father. My father became deathly ill in 1998, and I suppose that was where he met his conqueror. The doctors had no diagnosis for his condition, but I knew the answer; he was suffering from all his transgressions. He had been made to suffer for his indomitable implications in many high profile cases, where the police had not considered him as suspect. Paradoxically his unmerciful killings would not go unpunished. He had a higher power to answer to, and he was coming to collect. I forgave my father many years ago for selling me to Steven, but I could no longer sit back and watch him ruin another person's life."

"Your father was a calculated coldhearted snake. I will find it easy to forgive him because I had already forgiven myself of all my indiscretions. Surprisingly, I hold no ill feelings toward your father, only pity. I cannot take away his powerful strength because the good Lord beat me to it. Your father is gone now and there is no use resurrecting his spirit. So, I will let it go in order to keep the peace within me," Evelyn fervently stated.

Melissa quickly clinched her with a hug and whispers, "Can you ever forgive me?" A muffled whimper penetrated through Evelyn's head, as Melissa's lips smothered the side of her neck.

"Forgive you for what?" Evelyn asked.

"Forgive me for what my father did to you." Tears fiercely moved down her cheeks, rolling onto Evelyn's chest. "And forgive me for lying to you about my husband."

"Oh dear, please. There is nothing to forgive. The only person that I needed to forgive was me. It's okay, Melissa. I am grateful to you. It is because of you that I am a free woman. Had it not been for your courage and persistence, I would be miserably decomposing away in some jail cell examining my case for yet another appeal. There is nothing to forgive; I appreciate, with every beat of my heart, the things that you've done for me."

Evelyn, staring blankly onto the wall straight ahead, exhaled, and comfortably held Melissa in her arms releasing all regrettable gestures and with agreement Melissa hugged her back.

Chapter

18

Back to The Present

"I AM glad that you will be alright," Evelyn said as she walked into the hospital room.

"Yes, I will be fine," Melissa confirmed with a smile.

"I guess you are my guarding angel!"

"Not really. Everything was happening so fast and before I knew it, I was bleeding. I still wonder why that lady brought a gun to the meeting. I guess it saved both of our lives." Melissa looks away from Evelyn for a moment and glanced at the array of light shining through the window bouncing off the foot of the bed and added, "I am deeply sorry about your sister though."

Evelyn's eyes filled with sadness, but she remained silent.

Expecting the emotion, Melissa paused for a moment with hesitation, and then she continued, "I am truly sorry and I want you to know that it wasn't your fault."

"I am not so sure about that Melissa," Evelyn said in total disagreement.

"You can not take the blame for everything that happens in your life."

"But, this one falls right in my lap. Veronica was right, I

could have done more." I know in my mind that you are right, but my heart will not accept that reasoning." Evelyn bows her head to the floor, looked up and continued, "I will somehow have to get past this. This may be the toughest adversity yet."

"In some way, I can relate to your feelings. I was overwhelmed with different emotions when I learned that my father sold me to the monster that shattered my life. I was not able to move past that until I met you."

Before Evelyn could respond, the door opened and in walks Renée.

Astonished was not an absent manifestation symbolically displacing the faces of Evelyn and Melissa. They were first disconcerted when Renée came into view but their susceptible hearts allowed her in the room and a look of unpredictability took over.

"Evelyn, I am so sorry. I didn't know. Please believe that I didn't know. I would never do anything to hurt you nor Melissa," Renée pleaded for them to believe her.

"It's okay Renée. Veronica had a lot of built-up anger inside of her and she had to get it out some way," Evelyn stated while taking a deep breath and releasing it in spurts.

"Melissa, are you going to be okay? You look okay!" Renée asked with much concern.

"Yes, I will be fine."

"This is all my fault ladies. I should not have brought her to the meeting. I can't believe I did not see this coming. Then again, I am not one to see too much of anything coming," Renée added with sadden words and sobbing eyes.

"Oh, don't blame yourself Renée," Melissa replied

"Well, you brought me Melissa so you shouldn't feel too

bad," Evelyn added with a smile.

Renée appearing puzzled and said, "What do you mean?"

"Let's just say that Melissa and I go way back." Evelyn kindly smiled and continued, "In the beginning, there was something special about this woman. I was drawn to her instantly. We never thought that our lives would be what they had become. It was faith that brought Melissa to me and it was *the strength of a woman* that kept her alive. We figured with all that we had been through, it was time for us to finally be truly happy and determining that happiness is not always found in the arms of a man or with sex, but through the heart of a friend. Our union together flows deeper than you could possibly imagine. We have been interlocked inside one another for several years now and it was evitable that we would share the rest of our lives together. Just as one life had been taken from me, God has brought me another sister. Our love extends beyond the ordinary friendship, but it is illuminated and enhanced through our remarkable journeys. With a strong appreciation of our indifference toward men and weighing qualities that the men in our lives were unable to fulfill, we embarked on a union beyond comparability. Which leaves us pondering the question…Was it ever really about the *man*? No…I don't believe it was. The strength we needed was always inside of us."

Renée softly scanned the face of Evelyn and Melissa, feeling to have missed something, yet again and said, "I have so much to learn, *starting with you two!*"

The women laughed and embraced themselves in a group hug.

Turn the Page for an Excerpt from

mrs. deveraux

A chilling novel available soon
By Alina

Intro to mrs. deveraux

The mysterious methodical and brutal slaying of five prominent Real Estate Developers left their prestigious communities and law enforcement baffled beyond belief. The killer evaded police so swiftly that they considered he may be among one of their own. With community leaders, the media, the Mayor of Bloomfield Hills, the governor and the FBI crawling down the backs of local authorities, it was imperative that they solved these cases and fast.

Just when the police thought they had a viable suspect, Mitch Cooper, he turned up dead too. The killer seemed two steps ahead of law enforcement until a Forensic Psychologist noticed a similarity in one of the signature clues from a murder that occurred six years earlier. Local authorities finally thought they were on to something. After tracking down the lead, they soon realized that the suspect in the murder six years prior was one of the first developers found dead in his home—with a single gunshot wound to the head and his body dismembered.

Who, within this prominent community was a killer? Who would have the motive and accessibility to murder these powerful people and get away with it? Plastered on the TV screen, was the gorgeous face of a prominent Real Estate Developer, Judith Ann Deveraux, who had announced that she too feared for her life. But there was something questionable about Mrs. Deveraux that captured the attention of the police. Was Mrs. Deveraux fearing for her life or should the community be fearful of her?

Intro to mrs. deverauX *cont...*

As the focus of the investigation took a stunning turn, Mrs. Deveraux found herself scrambling for the truth. Authorities now believed that her husband was somehow involved with the murders and that she aided him in one of the biggest twisted cover-ups in Michigan's history. Mrs. Deveraux hired a private investigator to get to the bottom of these allegations and what he uncovered would shock the community, hinder the investigation and lead the police on a wild goose chase. Authorities were now on a mad hunt for the truth and a race against the clock to find a meticulous killer...before other victims were discovered.

An Excerpt from mrs. deveraux

It happened way before the movie started. It happened before the Coopers had burned the midnight oil. It happened just before the celebration began. It was around five p.m. when the first blow hit. Mitch could not have seen it coming but Carol was too stunned to move. You could see the dusty yellowish glow from the rising sun beam through the Cooper's master bedroom window, squinting at Carol's white purplish and pale cheeks as she lay diagonally across the master bed. Her eyes were slightly opened and had stiffened with the passing hours. Decomposition had settled. Her lips were dark blue and purple. They were cracked from dehydration and no air circulation. She was shot at point-blank range.

They found their bodies in the master bedroom. Carol was on the master bed and Mitch's body was scattered across the floor. Mitch's legs had been severed and placed on the floor at the foot of the bed next to his arms which had been cut off first. The killer had started cutting the body into multiple pieces but had not finished for some apparent reason. The homicide detectives had concluded this because the killer had not neatly lined the body parts up as he had done before. Perhaps the killer was disturbed by someone or something. Startled by a voice or a muttered sound of some sort. It's hard to tell, but it stopped the killer in his tracks.

Mitch was ambushed by the assailant and forced to concede as a Nine Millimeter Beretta penetrated his temple. Within seconds, the killer forced Mitch inside the house as he came from his afternoon jog; shoved him onto the living room leather sofa and shot him between the eyes at close range. The blast pierced through the ears of Carol as she frightfully rushed to the top of the spiral staircase. She saw the killer hovering over her husband with

1

inquisitiveness. Carol watched for a moment as the killer seemed mesmerized by the blood that slowly ran from the gaping hole in Mitch's head. He seemed overwhelmingly occupied by the slow puffs of breath that Mitch took as his body slipped into death. The killer slowly reached inward to get a closer glance, slightly tilting his head for an angled view. At first, he didn't see her, but the noisily gasped that released from her body took the killer out of his trance and focused his eyes on her. She nurtured her mouth with a delicate touch of her hand and immediately dashed for the master bedroom. The killer quickly ran up the stairs in search for Carol. The killer entered two other rooms before finding Carol balled into a corner of the master bedroom. She was too shocked to put up a fight.

She never heard the gunshot blast. She didn't feel the bullet penetrate through her flesh. Suddenly she saw flashes of her life in full view as if she was watching a movie. She pictured the first time she danced with her husband, in the Greenwich Ballroom of the Valley View Country Club. She could still see the romantic sparkle that shined in his eyes as he stared into hers. She could not smell the flesh that burned in her chest from the powerful bullet that ripped her skin apart. Her mind had nearly escaped that scent. Instead, what flowed through her nose was the enchanting aroma of the rare Bird of Paradise floral arrangement that Mitch surprised her with the night before this horrific event. Suddenly, her mind was clasping with her body and soon she would fade into a deep dream that would last forever.

www.ingramcontent.com/pod-product-compliance
Lightning Source LLC
Chambersburg PA
CBHW071243170626
46809CB00001B/75